A Highlander Is Coming to Town

A Highlander Is Coming to Town

LAURA TRENTHAM

St. Martin's Paperbacks

This is a work of fiction. All of the characters, organizations, and events portrayed in this novel are either products of the author's imagination or are used fictitiously.

First published in the United States by St. Martin's Paperbacks, an imprint of St. Martin's Publishing Group.

A HIGHLANDER IS COMING TO TOWN

Copyright © 2020 by Laura Trentham.

All rights reserved.

For information, address St. Martin's Publishing Group, 120 Broadway, New York, NY 10271.

www.stmartins.com

ISBN: 978-1-250-31505-2

Our books may be purchased in bulk for promotional, educational, or business use. Please contact your local bookseller or the Macmillan Corporate and Premium Sales Department at 1-800-221-7945, ext. 5442, or by email at MacmillanSpecialMarkets@macmillan.com.

Printed in the United States of America

St. Martin's Paperbacks edition 2020

10 9 8 7 6 5 4 3 2 1

This book is dedicated to Claire Scott, the nicest Scottish lass I know. She answered any and all questions this American Southerner had about words and customs. I so appreciate her support!

Chapter One

Claire Smythe, her chosen nom de guerre for her time on the road with the Scunners, her former Scottish rock band, heard a clamor coming from the far end of the narrow alley that opened to Main Street. She hesitated, weighing her options. Stepping into the crowd would go against her number one rule: Avoid people.

On the other hand, if she abandoned her errand, she would have ridden miles for nothing and would have to turn around and come back the next day. If she and Ms. Meadows wanted something heartier than canned vegetables, then she would need to head to the shop. While leaving might be prudent, it was impractical.

A brisk December wind cut down the alley, gaining in intensity and slicing through her many layers. Her wardrobe wasn't anywhere near winter-ready. She hadn't had the money to supplement her clothes with a decent jacket. Luckily, though, the Georgia winter was proving to be mild by her Scottish standards.

Leaving her bike leaning up against the brick wall of the alley, Claire peeked around the corner. A large crowd was gathered in front of a newly painted HIGHLAND

ANTIQUES sign. A woman's voice coming through a microphone quieted the crowd noise.

While she couldn't see over or through the crowd, she assumed the voice belonged to Anna Maitland, the newly elected mayor of Highland, Georgia. Claire hadn't paid close attention to local politics. After all, she wasn't going to be in Highland much longer, but Anna Maitland's name had stuck out because she had also been the woman in charge of last summer's Highland festival. And the festival had been Claire's last performance as lead singer of the Scunners.

She flipped the hood of her sweatshirt up before stepping out of the alley. With her eyes on the pavement under her feet, she made her way toward the shop, doing her best to blend in unnoticed. It was a far cry from her days strutting around onstage, doing her best to draw every single eye in the crowd.

Anna Maitland thanked everyone for coming to the ribbon-cutting ceremony and welcomed the new business to Main Street. A smattering of applause followed.

"I also want to invite everyone to our first annual Burns Night holiday celebration the Saturday before Christmas. Main Street will be blocked to vehicles. Families will be free to enjoy music and shopping and food trucks. It's going to be a great time!"

Excited murmuring erupted throughout the crowd at the announcement. In Scotland, Burns Night celebrations were typically held in January after the holidays and during the dismal stretch of winter. As a Scottish singer, she'd been to her fair share and lent her voice to honor Robert Burns. The Highland, Georgia, version sounded more elaborate and fun.

But of course, she wouldn't attend. A pang of remorse infiltrated her heart even though she was the one avoiding making friends in Highland. Contrary to current appearances, she wasn't naturally a loner.

Claire slipped into Highland Drug and Dime without attracting any interest from the crowd. She pushed her hood back and pulled Ms. Meadows's list from her back pocket. Along with the typical staples of cornmeal, eggs, and bread, she had been tasked with getting some easy canned soups and pastas and peanut butter.

The shop wasn't as big as a typical American grocery store, but it carried all the basics, and without a car it was her only easy option. She gathered the items into a handheld basket and headed toward the checkout. Mentally, she parsed the items into the bags she used on her bike. It would be tight, but she should be able to manage without squashing the bread.

The total on the register ticked up with every purchase. Claire pulled the wrinkled cash out of her pocket and bit the inside of her mouth, willing the numbers to quit rising so high. In the heated shop, her multilayers of clothes were stifling, and a damp sweat had broken out across her shoulders and forehead.

The tax put her over by less than two dollars. A queue had formed behind her and her neck burned, but she didn't dare turn around. Leaning over the counter, she picked out two cans of ravioli and lowered her voice. "Could you take these off, please?"

The lady behind the counter cast a cutting gaze over the register, her expression neutral, yet Claire couldn't help the shame that roiled through her stomach. Being poor was the same ignoble experience on either side of the pond. That she was currently poor by choice didn't alleviate the humiliation.

"You can put those on my bill, Sandra," a man said behind her.

Claire snatched a quick glance over her shoulder, ready to bluster her way through the situation, but her excuses died when she met the kindly eyes of Preacher Hopkins.

While he didn't know everything about her, he knew more than most. After all, he had recommended her for the position with Ms. Meadows. His smile, along with the half-moon reading glasses perched on his nose, gave him a benevolent air of wisdom. His Afro was clipped short and graying, and his navy blue pants, white dress shirt, and red plaid bow tie gave him an air of neat professionalism that made her painfully aware of the frayed cuffs of her sweatshirt.

"Thank you, sir." Claire cast her eyes back toward the counter, where Sandra packed up her purchases in two paper bags. Escape was only seconds away, but before she had even taken two steps toward the door, Preacher Hopkins touched the back of her hand.

"I'd like a quick word if I may, Miss Smythe." He laid his few items on the counter.

Considering he had just paid for her dinner, she could hardly say no. Nodding stiffy, she retreated to a deserted aisle, out of the probing eyes of Sandra and everyone else in the line. Her shoulders and arms were already feeling the strain of the bags.

Preacher Hopkins joined her. "I hear tell you and Ms. Meadows are working out fine."

While she wanted to ask who had been talking about her and what had they said, she controlled the panic in her voice. "Aye, we rub along well."

A middle-aged woman entered the aisle and greeted the preacher. Thankfully, he didn't introduce her to Claire. "If you need anything, you still have my number, I hope?"

"I do, yes." Not that she planned to use it, but it was

comforting to know she had it in case of emergency. The past few months she'd lived without a safety net, and it had proved deuced uncomfortable.

She sidestepped away from him. His gaze bounced between the door and her, a thoughtful expression knitting his brow. She could almost see the questions formulating.

"If there's nothing else, I'll be going, sir," she said before he could ask her anything else.

"Tell Ms. Meadows I'll stop by for a visit soon."

With her hands full and her forearms burning, she nodded and strode to the door, stopping only long enough to prop one bag against a shelf to raise her hood against curious gazes and the wind. She juggled the bags on her hips, her grip clumsy and becoming more so the longer she carried them.

She stared at the entrance to the alley. Almost there. She would load her purchases and be back on the road in no time. A cuppa when she got back would restore her, and the groceries would keep them for the next week or so.

A crack in the asphalt caught the toe of her shoe at the mouth of the alley. She staggered to catch her balance, her left shoulder bumping into the wall and the bag scraping along the bricks. The load she was carrying lightened with an ominous rip. Groceries thumped and scattered. One of the ravioli cans rolled off-kilter toward the middle of the alley, the aluminum dented.

She checked around her feet with a sigh of relief. It hadn't been the bag with the eggs. She might not cry over spilt milk, but she would weep like a ninny over cracked eggs. A muttering of Gaelic-flavored curses made her feel better even if it wouldn't repair the bag. Squatting, she put the good bag down and shifted the torn bag like a babe in her arms to keep anything else from falling out. She gathered the closest item.

"May I help?" a man asked from behind her.

Still on her haunches, she whirled around, holding a bottle of generic aspirin at the ready. Not that it would do much to fend off a grown man. "What do you want?"

She tried to avoid speaking in town. Even with Highland, Georgia's summer festival and town motto of "The Heart of the Highlands in the Blue Ridge," her Scottish accent counted as unusual and invited too many questions for her comfort.

The man held his hands up and spoke as if she were a spooked horse. "Just offering to help you gather your groceries."

"Were you following me?"

"Of course not." He scooped up a can of soup that had rolled to his feet and held it out. "Thought you looked familiar, and I was trying to place you."

His smile was . . . nice. Which immediately drew her suspicions. She rose, took two steps, and snatched the can out of his hand, retreating like a skittish dog. Her jerky movements shifted the bag, and a jar of peanut butter fell and cracked against the concrete, the plastic lid splitting in two.

She would salvage what she could. She could skim any grit off when she got home. The rest would be fine. Buying a new jar was out of the question. Peanut butter was expensive, and she had used all the money Ms. Meadows had given her and then some.

It had happened. Rock bottom. The situation was even worse because she was choosing this life. She could go home with her tail tucked and her pride in pieces. She just wasn't ready to face her parents or her cousin Lachlan. Not yet.

The man moved closer. "Let me—"

"I don't need your help." Her steely tone was weakened by the sound of the bag rending further.

Not waiting for her permission, he plucked the torn bag out of the crook of her arm and cradled it with his big hands so nothing else could escape. "Of course you don't, but Mama would tan my hide if I didn't help anyway."

They faced off in an impasse. The man's nice smile had rematerialized with a crooked charm she most certainly did not find irresistible. Not even close. Okay, maybe his smile was within shouting distance of irresistible.

He looked familiar, but she found it impossible to place his face. His eyes were shadowed by a baseball cap, as so many American men favored. The hair curling at the edges was a dark blond.

Her gaze trailed lower, taking in broad shoulders and a frame that made her heart kick, not from fear but from awareness. His jeans fit snug and emphasized his muscular legs. An image tickled the edge of her memories. She stripped his pants off—mentally, not physically, unfortunately—and superimposed a kilt.

He was the man who had won Laird of the Games at the Highland festival over the summer. She had watched him throw the hammer and toss the caber with no small amount of admiration. While countless men had worn kilts during the festival, this man had worn his better than all of them. Not that she planned on telling a virtual stranger his thighs had featured in her dreams.

She picked up the intact bag and headed to her bike where it leaned up against the wall. She never bothered to lock it up. Highland was a small, safe town, part of the reason she had stayed on after the festival. Even besides the lack of crime, the bike wasn't the stuff of a thief's dreams.

The rims were rusty, and one side of the handlebars had lost its grip, leaving an exposed metal rod. Third gear was iffy, and the brakes squealed. Still, it was better than walking, and between the front basket and a canvas saddlebag, she was able to fit a good amount of groceries.

She repacked the items from her bag into the front basket, including the eggs, a loaf of white bread, a half gallon of milk, and tea bags among other staples. Nothing that could be considered an indulgence, except for maybe the tea.

He followed her and without a word, she packed the items out of the bag he held into the back satchel. This included the peanut butter, baking potatoes, cans of soup and the ravioli, and an assortment of ramen noodle packages.

"I guess I should thank you," she said grudgingly. Her etiquette teacher would be horrified.

"You're welcome." He crumpled the ripped paper bag and continued to fiddle with it even after it was a compact ball. His hands were strong and looked like they were used to a different sort of work than her musician friends. What did he do when he wasn't tossing cabers?

The question almost made it to her lips before she stopped herself. Small talk was an invitation to disaster. She gave him a brief nod, straddled her bike, and pedaled away. Was he still watching?

She didn't look back—more because of fear of crashing and breaking her precious eggs than pride. When she made the turn onto Maple Street, she allowed herself a peek. The mouth of the alley was empty. Of course he wasn't there. Good. She didn't want him looking at her and wondering about her.

Letting go of the tiniest niggle of disappointment, she focused on the road. Yellow and red leaves canopied the street on long branches and danced in the wind. Some of them jumped and twirled to join their brethren on the ground. The carpet of different colors was breathtaking and reminded her of the handstitched quilt on her bed at Ms. Meadows's house. Autumn in Highland had proved to be unexpectedly lovely.

She made another turn, this time onto a narrow country road. Trees hemmed her in on the left while open fields and fences stretched to her right. Cows and horses grazed and farmhouses stood sentinel in the distance. The solitude was comforting after the unexpected crowd in town and the run-ins with the preacher and the mysterious Laird of the Games.

Claire took a deep breath. The faint scent of woodsmoke hung in the air over the loamy forest. Every turn of the pedals unwound a portion of her tension. She wasn't sure when she had started to think of Ms. Meadows's little house as not just a haven, but a home. She loved her cluttered, cozy room and the shabby comfort of the old house in general.

Her front wheel bucked to the side and jerked her wandering thoughts back to more practical matters, like her less-than-reliable transportation. She slowed to a stop and bent over the handlebars to take stock. Her front tire was flat. She should have stayed in bed today.

She pushed the bike along the verge, cursing everything from the universe to the rocks along the side of the road. How far was she from Ms. Meadows? Farther than she'd like, but it was walkable even with a bike heavy with groceries.

She trudged along for what felt like hours, but was probably only ten minutes, the exertion combining with her many layers of clothes to make her uncomfortable. Just as she was considering stripping off her sweatshirt, the sound of a truck roared behind her. She guided her bike onto the grass and paused to let the truck pass on the narrow road, keeping her head down.

Ignoring her *leave me alone* body language, the driver pulled the behemoth next to her and idled, the diesel engine loud.

"Can I give you a ride?" The rich honeyed voice was only too familiar considering she'd replayed her brief conversation with him twice already. He was making it habit to catch her in vulnerable positions. Was it dumb luck or punishment from the universe?

"No." She glanced his direction to assess his reaction to her rudeness. She wouldn't blame him if he told her off and drove away.

Instead, he smiled. It was both reassuring and unbalancing. "I'm basically harmless. I promise."

She couldn't stop the sass. "*Basically* harmless? Not exactly a resounding recommendation. I find it creepy that you're following me."

"I'm not following you." He gestured toward the windscreen. "I live five or six miles down the road."

She waffled between wanting to remain aloof and begging him for a ride.

"I can't rightly drive off and leave you here. People fly up and down this road, and there's hardly any shoulder. Either you let me give you a ride, or I'll trail alongside you until you get home. How far do you have to go?"

"Not far."

"It will go faster for us both if you let me give you a lift. How 'bout it?"

She debated the merits of accepting. He would know where she was staying, which she'd prefer to avoid. On the other hand, she'd already been gone longer than she liked and his ride would get her back to Ms. Meadows faster, which was good. She would also avoid blisters, which was even better.

All considered, she gave him a nod. He maneuvered the truck ahead of her, one half in knee-high scrub grass. After loading her bike into the bed, he opened the passenger door and pushed his own shopping bags to the middle to make room.

She took a quick inventory. Beer, frozen pizza, and a banana cream pie. While the beer and pizza didn't interest her, her mouth watered at the thought of the pie.

The truck sat high off the ground. How in blazes was a normal-sized human supposed to get in? She grabbed the side of the seat and attempted to haul herself up, but her arms were jelly-like after carrying the groceries earlier and pushing the bike up the rolling hills.

She tried twice and failed, every nerve ending conscious of the man behind her. Without warning, the hands she had watched so intently in the alley clamped around her waist and plopped her on the seat. She turned on him with her fists raised, but he didn't try to cop a feel like some blokes would have.

He took two stumbling steps backward, windmilling when his heel caught on a divot of soft ground. After he regained his balance, they regarded each other like prey and predator.

He held his hands up as if surrendering. "I didn't mean to scare you, miss."

By the devil, he was strong. And attractive in the most American way possible with his jeans and ball cap and smile.

"Keep your bloody hands to yourself next time."

The quaver in her voice wasn't from fear, but she had no time for a flirtation, much less a dalliance. She barely stemmed a sound of disgust at herself before slamming the door shut.

He circled around the front of the truck through the high grass and climbed into the driver's seat. Once he got them back on the road, he asked, "Where am I dropping you?"

"At the top of Meadows Lane."

The truck lurched, telegraphing his surprise. "Are you staying with old Ms. Meadows?"

"Aye." Curious at his reaction, she shot a glance in his direction even if it meant accidentally meeting his gaze.

Claire had taken a position as live-in helper for the housebound elderly widow. While Ms. Meadows could still do the basics for herself like washing and dressing, Claire had taken over the tidying and shopping and cooking. Although it had taken a few frustrating weeks for her to learn to prepare the dishes Ms. Meadows liked. Claire had never made turnip greens or okra or corn bread. Now she did a bang-up job with Southern staples.

The house sat in what Ms. Meadows called a holler surrounded by woods. The setting was the stuff of a Brothers Grimm tale, but Ms. Meadows was nothing like an evil witch. In fact, the longer Claire stayed, the more the old lady resembled a fairy godmother. Albeit a cranky, sharp-tongued one.

"I'm Holt Pierson, by the way. What's your name?" he asked.

She hesitated, loath to surrender any more information than she already had, meager though it was. "Claire."

"Nice to meet you."

She made a throaty sound of acknowledgment but didn't return the sentiment. "Do I take it your skills don't extend to the kitchen?"

"And what would you know about my skills?" The tease veered naughty. Or was that merely her imagination? After all, she had been the one examining the way the denim of his jeans hugged his thighs earlier.

The curse of the fair-skinned struck as heat washed over her. "I remember where I've seen you before. You competed at the festival this summer and won Laird of the Games. That's all I was referring to, I can assure you."

"Isn't that a coincidence? I watched you perform at the festival too." He tossed a leading glance toward her, but she forced herself not to react.

"Are you sticking around Highland for a while?" he asked.

"Here it is. You can let me out at the top, thanks." She pointed to where overgrown bushes camouflaged the start of a gravel lane. The old mailbox needed a coat of paint and legible numbers, and the red flag dangled toward the ground like the standard of a defeated army.

Claire found sliding out of the truck easier than climbing in, but Holt still beat her to the truck bed. He lifted her bike out, replacing the grocery items that had fallen out of the saddlebags and basket.

Their hands brushed when she took the handles from him. Just lovely. His large hands were going to join his thighs in her dreams tonight, which was dangerous considering how much more nimble hands were than thighs.

"Thanks for the ride." She ducked between the bushes.

"Maybe I'll see you around!" Holt called out.

"Maybe." Not a chance. Holt Pierson already knew more about her than she was comfortable with.

Only when the growl of his truck grew distant did she relax. Disaster averted.

Chapter Two

The bang of the screen door sent a mild shot of adrenaline through Claire. Her run-in with Holt Pierson the day before had shaken her sense of safety. The clack of Ms. Meadows's cane against the wood floors smoothed her frazzled nerves. The two-plus months she'd spent taking care of Ms. Meadows, and having Ms. Meadows take care of her, had provided a much-needed refuge for her to consider and plan away from the machinations of her family. She'd grown comfortable. Perhaps too comfortable.

She had thought herself nearly invisible on her weekly run to the shops in Highland for food and sundry items for the house. No one had recognized her from the festival. Except for Holt Pierson. Which made her wonder what else he saw when he looked at her.

She ran a hand through her now shaggy hair, hardly even missing the spiky pixie cut she'd maintained for her stage persona as lead singer of the Scunners, the band that had played the Highland summer festival for two years running. She was a long way from the woman who'd strutted the stage and commanded an audience with a confidence she'd never been able to manifest out of the spotlight.

Ms. Meadows clacked her way into the kitchen, her cane and uneven gait playing out a rhythm that had become oddly comforting. "What's for lunch, girl?"

Claire had put together a simple tuna salad using canned tuna and the last of the mayonnaise, which meant another trip to town soon. Plus, she'd somehow not made it home with the precious jar of peanut butter. Blast Holt Pierson and flimsy paper bags.

"Tuna salad sandwich." Claire carefully set out the delicate china plates Ms. Meadows insisted they use for their meals, then helped Ms. Meadows onto the wooden chair before taking the seat across the table.

The china pieces weren't as old or expensive as the dishes Claire had grown up with, but they were priceless nevertheless. Ms. Meadows's mother had received them as a wedding present and passed them along. The sentimental value made Claire handle them like mini primed bombs.

Ms. Meadows took a bite of the sandwich and made a little sound Claire took as satisfaction. The weeks of daily lessons had taught Claire how to cook to Ms. Meadows's standards, which would have satisfied even Gordon Ramsay.

Claire had never seen her mother enter the kitchens except to hand a menu to the cook and housekeeper. As a result, Claire hadn't learned how to do anything useful. Only in retrospect did she recognize that while her mother lived a life of leisure by anyone's standards, it had not been easy. Strain and anxiety had taken a toll. Her father was not an easy man, and Claire had not been an easy child. She had been more burden than joy and treated thusly.

Her father was aloof and consumed with running the family business. Her mother spent her time organizing various charity functions, many of them to better the plight of sick or impoverished children around Britain and the world. In comparison, Claire had been pampered. She had attended the finest boarding school in England. She had been given an allowance for clothes. She had never worried about where her next meal would come from.

She'd had nothing to complain about growing up. Except for the constant ache of loneliness.

Now that Claire was older—wiser was up for debate—she had gained a new understanding of her mother and father. They were good people who should never have had a child. Claire would have given up her allowance and her posh boarding school and her fancy clothes to have dinner with them every night or go on silly outings together.

What would happen when the mechanism of her inheritance began to turn on her twenty-fifth birthday? The freedom and anonymity she'd enjoyed the last few years would be over, but then again, she'd grown tired of the road and staying in hotels night after night. Settling down felt less like a prison sentence than it had at twenty. Still, she wasn't anxious to join the cutthroat power plays her family dealt in like currency.

"Not bad," Ms. Meadows said between bites of her tuna sandwich. "You're a fast learner, girl. I'm proud of you."

Ms. Meadows never called her Claire. At first, she'd simply been *you'un. Girl* seemed a step up. Even better, the warmth the compliment inspired was a novel feeling for Claire. "Thank you, Ms. Meadows."

They ate in relative silence. It wasn't a hundred percent comfortable silence, but the awkwardness marking her first few weeks helping Ms. Meadows and living in her house had mostly dissipated.

"I met someone yesterday in town. Holt Pierson. Do you know him?" Claire kept her voice casual and gauged Ms. Meadows's reaction from the corner of her eyes.

Ms. Meadows let the sandwich drop to her plate, her face tight with an unexpected anger. "You stay away from that boy."

The vitriol shocked Claire. While Ms. Meadows had a biting wit and sly sense of humor, she wasn't mean-spirited and had been kinder than Claire felt like she deserved. "Is he dangerous?"

"His family is a boil on the butt of Highland. The Piersons are sneaky and untrustworthy. Holt's daddy tried to run me off my own land." Ms. Meadows picked up her sandwich to take a vicious bite, then stared at the innocent tuna as if her soured mood had transferred to her food. She pushed her plate away with her sandwich less than half finished.

"That's terrible," Claire murmured. While it was difficult to square her impression of Holt with the accusation, she had no reason to doubt Ms. Meadows.

"What did that boy do to you? What did he say? Do I need to call the sheriff?" Ms. Meadows was growing more and more agitated, her face flushed and her voice strident.

Claire rushed to soothe her. "Nothing of the sort. I dropped a bag of groceries. He helped me gather them and tuck them into the basket of the bike. He was perfectly nice and polite. I didn't realize . . ." She bit her lip, deciding it was best not to mention the lift home in his truck.

Ms. Meadows harrumphed. "Well, now you do. Stay away from Holt Pierson."

She nodded. It should be easy enough considering how rare her sojourns out of the house were. What were the chances she would run across him again? "I'll need to fix the bike before I can go into town again. I don't suppose you have a spare tire and a pump?"

"Don't know what all is out in the shed. You're welcome to take a gander. If you can't find what you need, call Preacher Hopkins. He'd be happy to help." Ms. Meadows braced her cane on the floor and gripped the edge of the table with her other hand in preparation to stand. Claire hopped up to take her elbow in a steadying grip.

Ms. Meadows let Claire assist her into the living room and her favorite chair. It had been clear from the beginning of their association that Ms. Meadows was loath to accept help, but it was also clear she needed it. Claire had more sympathy than she could express. They had found each other at a most opportune time.

After tidying the kitchen, Claire verified that Ms. Meadows had dropped into her afternoon nap in front of the telly. Closing the screen door softly, Claire slipped outside and took a deep breath of air. The brisk winds of the day before had torn most of the leaves from the trees. Fading remnants of yellow and orange smudged the trees stretching in all directions from Ms. Meadows's house. Steel-gray clouds scooted along as a backdrop.

The damp smell of dirt and decay wasn't entirely unpleasant, but it was foreign. She'd been raised in Glasgow, surrounded by centuries-old stone and manicured gardens. The woods were mysterious. She shuddered.

She'd seen enough horror movies to know what

happened to the girls who wandered into dark woods. Except for her trips to town, Claire didn't let the house out of her sight. Was she a coward? No doubt, but at least she was a live one.

Claire lifted the latch on the shed door and pulled. It bowed out slightly in the middle, but the top and bottom edges were stuck. After checking for other latches and finding none, she braced a foot on the jamb and put her entire weight into pulling.

"Come on, you bloody nob of a door," she muttered before throwing herself backward once more.

The top of the door gave way with a pop. Her hand slipped off the handle, and she landed on her bum, catching herself on her elbows. The jarring fall left her stunned for a few breaths.

"Well, that was dramatic. You okay?" A familiar baritone sounded behind her.

She tilted her head back and Holt Pierson came into view upside down and over her. She scrambled to her feet and brushed at the leaf litter and dirt coating her hands and jeans.

Why the devil did Holt have to show up when she was dropping things or falling on her arse or otherwise breaking down?

Ignoring her stinging palms, she asked, "What are you doing here?"

The question came out with more accusation than she intended, but he didn't seem offended or defensive, which left her battling surprise and suspicion. What sort of game was he playing? What was the prize? In her experience, men had ulterior motives for any kindness bestowed. Motives such as getting in her knickers.

His smile was open and charming and left her feeling nonplussed. He held up a jar of peanut butter. "I found your peanut butter busted up in the bed of my truck after I dropped you off. I chucked it and got you a new jar. Didn't want you to have to go without one of the major food groups."

"Thanks. That was really nice of you." She took the offering and turned the brand-new jar in her hands, pretending to examine the label. She didn't have to scrape grit off the top. "I'm sorry if I sounded rude. It's just that you surprised me. We don't get too many visitors."

His simple kindness filled her with enough warm fuzzies to cushion any rock bottom. Was he being nice because he was a nice person? In light of Ms. Meadows's dire warnings, she dismissed the thought as impossible.

Ms. Meadows would be horrified a Pierson had stepped foot on her land. Yet . . . Holt was like a warm breeze on the chilly day. His easygoing manner and general air of competence were undeniably attractive after she'd spent her last few years with musicians who qualified as neither.

Before she could tamp down the weakness of wanting to lean on him, he sidestepped around her to the stuck door. "Need some muscle?" Without waiting for her answer, he pushed up his shirtsleeves, grabbed the handle, and yanked.

Did she *need* muscle? No, but she wasn't going to complain about the view. Holt's biceps bulged in the green Henley pushed up almost to his elbows. His ropy forearms were attractive in a way she'd never noticed on a man. This is what came from not being around men for months. She was acutely aware Holt wasn't simply a bloke; he was a man.

The door surrendered to him with a scrape of metal on metal. Only the first few feet inside the shed were visible. From her vantage point she could see the outlines of a lawn mower, a chain saw, and bags of garden soil and fertilizer. The corners remained in creepy shadows. How many spiders lurked in the rafters? The hair on her nape raised.

She was ready to swallow her pride and call Preacher Hopkins when Holt took a step inside and waved his arm in front of him, a distaste pulling at his mouth. "I hate cobwebs. Are you after something in particular?"

"I need to fix the bike. Ms. Meadows thought there may be a tube and pump." While Claire didn't want to become further beholden to Holt, neither did she want to be the one who ventured into the spider breeding grounds looking for something that might not even be there. If he wanted to play knight-errant, she would let him in this instance. God, she was a hypocrite.

But she would be a non-spider-infested hypocrite. She glanced over her shoulder. Ms. Meadows would be napping for a good while yet.

Holt took off his ball cap and scratched the back of his head while staring into the abyss before replacing the cap with a decisive tug. "I can take a gander, but even if I find a tube, it'll probably be rotted."

He ducked farther into the shadows, shuffling around the garden implements to rows of shelves in the back. Claire stepped just inside the door, keeping her eye out for any beasties dropping from the ceiling. When nothing attacked, she took in her surroundings. Water-damaged packets of flower and vegetable seeds were stacked on the flat blade of a hoe. Sifting through them, she noticed some had been opened and part of the packets used.

Scraggly bushes lined the back of the house and the packed-dirt yard between the shed and door. How long had it been since Ms. Meadows had been well enough to hoe and plant a garden? Seeing her house and yard slipping further into decay and neglect must be breaking Ms. Meadows's heart a little more with every season that passed.

Claire tried to keep herself from caring too much. Her plan from the beginning had been to lie low with Ms. Meadows until she turned twenty-five on Boxing Day. Hopefully, she would have decided on a plan for her future by then. Unfortunately, the peace and clarity she sought had remained elusive.

And now there was Ms. Meadows to worry over even though Claire told herself she was merely her employer. When Claire left, Ms. Meadows would simply hire another girl. Claire wasn't special.

Amid the utilitarian mess in the shed, one item stood out like talisman. A medium-sized silver box on the end of a narrow wooden shelf drew Claire closer. A layer of grime muted the shine, but a decorative vine pattern on the lid and around the sides was visible. It belonged in pride of place on a mantel and not left to deteriorate in the elements.

Unable to resist the call of a shiny object, she turned the box around so the latch faced her. Her fingers left streaks along the top and exposed the patina of tarnish.

She glanced toward Holt, who was still rooting around along the shelves at the back of the shed. Her imagination churned. What was inside the box? She could imagine that Ms. Meadows's distrust of people extended to banks. The old lady was the type to squirrel cash away under mattresses or in sheds.

Her hands twitched. Yes, she was as poor as a beggar at the moment, but she didn't need the money. Or wouldn't in a matter of weeks at any rate. She was sorely tempted to open the box for another reason altogether. Her unmitigated curiosity.

Ms. Meadows was a widow, but for how long? Had

she loved her husband? Had she had children? And if she had, why weren't they here taking care of her? Any questions Claire had posed in that direction had been shut down in a trice by Ms. Meadows.

"Found a pump, but no tube." Holt's declaration ended the internal fisticuffs going on between her anemic conscience and her thirst for information.

She turned away from the silver box and waited outside for Holt. Brushing cobwebs off the brim of his cap, he held out an old-fashioned rusty metal implement she didn't recognize as a pump.

Practical matters overtook her earlier speculation. Claire estimated how long it would take her to walk into town and back—two hours at a brisk pace. Assessing the stacked gray clouds, she calculated the odds of a soaking. Near a hundred percent.

Damp, chilly weather had been a staple during her years in Glasgow. She'd basked like a cold-blooded reptile in the Southern summers the last two years. Even the autumn months boasted several warm sunny days.

Unfortunately, today was not one of those days. The sooner she set out, the sooner she'd get back. First, though, she had to get rid of Holt before Ms. Meadows caught wind of him. She pushed the shed door almost to a close, leaving it open a sliver so she could get back in later if need be.

"Thanks for the peanut butter. It was exceedingly kind of you and I really do appreciate it." Picking up the new jar of peanut butter, she shifted it from hand to hand, still uncomfortable with the thought of accepting the gift. Did it make her beholden? "I've got things to take care of now, so you can take your leave."

When had she become a rude git? It didn't seem

that long ago when she was carefree and happy and wild. That girl was being held hostage by the cautious woman she'd become.

"If the thing you're taking care of is your busted tube, you'll need a ride into town." Holt was like rubber, her discourtesy bouncing off him harmlessly. "Unless Ms. Meadows has a car stashed somewhere?"

The big American-style coupe parked on the other side of the house was a giant squirrel nest. Weeds had grown up around the flat tires, and leaves covered the bonnet. Claire had no idea the last time it had been driven, but *ashes to ashes and dust to dust* didn't apply only to people. The car was disintegrating back into nature.

"Not one that runs." Not to mention her lack of a valid license to drive in the States. "I can walk."

"I know you can walk, but once again, I'll point out that you don't have to. I'm headed into town anyway. Come on." He nudged his head toward the front of the house, stuck his hands in his pockets, and strolled away.

She was left to follow in his wake, knowing her practical streak was stronger than her pride. Even a one-way trip would save her loads of time and keep her from getting blisters. Her military-style boots were tough to look at and even tougher on her feet. Now that she'd made her decision, she picked up her pace. They needed to leave before Ms. Meadows woke.

"It would be churlish of me to turn down your kind offer of a lift to town. Therefore, I accept gratefully." Her voice was stiff and as formal as if she were accepting an invitation to share tea with the queen.

Which she had once when she was five years old. It was a blur in her memories. All she remembered clearly was losing her balance on her curtsy and a white-haired woman wearing a pillbox hat smiling at her in a kind but distant sort of way.

"Exceedingly churlish." While his voice was equally as formal, his blue eyes sparkled with laughter she suspected was aimed at her.

"Let me leave Ms. Meadows a note." While she stepped toward the house, Holt stowed her bike in the bed of his truck.

The front door creaked open before she even made it to the bottom of the porch steps. Claire took a hair too long to decide whether to call out a warning to Holt or something reassuring to Ms. Meadows.

"Are you stealing Claire's bike, you low-down, dirty thief?" Ms. Meadows yelled from the shadows of the porch. The barrel of a hunting gun came into view. Ms. Meadows shuffled out, balancing on her cane and holding a gun under her arm. It waved unsteadily.

Holt raised both hands in the air, a tense smile coming to his face. "It's Holt Pierson, ma'am. I'm not here to steal anything. Just being neighborly."

Ms. Meadows snorted. "Is that what you Piersons call it when you try to steal my land right up from under me?"

"No one is trying to steal your land. My daddy has made fair offers in the past. You've declined every one and that's been the end of it as far as I know, ma'am."

"Fair? Attempted chicanery is what it was. Which is what you're trying to pull now unless my eyes deceive me."

"I don't think chicanery falls under high crimes." Even though his hands were still in the air, his stance relaxed.

Ms. Meadows tucked the gun higher under her arm. Considering Holt's truck was big and shiny and expensive, the accusation of being a bike thief would have been almost comical if it hadn't been for the gun aimed at his heart.

"Don't get her fashed. She might accidentally pull the trigger," Claire muttered, then stepped forward into Ms. Meadows's line of sight, but not the aim of her gun. "Holt wasn't stealing the bike. He offered to run me into town to get a new tube for it. We didn't find a replacement in the shed."

Ms. Meadows stared at Claire while still keeping the gun trained on Holt. "We? Was this man rooting around in my things?"

Damn and blast. She should have tossed Holt out on his ear the second he made an appearance. Ms. Meadows's feelings had been clear, and Claire had agreed to stay away from him not a half hour earlier. Although surely, a mere nod didn't qualify as a blood oath.

She glanced toward Holt before inching toward Ms. Meadows. "You told me I could look in the shed for a tube."

"You. Not him." The barrel of the gun dipped toward the ground. "You promised to keep your distance from him."

Ms. Meadows had nailed her there. "Holt did nothing untoward, I promise. He merely offered me a lift into town to get the bike fixed. But if you'd prefer, I can walk the bike to town this afternoon or tomorrow to get fixed. It will take me quite a bit longer than usual, though."

Ms. Meadows set the gun down to lean against the porch rail. "The Drug and Dime called to let me know my medicine is ready to be picked up."

That explained why her nap had been cut short. Claire could only hope the rain held off. "Of course. I'll set off now. Can you take the bike out of your truck, Holt?"

Instead of moving toward the bed of his truck, he took two ground-swallowing steps toward the porch and Ms. Meadows, removing his hat and shuffling the brim through his fingers. "This is crazy. You and my family have attended the same church for years. I promise I'm not here for your land. I met Claire in town yesterday and simply aim to be neighborly."

Ms. Meadows barked a laugh. "You've never offered to be neighborly before, but now that a pretty girl is living with me, suddenly you're the soul of Christian kindness, eh?"

Pretty? Claire's toes curled in her battered boots as she fought the urge to tug at her ragged auburn hair. Between her hair, lack of makeup, and boyish wardrobe, she veered more plain than pretty, which was what she'd been going for. She braced herself for Holt to scoff at the suggestion, but he didn't. She stole a glance at him under her lashes.

His cheeks were flushed, and he hung his head, the picture of contriteness except for the roguish tilt at the corner of his lips. "You're right to chide me, ma'am. I can only blame youthful ignorance for my behavior toward you all these years, but I'd like to do better now. If you'll allow it, I'd be happy to give Claire a ride to get her bike fixed. There's no shoulder until you hit city limits, and it's fixing to rain."

"I won't be beholden to you or your family." Even though the words were harsh, Ms. Meadows's voice had softened the tiniest bit.

"I don't have a hidden agenda, and I don't expect anything in return."

Holt and Ms. Meadows held each other's gazes for a long moment. Claire might as well not have been there. Although she was the focus of their argument, their animosity had nothing to do with her. She recognized old hurts when she saw them in others or in a mirror.

"I know where to direct the sheriff if anything happens to the girl." Ms. Meadows crossed her arms over her chest in a grudging surrender.

Claire couldn't help but feel like a pawn in an old feud, yet Ms. Meadows's prickly defense also made warmth bloom in her chest.

"Yes, ma'am. I'll take good care of her." Holt kept his face and voice bland, but the omnipresent twinkle in his eyes was ready to spark into a laugh.

"I can take care of myself, thank you very much," Claire returned tartly. The statement landed disharmoniously in her ear. If she could take care of herself, why was she avoiding her life by hiding out in an old woman's house? A question to examine another time.

Holt retreated to the truck and climbed behind the wheel. Ms. Meadows held on to the porch rail and took the steps one by one. Claire met her at the bottom to offer a hand. Ms. Meadows took it and squeezed. "You be careful now."

"Do you really think Holt Pierson would hurt me?" Claire glanced over her shoulder at the truck.

Ms. Meadows rolled her eyes and sighed. "No. He was a hell raiser when he was young, but no worse than most young men, I suppose. You do know what to do if he gets handsy, don't you?"

Claire blinked at the turn in the conversation. She had handled her fair share of handsy men while playing gigs all over the UK and America, but couldn't help but be curious as to what Ms. Meadows thought was appropriate. "What would you suggest?"

"Punch him right in the balls." Ms. Meadows nodded sagely. "Works every time."

A laugh born of shock popped out. How many times had Ms. Meadows had to employ the method? The thought dried up any humor. Had nothing changed for women over the generations? "Don't worry, his bollocks will be forfeit if he acts inappropriately."

"Good girl. Now, since you're going into town anyway, do you mind running by the Drug and Dime to pick up my medicine?"

"I don't mind a bit." Claire didn't add that running errands was in her job description.

"Let me get my pocketbook." With another squeeze of her hands, Ms. Meadows retreated to the house, then returned with an old-fashioned patent-leather purse, the shine gone from the worn edges. "Take this to pay for the bike repairs and my pills."

Claire tucked the folded bills into her front pocket and walked slowly toward the truck, fighting the feeling that danger did indeed await her with Holt Pierson. Just not the kind Ms. Meadows was worried about.

Chapter Three

Holt watched Claire and Ms. Meadows discuss something, probably how best to murder him and dispose of his body. Relief squashed a portion of the adrenaline still coursing through him. He'd never had a gun pulled on him at all, much less by an octogenarian who strained to even hold it up. Later he would laugh about it, but at the moment his focus was on not scaring Claire off.

She disappeared from view as she circled the truck. He forced himself to unclench the steering wheel and toss her a smile on her awkward climb into the passenger seat. After her reaction to him lifting her in yesterday, he didn't want to risk her wrath. He turned the ignition and the diesel truck rumbled to life, the noise doing a good job filling the silence.

The tires skidded on the gravel of the lane as he pulled onto the main road. Halfway to town, raindrops splattered the windshield, picking up in tempo.

"It would have been a nasty walk to town." The awkwardness he battled around Claire was something new.

Charming girls had been a skill he'd developed at

an early age. Maybe he was just out of practice. While he was hardly a Lothario, he'd dated extensively in high school and his early twenties. Mostly local girls who were fun and nice and familiar. Girls he'd known all his life and who had known him. His relationships never ended in a blaze, but petered out into uncomplicated friendships. It could be worse. At least he didn't have to dodge wrathful exes every time he went to town.

Claire was many things—secretive, mysterious, puzzling—but not familiar or boring.

"I'm used to nasty weather," she said.

"My friend Izzy moved to Scotland a year ago. She said the weather is unpredictable."

Claire made a sound that might have been a laugh. "*Unpredictable* is a nice way of putting it. Winters are exceedingly dreary. At least in Highland, you get sunshine and blue skies on occasion."

"Is that why you decided to stick around? Because of the weather?"

"Not exactly." She crossed her arms over her chest. He didn't need to be a body-language expert to recognize the *fuck off* vibes.

"How did you and Ms. Meadows get hooked up?" He flicked a glance in her direction, trying to read behind the meager words she offered.

She had mastered her tongue, but had less control over the emotions flitting across her face. Worry or perhaps fear had her chewing on her lip. Was she afraid of him or someone else?

"Did your father really try to steal her place?" As a defensive strategy, her lobbed question was good. He could hardly ignore it.

"Steal, no. Buy, yes. Our farm abuts Ms. Meadows's land. A little creek bisects her land beyond the woods.

It would be nice to have access to that water." Holt couldn't say much more because he didn't know much more. The animosity between his dad and Ms. Meadows had exploded when he was young, and he hadn't paid it much mind. His teenage self had been fixated on the issues that had mattered at the time, namely football and parties and girls.

"Ms. Meadows doesn't like you." Her lilting tone was speculative. Had she been the girl who dated the bad boy to spite her parents?

It was a shame Holt didn't qualify as a boy or particularly bad. His list of transgressions harked back to high school and included minor rebellions like drinking and toilet-papering his principal's yard.

"No, she doesn't, but I think it's my family name she takes issue with and not me in particular. Considering you're sitting here, you must not share her poor opinion."

"I've yet to decide about you." Her voice veered surprisingly flirty. As if she noticed the breach, she sniffed and added, "But Ms. Meadows is probably right. Men like you are nothing but trouble."

"Men like me?" He made the turn onto Highland's main drag.

Over the last day, seasonal decorations had gone up. Reindeer and Santa hats that would light up at night were clamped to the wrought-iron poles lining the street. Each pole was wrapped in white twinkle lights and topped with a giant red bow.

The windows of the businesses were decorated in greasepaint drawings of Christmas scenes. Some looked professionally done and some looked like they'd given free rein to a class of kindergartners. In short, it looked like Santa's elves had had a drunken midnight party.

Highland had always dressed itself up for Christmas, but this year, with Anna in charge and the first annual Burns Night Street Party fast approaching, the level of Christmas Crazy had reached new heights. Literally, considering the giant evergreen tree taking up the fountained alcove smack in the middle of town.

Jessie Mac and Jessie Joe stood at the base of the tree in red rain jackets untangling a string of lights. Jessie Mac was pointing up at the tree while Jessie Joe nodded. The cousins had been a Highland fixture for as long as Holt could remember. Given any task, they would get it done.

"It's lovely." Her eyes were wide with wonder and an innocent joy that surprised him. She wore the persona of a jaded tough woman so well. Was it all an act?

"You don't think this is a step beyond what's normal?" Holt asked. While he hadn't forgotten about her *men like you* statement, he decided not to press her. There would be time to delve deeper into her psyche. He hoped.

"Maybe, but there's enough drab and depression in the world. Why not spread color and joy?" She craned her neck to see back down the street.

He recognized her statement as rhetorical, yet couldn't help but probe for more. "You've experienced gray, depressing times?"

"I've had my share." If she'd known her clipped, defensive answer only made him more curious, would she offer the truth? "And you?"

He hadn't expected her to ricochet the question, and he had the urge to squirm. "I suppose everyone does."

Her attention swung to him, her dark-green eyes crystalline and cutting. "You live in an idyllic village on your family's farm. You must be doing well to afford a truck like this. You don't have everything you desire?"

Now he was the one attempting to hide the desert-like stretches of his soul. "Not everything," he said quietly.

Her gaze continued to excavate through his silence until he turned into the parking lot of Wayne's Fix-It shop at the end of the street. She squinted through the rain pelting the windshield. "They carry bike tubes?"

"Wayne does a little bit of everything and can fix about anything." He shrugged out of his rain jacket and tossed it on her lap. "Put that on so you don't get soaked."

She was wearing jeans and at least three shirts, all made of cotton. The top was a green-and-brown-plaid flannel that looked warm enough but wouldn't do anything to protect her from the rain. She hesitated as if the jacket finally exceeded her limit of accepting aid, but slipped her arms into the too-long sleeves.

Pulling the hood up, she hopped out of the truck. He did the same, beating her to the back of the truck to lift her bike out.

"What are you doing?" Rain dripped off the edge of the jacket's hood as she blinked up at him.

"Helping you get the bike inside." He ignored her huff and took off at a jog with the bike, stopping under the overhang at the door to shake the water off his cap.

"Why did you give me your jacket if you were getting out of the truck too?" she asked when she joined him.

"So you wouldn't get wet. Duh." He gave her a smile to indicate he was teasing, but she didn't smile back.

"That was really nice of you." Suspicion added tartness to the pronouncement, but far from being offended, he fought the urge to smile.

"No problem. It's all part of my evil plan."

Her eyes flared and he could almost see her tallying up his deeds, both good and bad, before the hint of a smile lightened her countenance. "So you do admit you have an evil plan."

He faked a gasp and covered his mouth. "Oops, I didn't mean to say that out loud."

"Now that you have, you might as well fill me in on the details." The suspicion had been replaced with a much more interesting flirtatious tone. Still, even when she was inserting daggers into her voice, her Scottish lilt was sexy as all get-out.

"What if my evil plans include taking you out to dinner one evening?" He might as well shoot his shot while she seemed receptive.

Her initial reaction gave him hope. Her body leaned forward, and excitement sparked in her face. His shot turned into an air ball when her mouth firmed and her teasing gaze fell to her flat tire. "I don't feel comfortable leaving Ms. Meadows for a frivolous reason."

She pulled the door open, and he wheeled the bike inside, the wet tires squeaking on the linoleum. It was a rejection, yes. But he hadn't imagined her interest. Was her concern about leaving Ms. Meadows real or was it an excuse to keep him a safe distance?

One side of Wayne's Fix-It shop was filled with aisles of broken electronic equipment that Wayne cannibalized for parts. The other side was lined with a cornucopia of items to meet a small town's electronic needs, like cables and wiring to laptops and batteries. He fixed cell phones and computers behind the counter running the length of the wall in the back of the shop, and in the backroom he repaired larger equipment like lawn mowers and leaf blowers.

Wayne Bocephus was somewhere between a red-neck savant and a mad scientist. In his mid-fifties with a full head of snow-white hair and an untamable cowlick in the middle of his forehead, he had the air of a distracted college professor and the build of a retired pro wrestler.

As Holt pushed the bike through an overcrowded aisle, he spotted Wayne sitting on a stool behind the counter, hunched over a cell phone with its innards exposed. His thick fingers looked incongruous holding the smallest soldering iron Holt had ever seen.

Wayne didn't immediately acknowledge their presence and Holt waited until he looked up, the pair of magnifying glasses he wore making him look comical. "What can I do for you, Holt?"

Holt thumbed toward Claire. "This here is Claire, and she needs a new tube and general tune-up of her bike. I don't suppose you can get to it this morning?"

"Howdy do." Wayne pushed his magnifying glasses to the top of his head and held out a hand toward Claire. His razor-sharp gaze lingered on her face, and he shook her hand for a beat longer than was polite. "Have we met before?"

"I don't believe so. Pleased to make your acquaintance, sir." The formality in her voice sounded as practiced and rote as the dances and manners he was forced to learn when his mother had made him attend cotillions when he was young.

"Likewise." Wayne nodded his chin toward the curtained door behind him. "Roll it out back, and I'll give one of the kids a holler. Give us an hour."

Working for Wayne was better than attending a community college class, and he routinely took on young men and women interested in working in auto or HVAC or as electricians. In fact, a stint working for Wayne was regarded as more qualifying than an associate's degree.

Holt deposited the bike out back, where a young man with a constellation of pimples on his cheeks took it out of his hands with a nod and smile.

Holt led the way back outside, but stopped under the overhang. "We've got an hour to kill."

"I've got to pick up a script for Ms. Meadows at the chemist, but you don't need to accompany me." She shrugged his rain jacket off her shoulders. "You should—"

"No, I shouldn't." He grabbed the lapels, lifted the jacket back over her shoulders, and pulled the edges together at her chest. The position was unintentionally intimate. Instead of breaking the contact, she tipped her face up to his. Her lips parted as if she had a secret to impart. He tensed. A raindrop fell from the brim of his cap to land on her cheek and coast down like a tear.

The moment fractured and she stepped away, scrubbing at her cheek with the heel of her hand. He wanted to draw her back around to look at him, but he didn't. She was strong, yet fragile. Under the flashing neon FUCK OFF above her head was a HANDLE WITH CARE in small print.

"Follow me." Holt plotted a course to reach the Drug and Dime by sprinting from store overhang to store overhang. Claire's giggles were contagious, and both of them were breathless and laughing by the time they reached the last overhang and had to make a break across the street.

He reached for her hand and tugged her from out of relative dryness into a jog across to the Drug and Dime. Water seeped through the shoulders of his plaid button-down and Henley T-shirt. Even after they were across the street, he didn't drop her hand, but more surprising was the fact she didn't pull free.

"After you." He reluctantly let her go to open the door.

The chill of the pharmacy incited a course of shivers. He tagged after her, not needing to pick anything up. Claire pulled out a cache of small bills to pay for Ms. Meadows's medicine. As if sensing his calculating gaze on her, she shifted so he couldn't see her stuff the remaining money back in her pocket.

She tucked the white bag into the pocket of his rain jacket and gave it a pat. "Do you think my bike's ready?"

"Nope. And I need a drink."

Her eyes went wide and unblinking. "Isn't it early for a drink?"

"I meant a coffee. Or hot tea, if you prefer."

Her shoulders visibly relaxed. "Oh, yes. That would be brilliant."

"I've never been called brilliant before. I like it."

"Don't get a big head. In Scotland, it merely means exceptionally fine and is not commentary on the size or quality of your brain."

"Unfortunately, what's not so brilliant is that the Brown Cow is back thataway. Come on." Once again, they held hands on their sprint back across the street.

Holt made sure not to even glance toward their joined hands. If he mentioned the insurgency taking place, he had a feeling Claire would snatch her hand away and deny any pleasure at his touch. Once again, they only broke apart on entering the Brown Cow Coffee and Creamery. The creamery portion of the store was closed during the week through the slower winter months, but the scent of rich coffee had him heading straight for the line.

Locals filled the tables and milled about in conversation. Mr. Timmerman, the owner of the Dapper Highlander, a tailor shop catering to the kilt-wearing Scots wannabes, and Iain Connors were at the closest table.

As soon as Holt and Claire placed their orders—coffee for him and a mug of tea for her—Holt guided Claire over to where Mr. Timmerman and Iain chatted. The closer they got, the more she dragged her feet.

Iain stood to greet him with a handshake and slap on the back. The two of them had bonded over the summer Highland Games and had become good friends over the course of the fall. Iain was Anna Maitland's live-in boyfriend, which had caused quite a titter when she was running for mayor, but Holt expected they would make it official with a marriage license soon enough.

"Come and join us," Iain rumbled in his broad, thick brogue. He gestured to the two empty chairs, turning his smile toward Claire, who resembled a rabbit ready to bolt.

Mr. Timmerman turned in his seat to favor Claire with one of his jolly smiles, but she didn't smile back. Claire looked from Holt to the table and back to Holt before she acquiesced and perched on the edge of one of the empty chairs. Pulling off his ball cap, he took the fourth chair, ruffled his damp hair, and took a bracing drink of his coffee.

She scooched her chair closer to his until her knee brushed his. Aiming a tight-lipped smile at her tea, she took a sip.

"Claire, this is Mr. Timmerman, owner of the Dapper Highlander, and Iain Connors," Holt said, pointing at each man in turn and watching her from the corner of his eye. It was obvious she wanted to be anywhere else.

"Are you new to Highland, Miss Claire?" Mr. Timmerman asked.

"Fairly new," she said.

Iain perked up. "Ah, you're a Scot too. Where do you hail from?"

Holt ran a hand down his chin, trying to decide if this meeting was a stroke of genius or devastating to his cause of ferreting out her secrets. All three men looked at Claire with different levels of anticipation.

"Glasgow," she said shortly as if she were giving up the information under threat of torture.

"I worked in Glasgow for a bit. It's a big place," Iain said leadingly.

Not picking up the bait, Claire hummed, nodded, and didn't meet anyone's eye.

"You look familiar." Iain's brows were drawn low as he stared at Claire.

"No. I don't think so." Claire's body was strung tight, and she glanced toward the door.

Iain snapped his fingers and pointed. "You sang at the festival. The Scunners, am I right?"

"Yes. Yes. That's right. The Scunners." She was suddenly eager to answer and her relief planted a red flag for Holt. What was she hiding?

"Are you settling down here?" Mr. Timmerman asked.

Again, Holt stared at Claire, waiting for her answer to a question he'd wanted to ask too.

"No. Or . . . maybe? But, no, it would be an impossibility. I think." Her waffling wasn't offering any insight.

"Claire is living with Ms. Meadows doing chores and errands and such," Holt said.

"I haven't seen Ms. Meadows at church in a possum's age." Mr. Timmerman stroked his beard thoughtfully. "It's certainly kind of you to help her out."

"She's paying me," Claire said suddenly. "I'm not doing it out of the goodness of my heart or anything. It's a job."

Awkwardness descended. Claire firmed her chin and sat back in her chair. She was like a turtle trying to protect a soft underbelly with a hard outer shell of indifference. He noticed something else, though. Her accent was the same, yet different from Iain's. In fact, Claire's accent more closely resembled that of Alasdair, who had been raised in both Scotland and England and with money. Yet another mystery to explore.

But not in front of Iain and Mr. Timmerman. Holt cleared his throat. "How're are the plans for the Burns Night festival coming along?"

Claire visibly relaxed into her seat.

Iain turned his attention to Holt. "Great, actually. Anna has everything well in hand. Except this blasted rain. The tree was supposed get decorated today, but it doesn't look like that's going to happen."

"Forecast is calling for a gully washer tonight. High winds too. I hope Jessie Mac and Jessie Joe secured the decorations along the street." Holt's thoughts turned to the farm and any preparations he should tackle.

Mr. Timmerman shook his head, a wry smile breaking through his well-trimmed beard. "The cousins might do things their own way, but they don't do a shabby work."

Holt finished the rest of his coffee and turned to Claire. "You ready to go see if Wayne and the boys are done?"

She stood and surprisingly stuck her hand out

toward Mr. Timmerman and then Iain, shaking both hands. "It was nice to meet you both."

"I don't believe I caught your last name," Iain said.

"Claire . . . Smythe." The hesitation was slight and he might have missed it altogether if his senses weren't attuned to her. Iain and Mr. Timmerman didn't seem to notice, turning back to their conversation after nodding and smiling them off.

Holt ushered her out the door. This time, Claire didn't take his hand as she began the sprint from overhang to overhang. The connection had been severed by the conversation with Iain and Mr. Timmerman.

Other, more practical worries surfaced. If the pelting rain continued all day and night, the south pasture might flood. Should he move the animals? If his dad had been there, they could have discussed the merits, but he was on his own.

By the time they ducked into Wayne's shop, Holt fought shivers. Her bike was leaning against the side of the counter in the back of the shop. Not only had the flat tube been replaced, but a new grip covered the formerly exposed metal of the handlebar and the chain had been oiled and tightened. No one was there.

A note had been taped to the seat, the printed handwriting almost childlike. *Bike done. Easy fix. No charge.*

"He shouldn't have fixed the handlebar. How much is he charging me?" Claire stuck her hand into her pocket and pulled out a few crumpled bills.

Holt took the note and handed it to her. Bewilderment flitted across her face. "What about the new tube and the labor? Surely this is a mistake."

"Knowing Wayne, he appreciates getting some spare parts out of the way while giving one of his trainees some practice. He's a nice guy."

Claire harrumphed and shot him a teasing side-eyed glance. "Highland seems to be chock-full of those."

Holt grinned, took the bike by the handles, and rolled it toward the door with Claire on his heels. Making quick work of loading the bike in the bed, he cranked the heat as soon as he was behind the steering wheel. He peeled off his outer shirt and took off his dripping hat while Claire stripped off his rain jacket, folding it neatly at her side. The front of her jeans was wet, but at least she had on leather boots.

"Do you think he's angling for something?" Claire's brow knitted, her confusion obvious.

"Who?"

"Him." She pointed at the shop. "Wayne."

Her question left him nonplussed. His experience growing up in Highland had left him with a healthy respect and appreciation for the capacity of people to be generous to their neighbors and to strangers alike.

Not that people didn't fight and argue and gossip—his dad's feud with Ms. Meadows was a prime example—but if someone needed a tarp on a roof that had been ripped off by a tornado or if their house burned down, people would turn up to help patch the roof or with clothes and food without being asked.

He wasn't naive, though. The world wasn't always such a kind place. "I doubt he wants anything from you, but if makes you feel better, I'll drop by later and slip him a few bucks."

She dug in her pocket and held out what looked like less than five dollars. "Do you think this would cover it?"

He wanted to tell her to keep the money, but pride was delicate and wounded easily. He could try to explain the psyche of a typical Highland resident, but it would be like explaining to a child why the sky was blue. "That's plenty. Tuck it into my dash."

She did, and then sat back with crossed arms and a tapping foot. Casting her a glance from the corners of his eyes, he asked, "Hasn't anyone done something nice for you just because?"

Her shrug left her shoulders in a tense scrunch. "I've found most people have ulterior motives."

"Even your family?"

Her bark of laughter held only irony. "Especially my family."

An unhappy childhood then. He couldn't relate. His parents were great. Oh, he'd gotten in his fair share of hell-raising trouble as a teenager, and they'd shown him tough love, but always love. He'd known he could count on them no matter how much of a rebellion he'd staged back then.

While he searched for something to say that didn't sound like a pathetic platitude, she surprised him by offering more crumbs. "My parents didn't beat me or anything—I don't want to give you the wrong impression—but sometimes I wonder if they only had me because it was the thing to do."

"How do you mean?"

"You know, after university, you get married to a suitable partner, then after three years of marital bliss, a child should follow. That child should be attractive and accomplished. I don't think I was what they expected." The brittleness in her voice made him want to stop the truck in the middle of the road and draw her into a hug, but he didn't.

"I'm sorry."

"It's not your fault."

"I take it you aren't close with them?"

Rain pelted the truck and filled the silence with white noise. When she spoke, he had to lean over to hear her. "I'm not sure how to answer that. They don't understand me, and I don't understand them. It's like I was a changeling child."

The rain weighed down the overgrown bushes and obscured the lane leading to Ms. Meadows's house. The mailbox acted as the beacon guiding him onto the lane. He inched forward, the branches scraping along the sides of the truck.

"Thank you for giving me a lift. I'm sure you had other things to do." Her speaking pattern slipped into the same formality she'd adopted in the Brown Cow faced with meeting Iain and Mr. Timmerman.

"You're welcome. I head that direction several times a week. It wouldn't be a bother at all to give you a ride. You should put my number in your phone."

She tucked her hands under her legs. "I don't have a mobile."

He did his best to hide his surprise. "Well then. I'll bet Ms. Meadows has a landline."

He pulled to a stop in front of the house. Reaching across her, he opened the glove box, not missing the slight intake of breath or the tensing of her body. He tore off the flap of an envelope, grabbed a pen, and jotted his number down. Their fingers brushed on the handoff. She blinked at the number for a long moment before stuffing it into the front pocket of her jeans.

Ms. Meadows came out using the shotgun as a cane. She stared toward the truck as if she had developed Superman's ability to laser people in half.

Claire cracked the door open, but before she could slide out, he caught her wrist. She turned with an unvoiced question in her eyes.

"Are you in trouble?" he asked in return.

Her lips parted and everything about her suspended except for her pulse, which fluttered faster against his thumb. When she finally spoke, her gaze dropped to where his hand circled her wrist. "Not exactly."

She pulled free of his loose hold and jumped down. Before he could even exit the truck, she hauled the bike out of the bed and pushed it across the puddled driveway, lifting it up the steps and into the shelter of the porch. Claire and Ms. Meadows had a brief exchange of words before the old woman hobbled through the screen door. Claire held a hand up in a wave before disappearing inside.

He shook his head. Why couldn't she have answered with a simple black-or-white yes or no? Why did she have to be frustratingly confusing and downright fascinating?

Chapter Four

Claire sidled over to the window and, half-hidden by the threadbare curtains, watched Holt. She'd had years of keeping her own counsel. Why then did she find her tongue loosening around Holt? Her toes scrunched in her boots, her feet cold and numb in her damp socks.

Her run-in with Iain Connors had been hair-raising. Who would have thought she would cross paths with another Scot in tiny Highland, Georgia? It defied logic and probability. If anyone might have recognized her, it would have been him. Her family was well known in Scotland, and the product of her family's fortunes, Glennallen Whisky, was familiar the world over.

Her picture had been in the papers and m̶ spreads more than she would have liked gr̶ Of course, the lifestyle described by the ̶ exposés had been a projection of what he̶ envisioned, not reality. Claire hadn't eve̶ but they always trotted one out for a ph̶ Was there anything more British tha̶ heiress and her pony?

But Iain hadn't shown even a fl̶ beyond her stint in the Scunner̶ with her truth still hidden. Or, less charitably put, with her lies intact. She was daft for worrying.

Her years on the road with the Scunners had distanced her from her posh upbringing. None of her old friends would have recognized the woman she'd become, strutting and preening onstage. She'd loved the anonymity. The hard partying and travel had held their appeal too. Until they hadn't.

The truck backed out of the lane with a roar and disappeared. Part of her had hoped he would change his mind, march to the door, and demand answers to the questions he hadn't asked but she could sense brewing. That same part wanted to tell him everything. It was a good thing he'd left, because she was feeling especially vulnerable. Tomorrow, she would be strong again.

The engine noise faded and tension unwound from her shoulders. She pulled out the piece of paper he'd written his mobile number on. The last three numbers had smudged beyond all recognition in her wet pocket.

She told herself she was relieved the temptation to call him was off the table. A wash of disappointment proved she was a liar.

"Did young Mr. Pierson behave himself?"

Ms. Meadows's voice right behind her made her start around. How had the old woman snuck up on her?

"He did." He did more than behave himself, he had been . . . kind. At least, she thought it was kindness. As she had so little experience with the motivation, she couldn't be sure.

Meadows cocked her head to the side. "You ___"

"___on't. He was convenient. That's all." Her ___ warm and her gaze darted toward the ___ for an excuse to change the subject.

Even though she'd done her fair share of lying over the years, she'd never become an expert.

Ms. Meadows's hum transmitted sarcasm. "I'm old, but I ain't dead, girlie." She turned and tottered away without the gun or her cane.

Claire hustled to her side and offered a steadying arm as they made their mincing way toward Ms. Meadows's chair and the telly

"Could you put the gun back in the closet?" Ms. Meadows waved a hand toward where the gun was propped against the wall.

Claire tucked the gun into the farthest corner of the closet. "Why do you have a gun? Did you used to hunt, Ms. Meadows?" Claire's father had been a weekend hunter. She had never understood the appeal of shooting at birds for sport.

"Goodness, no. My husband kept it around to chase off varmints and for protection, I suppose, although no one ever bothered us out here. Only time I had to pull it on a person was Holt's good-for-nothing daddy. The junk drawer ate the ammo years ago."

Ms. Meadows didn't often mention her husband, and even though she didn't want to be interrogated in return, Claire couldn't help but be curious. "How long has he been gone?"

"Thirty years this Christmas." Ms. Meadows's voice was completely matter-of-fact.

Thirty years. It was longer than Claire had been alive. A pang of echoed loneliness seemed to resonate between them.

"I'm so sorry," Claire said softly enough that Ms. Meadows could choose to ignore or recognize the sentiment.

"I'm sorry too. Samuel was a good man."

"What happened?" Claire snapped out of the line of

questioning before Ms. Meadows could tell her off for being so nosy. "You don't have to—"

"Heart attack," Ms. Meadows said brusquely. Claire didn't move or speak, afraid Ms. Meadows would slam the door that had opened between them. In a softer voice, she continued. "It was sudden. He was only fifty-five. I suppose that seems old to you, but he was young. It happened right outside at the bottom of the porch. I can still remember being confused at the way he was lying there so still."

Ms. Meadows reached out a hand as if touching a photograph that existed only in her mind. Claire's chest hurt and tears stung her eyes. Keeping her distance from Ms. Meadows should have been a snap. After all, the old woman hadn't inspired warm and fuzzy emotions when Claire had first met her. She had been short and a bit cold and had only grudgingly admitted to needing help.

Bit by bit, Ms. Meadows had softened toward her. Claire supposed you couldn't live with someone, eat with them, spend day after day in each other's company, and not unbend. Claire's own defenses were rotting away in the comfort of Ms. Meadows's home.

Claire reached out a hand with a tentativeness that reflected her fear of getting it slapped away. Ms. Meadows allowed Claire to give her arm a slight squeeze. Although Claire didn't let her hand linger, the moment veered awkward.

Ms. Meadows cleared her throat. "You should go take a hot shower and change into dry clothes."

Claire took the opening to retreat to her small room in the back of the house. If not for Holt's rain jacket, she would have been soaked to the bone.

Routine ruled the rest of the day and evening. After dinner, they played a few hands of cards. As casually as possible while discarding the six of hearts in their game of gin, Claire said, "I noticed a lovely silver box in the shed when I was looking for a bike tube. I'd be happy to bring it inside and polish it for you."

Ms. Meadows picked up the six and tucked it into her hand before discarding. "No, thank you."

Claire contemplated her next play, not in the game, but in the conversation. "Are you sure? It can't be good for whatever is inside to be subjected to the weather."

"I said, *no*." The word ended the conversation like a key locking a door. Before she could probe further, Ms. Meadows picked up Claire's next discard and lay her cards down, announcing, "Gin!"

Claire grumbled good-naturedly about losing again, then helped Ms. Meadows, wearing a fresh nightgown, settle down in her bed in front of a small telly sitting on her bureau.

The channels were limited to whatever the antennae on top of the house could pick up, and Ms. Meadows complained about the mind-rotting shows she had to choose from.

"Why don't you read instead?" Claire asked. "You have a bookcase full in your sitting room."

"Oh that I could. My eyesight has gotten too poor. I used to love reading." A wistfulness threaded the words.

"Audiobooks are all the rage, and there's certainly nothing wrong with your hearing. Do you want to try one?"

"I don't have the money to toss around willy-nilly on such extravagances. TV is free." Ms. Meadows sniffed, which Claire had come to recognize as the close of any conversation.

After saying their good nights, Claire lay down in her twin bed in the dark and listened to the rain patter on the roof. Her thoughts drifted like metal filings toward a Holt Pierson–shaped magnet.

The day had done damage to her recent theories on people—men in particular. Wayne had fixed her bike and seemingly required nothing in return. Not even her thanks.

In addition, not only had Holt *not* put the moves on her, but he'd come as near to offering her friendship as she'd experienced in a long time. It felt strange. But also nice. Except another dynamic was at play between them. One she wasn't immune to.

Holt was attractive. Not just attractive. He was sexy. Not in the bad-boy way she'd gravitated toward in the past but in a stable, and—dare she say?—mature way. He was an adult, and she was . . . not a grown-up. At least, she didn't feel like one, even if her age said otherwise.

She should have studied harder in school. She should have gone to university. She should have returned home to apprentice in the distillery. She shouldn't have picked the worst men to date as a rebellion. She shouldn't have thumbed her nose at her responsibilities. She shouldn't have joined a touring band.

Regrets made for poor bedfellows. She punched the pillow and turned over to face the window. On clear nights, silvery moonlight lent a fairy-tale-like quality to her room. Those were her favorite nights. Nights when she believed in redemption and forgiveness. Tonight, though, it was dark and her dreams would be full of shadows.

She cast off the covers, pulled on a pair of ratty sweatpants, and tiptoed through the quiet house, pausing at each squeak of the wooden floorboards. The telly was off in Ms. Meadows's room, and nothing stirred.

Once she was outside, she straightened from her hunch and took a deep breath. Her travels had taken her to fairs and festivals around the United States. They smelled of cotton candy and frying oil. The Glasgow of her youth had smelled of old stone and whisky.

The surrounding woods were rich with unfamiliar earthy scents. The wind in the trees spoke of decay and growth—an ancient cycle of life. Her shiver wasn't entirely from the cold. Had someone traipsed over her grave?

The sky spit out errant raindrops, but the worst of the deluge seemed to be over. Claire shifted the door of the storage shed open enough for her to slip inside. Fear crawled over her like all the spiders and beasties she was imagining hovering in the shadows of the shed. An irrational fear of being shut inside had her pushing the door open wider.

She put out her hands and shuffled toward the shelf with the silver box. Had this been her plan when she got out of bed? Yes. Right or wrong, she had known since the moment she'd seen it that she'd be unable to resist the call of her curiosity.

Her fingers brushed cool metal. She'd been anticipating it yet still jerked at the sensation. Tucking the cold metal box under her arm, she tiptoed back toward the house, fighting the feeling she was betraying Ms. Meadows. Whatever was in the box was none of Claire's business.

When she reached her room, she slipped the box under her bed and pushed it toward the wall. While there was little chance Ms. Meadows would notice the box gone from the shed, she didn't want Ms. Meadows to see it until she'd had a chance to polish it to a shine.

Sleep, when it finally claimed her, was restless. Her imagination soared in directions that were both fanciful and troubled. Pieces of her past mixed with whatever the box held captive.

Birdsong and the sun shining brightly through the window woke her. She rubbed her gritty eyes and lay there a moment to get her bearings in time and place.

Hauling herself up, she dropped into her typical morning routine. The perking coffee gave her a shot of vigor, and she enjoyed a cup before noises from Ms. Meadows's room signaled her wakefulness.

Claire knocked before cracking the door. "Need any help?"

"Good morning, girl." Ms. Meadows had already changed out of her nightgown and into one of her sack dresses, this time in blue with white daisies, along with woolen socks and brown clunky sandals. The combination of the old-fashioned dress with the irreverent footwear on an eighty-five-year-old woman never failed to make Claire smile.

"Let me do your hair." Claire moved a squat stool in front of the mirror hung on the closet door and steered Ms. Meadows to sit.

Ms. Meadows had resisted Claire's offers of hair care for the first month of their arrangement. When she had finally relented, it was obvious the pleasure she took in the attention. Ms. Meadows had a head of thick, snowy-white hair. Claire had given it a trim and kept it combed and curled.

"I can't believe you get to enjoy days like this in winter," Claire said while waiting for the curling iron to heat. "Glasgow is damp and miserable for a good six months out of the year." It was an exaggeration but not much of one.

"Speaking of Glasgow, you've never asked to use the phone to call home. Do you have any family left in Scotland that might be wondering what you're getting up to in Georgia?" Ms. Meadows arched a brow when Claire's eyes met hers in the mirror.

The question caught her with her guard down. Not just down, but decamped entirely. She made a few *um* and *uh* sounds that didn't jump-start her ability to come up with a suitable lie.

"My parents and I aren't close." The truth shot out before she could stop it. The more she thought about it, though, the more she wondered why she was keeping so many secrets. Who would Ms. Meadows tell?

"They're still in Glasgow?"

"Yes." According to the internet, they were still hosting fundraisers and smiling with peers and millionaires. What did her parents tell their friends about her? Maybe they didn't talk about her at all. Out of sight and all of that.

"I imagine they regret the distance as much as you do."

The observation rocked Claire's stomach, making her feel sick. Did Claire regret the distance? Of course she did. Especially as decisions that would affect everyone in the Glennallen family were approaching like the fall of a blade. That's how she felt some days. Her execution was nigh.

No matter what she decided, whether to sell her shares or return to sit on the board, people would be hurt. People she cared about despite the physical and emotional distance of the last few years. After all, she was the one who had left.

"I thought I might test out the new tubes and ride to town today as it's so pretty out. Need anything?" Claire finished curling Ms. Meadows's hair and unplugged the iron.

Ms. Meadows patted her coiffure and smiled. "Could you pick up a quart of buttermilk? I have a hankering for biscuits. It can be your next lesson, but I'll warn you, they are tricky little buggers to get right."

After making them both a breakfast of poached eggs and toast, Claire set out cycling to town. Although the air held a chill, the sun was warm and the sky was blue. The shimmy in her wheels had smoothed and the gears changed without a clang. With the wind roaring in her ears, she flew along the country lane, humming an old Scottish folk song. Her optimism soared like a hawk on the wing.

She made it to Highland in record time and left her bike leaning up against the brick wall in her usual alley. Occasionally, a couple of kid-sized bikes would be there, but not this morning.

Flipping her sweatshirt hood up to hide her face out of habit, she strolled down the street, window-shopping along the way. She would stop to get buttermilk on her way back, but first she had another mission.

The Highland library sat at the end of Main Street. It was a large two-story brick building that once might have been someone's house. Stone steps led up to the double doors. Claire had avoided the library, not sure how the system worked in the States.

Institutions usually required names and numbers and proof of existence. While her passport required her legal name, she didn't want to be flagged in Highland. Her family had the wherewithal to find her, and as the days ticked down to her birthday, she would imagine they were growing desperate.

Despite the risks, she hoped to gain access to audiobooks for Ms. Meadows, and sidled inside with a deep breath. The scent of paper and ink lingered over the more industrial smells of cleaners and technology. Rows of books formed a gauntlet between her and the librarian staffing the large circulation desk along the back wall. She wandered up and down the rows, letting her fingertips glide along the spines of mysteries and romances and science-fiction books.

A bank of computers made her stop short, and she glanced at the closest unoccupied cubby. The last person had left the browser open to a website with detailed knitting instructions. She waited for a few minutes, but no one returned to claim the computer. Glancing to either side of her, she slipped into the seat and was sure a librarian was going to ask what the devil she was about, but she was ignored.

Cracking her knuckles like before a fight, she typed in her parents' names. The social section of a Glaswegian newspaper was listed first. The post was only a month old. Claire clicked through the pictures. There were her parents smiling without a care and holding champagne flutes.

Did they worry about her? Did they scour the internet for any mention of her? Not that they would get any hits returned. She'd used a variety of stage names when she traveled with the Scunners. Her bandmates had chalked it up to artistic eccentricity. Unless her parents tapped friends in government to check the movements of her passport, they would have no clue she was even in the States, much less Highland, Georgia.

Next, she searched for her cousin Lachlan Glennallen. The under-thirty rising stars of the Glasgow business community had been announced for the year. With a head full of the Glennallen auburn hair, Lachlan smiled at her from the number one position. She smiled back, pulled up her email service, and logged in before she could think any better of it.

Saw the paper. Are you having to live in the garden because your head is too big to fit in the door? She didn't bother with a greeting or a signoff.

Her in-box popped up with a reply almost immediately. *You little git. Where are you?*

Claire hesitated a moment. Lachlan would be cleverer than her parents about tracking her. Still, she was on borrowed time already. *I'm somewhere thinking. Somewhere safe.*

You'd better be thinking how great it's going to be to partner up to run the distillery. I have gobs of ideas to market to blokes my age.

She and Lachlan—mostly Lachlan—had talked about how they would take over Glennallen from the old guard when they both came of age. Lachlan had turned twenty-five two years earlier and claimed his inheritance, which consisted of a percentage of stock. Without her throwing her support behind him, though, he wouldn't have enough power to accomplish anything.

Their plans had sounded good when she was twenty and twenty-five seemed a lifetime away. That lifetime now consisted of a few scant weeks.

Her fingers held over the keyboard before they put into words her fears. *What if I don't want to run the distillery?*

Why the bloody hell wouldn't you want to? Do you not like money?

Money might not buy happiness, but as she'd learned the last few months, not having any was miserable.

"Whatcha doing?" The whispered question came with a puff of breath along her cheek. She let out a squeal, which drew everyone's eyes toward her. Exactly the sort of attention she tried to avoid.

Holt Pierson was hunched behind her, his chin nearly on her shoulder. Her hood had hidden her from over-curious, prying eyes, but also masked his approach.

"You scared the dickens out of me. What are you doing in a library?" She managed to close her email, which left the online newspaper up. She laid her arm over the keyboard and half turned, hoping she was blocking most of the screen from his view,

The man in the next cubby tossed a disgruntled look in their direction, closed his textbook with a snap, and vacated the space. As if taking the silent admonishment to heart, Holt straightened, but he kept his hand on the edge of the cubby desk. She tilted her head back to see him, and her hood fell to her shoulders.

Sweet Jesus, after her windy ride then being stuffed under the hood, what did her hair look like? It shouldn't matter. She shouldn't want to appear attractive for Holt Pierson or anyone else. Yet her hand rose of its own accord to tuck her hair behind her ears and smooth the stray waves in the back. Growing out her pixie cut was a test of patience she wasn't sure she would pass.

"I *can* read. And write, when I put my mind to it. Shocking, I know." He winked. The tease in his voice was like a favorite shirt he wore with ease. Did the man ever get defensive or ruffled?

"That was badly done of me. Pardon," she said stiffly. "I shouldn't have assumed just because you look like you do, you don't possess a decent number of brain cells."

His eyebrows bounced up and his smile took on a wicked crook. He leaned down, and she caught the scent of fresh laundry and shaving cream. The slash of tanned skin between his collar and his jaw beckoned her closer. What would his skin feel like against her lips?

"A decent number of brain cells? You're making me blush," he said. "But I'm more interested in what I look like in your eyes. Do tell."

He looked like a delicious decadent treat she wanted to devour. Her gaze shot to his, and she immediately regretted locking eyes with him. Could he read her mind? She bloody well hoped not.

"You look like a . . . Viking?" She wanted to kick herself. Vikings spent their days conquering villages and seducing women. They were dead sexy.

"Do you like Vikings?" He took the empty chair from the vacated cubby and shifted to face her. Still too close for comfort but far enough away for Claire to gather a few of her scattered wits.

"Vikings were a dirty, foul lot who pillaged innocents." That was better. Much less complimentary than calling him a sexy beast.

He steepled his hands and pursed his lips as if really considering the comparison. "I can be foul and dirty depending on what chores I'm finishing up on the farm, though I try to avoid pillaging innocents. But you aren't an innocent, are you?"

Blast and damn. The heat radiating from her cheeks was answer enough. No, she was far from innocent, especially where it pertained to fantasies about him. *Foul and dirty* was an understatement. Her dream the night before skated on the edge of depraved.

"What I am or am not is none of your business," she said primly.

"True enough." He leaned the chair back on two legs and rocked, his legs spread wide. "Catching up on news from back home?"

Claire turned back to the computer and exited the browser. "Indeed I am. Ms. Meadows doesn't have internet access."

"Not surprising. I personally couldn't survive without it, but her generation lived a simpler life."

"I'm sure you'd find it difficult to live without your porn." She bit the inside of her cheek. Why had she said that? Not only was it insulting, but now she was imagining what sort of things Holt got up to while watching porn.

His reaction was one of delight and not outrage. He tsked and thickened his Southern accent even more. "Why, Miss Claire, I do declare. And you call me foul and dirty?"

"I . . . you . . . sorry," she mumbled.

"For your information, since my parents took off to discover America in their RV, I've been reduced to watching cooking videos."

Surprise squashed a portion of her earlier embarrassment and steadied the conversational footing. "What was up with all the frozen food the other day?"

"I haven't actually graduated from watching videos to making anything. Anyway, cooking for one is depressing, but so is eating frozen pizza night after night." He'd lost his smile, which made Claire feel a bit chillier than when she had basked in his teasing humor.

Holt was lonely. It was strange to think a man so enmeshed and integral to Highland could be lonely. They had more in common than she'd first supposed. Loneliness she understood.

"You should host a party."

"I'm a little old to be throwing a kegger in my barn," he said wryly.

"What's a kegger and why do you want to toss it around?"

"A kegger is a party featuring a metal barrel filled with cheap beer. Everyone gets trashed."

"That sounds . . . terrible actually. No, I meant a dinner party for your friends."

"A dinner party?" He sounded like she'd suggested he go full Monty at the local exotic bar. In her limited travels around Highland, she hadn't seen an exotic dancing bar. That sort of deviance was probably outlawed.

"My parents used to have them all the time growing up. It gave my father a chance to wear his tuxedo." Why had she offered that revealing tidbit? It was only after she ran away from home that she realized most men didn't own tuxedos, they rented them.

"The best we can do around here is a Canadian tuxedo. Or a fancy kilt."

The memory of Holt competing in the Highland Games flashed into her head. His kilt had been utilitarian. A sporran and jacket would have been in the way. Like the director of a movie reel, she panned in on the slash of muscled thigh he'd exposed tossing the sheaf or throwing the hammer. It had been strangely titillating.

Her gaze fell to his thighs, sadly encased in denim at the moment. "Fancy kilts are good too."

He rocked the chair on two legs and crossed his arms. "Maybe you're onto something. I could have Anna and Iain over."

He didn't say her name. And why should he? She cleared her throat and stood. "I should leave you to your planning then."

The chair banged to all fours and he stood too, shoving his hands in his pockets. "How's the bike?"

"A delight. If I didn't know any better, I would say Wayne switched it out with a new one."

"Glad to hear it." He fell into step beside her.

She cast a glance toward the circulation desk. "Does

the library only carry physical books or do they have a section for audiobooks?"

He scratched the back of his head. "I don't know, but we can find out easily enough."

She tried to grab his sleeve but he was already striding toward the intimidating-looking lady at the desk. Claire scurried to catch up.

"Hey there, Ms Coburn. How's the book business?" Holt leaned an elbow on the chest-high portion of the desk and sent one of his smiles toward the woman.

Ms. Coburn was a stereotype. Stern disapproval transmitted like radio waves. Her hair was scraped back into a tight brown bun, and her severe gray dress was buttoned halfway up her neck and at the wrists. She could have been cast as evil headmistress of an all-girls school or housekeeper of a creepy gothic castle.

Claire should have known not even a nunlike villain could resist Holt Pierson's charm. Ms. Coburn still possessed X chromosomes after all.

The woman's face turned from stone to pudding. "Business is brisk. Although I must say I'm surprised to see you in here."

Claire turned from Ms. Coburn to Holt and lifted her brows. So he wasn't a regular who happened by when she was there. Was that a blush creeping up his neck?

He cleared his throat. "I'm wondering if you can help my friend. She's interested in audiobooks. Do you carry them?"

Ms. Coburn turned her attention to Claire, who tensed expecting a stony assessment. Instead, the impression was one of intelligence and kindness. "Indeed. You'll just need to fill out some paperwork for a library card, dear."

"Oh, not for me. I'm staying with Ms. Meadows,

and she has a hard time reading print books anymore. I thought she might enjoy an audiobook. She gets tired of the telly."

Consternation drew Ms. Coburn's brows down. "Gail used to be a regular patron. I'm embarrassed to say I hadn't thought about her in quite some time. I should have . . ."

Ms. Coburn didn't finish the thought but turned to her computer and typed with a speed and efficiency that was impressive. Her gaze darted over the screen. "It looks like I can simply reactivate her card if she wants to come down to verify her address with a utility bill."

"She has a difficult time getting around, I'm afraid, and doesn't drive anymore. Is there any way I could take her one to try?" Claire asked with a smile she hoped looked trustworthy.

"We have some CDs on the shelf, but most are digital these days. I can give you instructions on how to sign up online and download one to an electronic device, but she'll still need to bring proof of residence to reactive her account." Ms. Coburn riffled through a stack of papers.

Frustration built inside of Claire. Had an evil fairy gifted her with roadblocks when she was a baby?

"Ms. Meadows doesn't have a computer or a smartphone or a car." Holt didn't seem bothered by the difficulties. "But this conversation has left me with a hankering to listen to a rousing tale of murder and mayhem. I think I'll check one out. My card is still valid, isn't it, Ms. Coburn?"

She tapped on her keyboard again. "Look at that. It is, Holt. Why don't you and your friend go pick one or two audiobooks out?" She gave them a wink before turning to a stack of books waiting to be checked in.

With a hand on her back, Holt guided Claire to the stacks to the right, where he pulled out an audiobook with a spy-thriller-type cover. "Do you enjoy murder and mayhem?" Claire asked.

"Not particularly, but considering Ms. Meadows enjoys threatening men with guns, I assume she'll eat it up."

Claire put her hand on his arm before he could sidle farther down the aisle. "Thank you."

He shrugged, his gaze still on the gun-toting spy on the cover. "The least I can do. I feel bad about the way my family has treated her all these years."

"It's hardly your fault. You were young when they fell out."

"Yep. But I'm not young now and haven't been for a while. If I was a regular at church, maybe the preacher would have nudged me."

"You aren't a regular?"

"Not for a few years now. Don't have anything against it, just don't feel called to attend. Maybe that will change as I get older."

"And closer to death? That seems to be a great motivator."

He barked a laugh. "Ain't that the truth. How about a classic Agatha Christie?" A Miss Marple audiobook found its way into her hands.

"Perfect." Claire turned her attention to the shelf. None of the books were recent releases, but she found a historical fiction book that had been a bestseller a decade earlier to add to her cache. Surely among the three choices, Ms. Meadows would enjoy at least one of them.

She turned back to head toward the checkout, but Holt stepped in front of her. "Hang on, do you know if she has a way to play CDs?"

She hadn't even considered it. Her shoulders slumped with her gusty sigh. "I haven't seen one, but she might have one stashed under her bed or out in the shed."

"My dad has an old one in his office to play his collection of Motown CDs. I'll drop it by. I need to check on the big house anyway. Haven't even cracked the door open in a week."

"I thought you lived on the farm?"

"I do, but not in the main house with my parents. I moved into a cabin on the edge of the property after high school. Didn't want to be one of those guys who was thirty and living in my childhood bedroom."

What did his cabin look like? She imagined rustic tranquility. Was he messy or neat? Was his furniture sophisticated or homey? Did animal heads or paintings hang on the walls? How big was his bed? Her wandering thoughts got stuck on the last question.

"It sounds lovely." Her voice came out breathy, and she cleared her throat to get a handle on her imagination.

"It's all right, I guess." It didn't sound all right. He sounded as unhappy as she felt.

She would give up her firstborn—not that she was likely to ever bear one—to plant her roots in a home. Not merely a house, but someplace warm and welcoming and comfortable. A home where she could be herself.

Her posh childhood had not been jolly. The freedom she'd achieved by running away hadn't satisfied her either. What would make her happy?

She wasn't sure, but since deciding to lie low in Highland, a mirage had appeared on the horizon; in it, she walked down a street that looked remarkably like the street outside, and she wasn't alone. A man with a smile to melt all the snows across the Highlands was by her side.

"Will your mum and dad be home for Christmas?" she asked to change the subject.

"I don't know. They're going to take in the sights and a few shows in New York City—Mom loves musicals—and then who knows? Florida maybe. Someplace warmer than here." He shrugged. Affection warmed his voice when he spoke of his parents, but she could also sense a tinge of hurt feelings.

"Let me guess . . . only child?"

The distance between them had closed inch by inch while they'd been whispering as if unseen forces were ratcheting them together. He was tall and broad and his scowl might have intimidated her if she didn't know him better. Her shiver had nothing to do with fear. Which was scary. She took a step back, but the shelves precluded a true retreat.

"What does being an only child have to do with anything?" he asked suspiciously.

"You're used to being the center of your parents' attention and you resent them for leaving you the entire responsibility of your family farm while they gallivant around having fun. Without you. If you had a brother or sister to share the burden—and attention—with, you might not be so resentful about their leaving."

She tensed, waiting for his reaction. He had every right to tell her to mind her own business. Instead, he opened his mouth and then closed it with a self-deprecating chuckle. "You didn't just put me in my place, you shoved me there with a well-aimed kick to my ass."

"You aren't angry?" She wanted to stuff the question back in her mouth when he narrowed his eyes on her and his smile diminished to a mere shadow.

"For telling me what you really think? Hardly. Most men appreciate the truth."

A guffaw escaped before she could muffle it.

"I take it your experience has been different?" His voice had softened even further, and he leaned closer with his whisper.

The silence in the library felt cathedral-like, and as if she were in a confessional, she answered him. "Quite different. Opposite, in fact. Men will say anything to get what they want, and after they do, they discard you like rubbish."

"Sounds to me like you've known all the wrong men."

"I can't argue with that. Musicians are notorious for bad behavior. It's one reason I wanted off the road." It wasn't a lie, but her father had been the first man to disappoint her.

"There are good men in the world."

"Are there?" Her voice lilted up into a question. A week ago, she could have said good men were close to extinction with a surety she now lacked, because the man standing in front of her was strong evidence to the contrary.

"I'll prove to you good men exist." His jaw had firmed with a stubbornness that was undeniably attractive.

She faked a lighthearted laugh. "I'm a lost cause. It would be like trying to convince a bairn who had seen Saint Nicholas take off his beard that he was real. In short, it will take a miracle."

His smile was slow and sexy and made his blue eyes dance. "You're in luck. Christmas in Highland is the perfect place for a miracle."

Chapter Five

Holt plucked the audiobooks from Claire's hands and strolled toward the checkout counter to hand them over for scanning, leaving Claire looking decidedly bemused. If their meeting in the library had proved anything, it was that the connection he felt wasn't one-sided. He'd only taken a half dozen steps toward the door when her shoulder brushed his arm as she fell into step beside him. He stole a glance down at her without tilting his head.

Slowly—very slowly—he was chipping away at her defenses, but if he probed too far, she would scurry back into her hidey-hole. What had made her so squirrelly? At least one asshole was involved, but her wounds cut deeper and wider than a couple of bad relationships. They went back to childhood.

"Okay, my turn. Are you an only child as well?" he asked as casually as he could manage. He wouldn't be surprised if she made a break for it.

Her hesitation left a palpable tension between them. While it wasn't sexual, he could extrapolate. Claire would bring the same tension and challenge into bed.

It was a heady, if inappropriate, thought to have pop into his head.

"Yes." Although the single word was curt and didn't invite further questions, he savored her answer as a victory, and was happy when she asked, "What led you to that conclusion?"

"Siblings are contractually obligated to get all up in each other's business. Yet you don't even have a cell phone to text anyone from back home. Ergo, it's just you and your parents." Another possibility inserted itself. "Or maybe they've passed on?"

At her silence, he stopped before they exited the library, guided her into the privacy of the stacks to his right, and stammered out an apology, but she cut him off by raising her hand. "My parents are still very much alive in Scotland."

"Are you planning on going home for Christmas?"

"I'm not sure. No. Maybe." She sighed and rolled her eyes, but her frustration seemed to be directed at herself. "As a matter of fact, I have some decisions to make."

"Regarding your family?"

"My family. My career. My future. They're tangled together. But I'm not ready to tackle it yet."

It wasn't much, but at least she was planning to stick around for a while longer. He'd have to make the days, and hopefully weeks, count. After all, he'd promised her to introduce her to a good man. Namely, one Holt J. Pierson.

"By the way, why are you here?" She gestured around them.

"Philosophically speaking? Are we here or is it all a dream?" Playing dumb was a terrible strategy, but better than the truth. He'd seen her walk down the street from where he'd been having a coffee with Dr. Jameson, the local veterinarian, at the Brown Cow.

"At the library, you daft man. Aren't you going to check something out for yourself?" She gestured toward the audiobooks he'd checked out for Ms. Meadows.

"Yep. Of course I was. I got distracted." Tumbleweeds filled his head. He glanced at the nearest books, which happened to be cookbooks. He grabbed a random one off the shelf. "A cookbook. I'll need to make something impressive if I plan a dinner party."

Her brows bounced higher. "You're really going to do it? I can't believe it."

"I'm full of surprises."

She nodded at the book. "Apparently so. What are you going to make? There's nothing better than a cheese soufflé."

He actually looked at the book. *Adventures in French Cuisine.* Lord help him. But her declaration had provided him with an opening. "Well then, I'll make you one."

"You don't—"

"How about Saturday evening?"

"But Ms. Meadows—"

"Will be fine on her own for a couple of hours. I'll make sure she has my number and if she needs help, we can be there in a jiffy. Anyway, you leave her alone to come to town often enough."

He could almost see her trying to come up with an argument against his logic. Finally, she threw her hands up. "Fine. Saturday-night soufflé sounds delish actually. Saturdays are always ham, beans, and corn bread for Ms. Meadows."

After Holt had checked out the fancy French cookbook, they strolled out of the library together, stopping to admire the Christmas tree dominating the small courtyard between the brick storefronts on Main

Street. Jessie Joe and Jessie Mac stood holding a giant star while staring at the top of the tree.

"What's up, boys?" Holt clapped Jessie Joe on the shoulder while shaking Jessie Mac's hand. "This here is Claire Smythe. She's staying out with Ms. Meadows."

"Nice to meet you, Miss Claire," Jessie Joe said. "Ms. Meadows taught me and Jessie Mac biology. Best teacher I ever had."

"What?" Claire gaped slightly at the two men. Holt was just as surprised.

"Yep. We all had a crush on her back then, didn't we?" Jessie Joe elbowed his cousin, who merely nodded. "It was a sad day when she quit teaching."

"Why did she quit?" Holt asked.

"Got married. Had a kid." Jessie Joe shrugged and turned his attention back to the tree. "We're waiting for the utility truck so we can use the basket to get the star on top. It's a mighty pretty tree, ain't it?"

"You've done a fine job." Christmas spirit flickered inside Holt like a partly screwed-in Christmas light. He had been feeling sorry for himself lately, but Claire had provided a jolt.

"You wait until it's all lit up," Jessie Joe said. "There won't be a Grinch left in Highland."

Even Claire took in the tree with a little smile on her face. The sound of incoming machinery had them saying their goodbyes to the cousins so they could top the tree with the star.

"Do you have a Christmas tree?" she asked once they were away from the noise.

"Not yet." He hadn't planned on putting one up, but he found his mind changing in an instant. Maybe he'd even trek out into the woods behind the cabin and cut a fresh tree to decorate. "Does Ms. Meadows have one up?"

"No, and she hasn't mentioned one either." She kicked a pebble off the pavement and watched it skitter under the tire of a passing truck. "Her husband died around Christmas, I think."

Holt racked his brain, but couldn't remember Ms. Meadows as anything but a widow. "It must have been a long time ago."

"Thirty years or more. She's been lonely a long time now." The melancholy in her voice telegraphed the fact Claire had come to care for the old lady even if it was against her instincts.

"They must have loved each other very much."

"I guess." Skepticism was rife in her voice.

"You don't believe in good men or love? That's pitiful."

"Or is it realistic?" With a philosopher's tone, she continued. "Falling in love is merely a confluence of hormones and pheromones and dopamine. Once it peters out, people generally find themselves stuck in a relationship where they regret their choice of partners."

"I was wrong, that's not pitiful; that's downright bleak." Holt wasn't sure if he was amused or horrified.

"Have you loved anyone? Truly loved them?" She shot him a glance.

He rubbed the back of his neck, running through the list of women he'd dated. He'd liked several and had fun with most, but he hadn't fallen in love with any of them. Many of his exes had gone on to marry other men, though. They seemed completely capable of falling in love. Was he deficient in one of three ingredients needed to actually love someone? Talk about bleak.

"No, I can't say that I have. What about you?" he asked.

"Me either," she said simply.

"Does it make you feel sad or bad or whatever?"

"It makes me feel glad. It means I'll never get hurt." She ducked in front of him.

He took her hand before she could escape. "How about I give you a lift home?"

"No, thank you. I have more errands and don't know how long I'll be. I'll see you later." The set of her chin signaled her determination to accept as little help as possible. While it frustrated him, he admired her spirit.

He dropped his hand. "Don't forget about Saturday-night soufflé."

"I'm looking forward to it." Her scrunched brows belied the words. Did she already regret agreeing? Well, too bad. He wasn't letting her off the hook.

With a quick step, she navigated the sidewalk, flipping her hoodie over her head and ignoring the people she passed. Her destination was the Drug and Dime.

Her words twanged like a tuning fork in his head. *I'll never get hurt.* No one who hadn't experienced heartache swore off love so adamantly. She had a story he wanted to hear, but more than anything, he wanted her to trust him enough to tell it.

Claire ducked down an aisle in the Drug and Dime while watching the front window of the store. Her view of Holt was impeded somewhat by the Santa Claus with his sleigh full of presents painted on the window.

What was he thinking after their weirdly philo-sophical conversation about love? And how in the world had he never been trapped in the obnoxious, painful state? He was practically perfect.

No. No one was perfect. That's what a person learned once the dopamine wore off and the cloud of pheromones cleared.

He strolled off with his head down and his hands

stuffed into the pockets of his jeans. She stared at his bum—which was perfect—until he disappeared.

Turning her attention to the shelves in front of her, she racked her brain to remember what Ms. Meadows had asked her to pick up. The Drug and Dime was a pharmacy that carried an assortment of groceries for customers who couldn't make the trek to the large box store on the edge of town.

It took a moment for her to realize she was staring at hemorrhoid cream. Definitely not on her list.

She backpedaled and bumped into someone's shoulder. The person stumbled to the side, items tumbling to the floor.

"Bollocks! Pardon me." Claire bent down to help the woman pick up the scattered boxes around their feet and did a double take as she straightened.

The woman wore heavy black combat-style boots similar to Claire's. The laces trailed to the ground as if she'd been in a hurry when she got dressed. In contrast, a light-as-a-cloud multicolored tutu puffed around her legs. Her sweatshirt was frayed at the collar with the letters UGA emblazoned in bright red across the front. A thick braid of red hair hung over one shoulder.

It was Anna Maitland. She had been a bundle of explosive energy running the summer festival. While she was still strikingly pretty, the dark circles under her blue eyes stood out against her wan complexion. She looked as if her last good night of sleep had been months ago.

"Ah! The lead singer of the Scunners. Claire, right? Iain told me he'd met you at the Brown Cow the other day." The woman's smile banished the shadows in her expression to the edges, almost making Claire wonder if she'd imagined the woman's weariness. "I'm

Anna Maitland. We met briefly over the summer during the festival."

"Aye, I remember."

"I own Maitland Dance Studio across the street." Anna pointed, but Claire didn't bother to turn and look. She'd seen the kiddies filing into and out of the studio.

"That explains your outfit."

Anna gave a rueful laugh. "I forget I have it on sometimes. I had no idea you were staying in Highland after the festival."

"Yes, well. I got tired of the musician's lifestyle. Highland seemed like a nice place to figure out what's next." Claire congratulated herself for telling the truth.

Anna squinted and tilted her head to see under Claire's hoodie. "You've changed your hair, haven't you?"

"I went back to my natural color. For shows, I used a temporary artificial red dye to stand out under the lights." Claire touched the hair at her neck, and the hoodie fell back to her shoulders. "I'm letting it grow out too. It's at that weird in-between stage."

"Does that mean you aren't performing anymore?"

A shock of pain spurred her heart faster. When she'd left the Scunners, she had left the road, but was that the end of everything? "I guess I'm not."

An awkward silence descended. Anna's gaze darted to Claire's hands, and her expression morphed into horror. Claire looked down. She held an item Anna had dropped.

"Pardon me." She held out the white box, the script coming into sharp focus the first time.

A pregnancy test. Anna snatched it out of her hand and held it along with two others close to her chest, the colors marking them as three different brands. Anna wore no wedding ring, which didn't matter in this day and age, but might explain the worry on her face at the reality of an unplanned pregnancy.

"It's not what you think," Anna said.

Claire held up her hands. "It's really none of my business."

Anna mouthed what sounded like a colorful American curse and ignored Claire's declaration to the contrary. "What am I saying? It's exactly what you think. Why else would I be in a pharmacy buying three pregnancy tests?"

Claire didn't want to get involved. She should wish the woman good luck, get on her bike, and follow Ms. Meadows's example and become a hermit in the woods.

"Can I help?" The offer popped out before Claire could stop it. A fellow woman was in need. A fellow redhead at that.

"I would be forever in your debt if you would buy these for me." Anna shoved the boxes toward Claire, who took them reflexively.

"I don't have enough money." Her face heated at the admission.

"I'll give you the money. I just . . . It's going to sound so immature, but—" Anna looked up and down the aisle to confirm they were alone. "Everyone knows me. If I buy these, the word will get around town before I even have a chance to pee on it. I could drive to the next town over, but I have classes all day and need to know. Now. I'm going crazy."

Claire had no social currency in Highland to bankrupt. No one knew her and she didn't have a reputation to lose. "I'd be happy to take them through the checkout."

Anna whispered, "Thank you," a dozen times while

fishing out two twenty-dollar bills. "Could you bring them over to the studio for the handoff?"

After Claire agreed, Anna swept out of the store and jogged across the street, the wind fluttering her tutu.

Three tests seemed like overkill, but it wasn't her money. Claire wandered to the grocery section of the Drug and Dime, finally recalling the buttermilk Ms. Meadows had tasked her with buying.

With an uncomfortable smile, she didn't meet the shopgirl's eyes as she rang up the tests and the quart of buttermilk. Claire made the purchases in record time and was back on the pavement, clutching the bags close even though she was confident no one with X-ray vision wandered the streets of Highland.

Electronic chimes announced her entrance into Maitland Dance Studio. Anna emerged from a door in the back, an expansive dance floor framing her.

"Thanks again. You're a lifesaver." Anna barked a nervous laugh and gestured her over. "A reputation saver at any rate."

Claire followed her into the studio space and held out the bag with the tests, putting her other things on a small table by the door covered in brochures for the dance studio. "No worries. Here you are."

Anna took the bag and checked inside, gnawing her bottom lip before slapping on an obviously fake smile and looking up. "Where are you from in Scotland?"

"Glasgow." It was the same lie she'd given Iain. Actually, it wasn't a lie, it just wasn't the entire truth. As soon as it was socially acceptable, Claire had been sent to boarding school in England.

She'd been homesick and wanted to return to Scotland. Her first school holiday home had reminded her how lonely she had been, though, and she'd gladly returned to school. All the girls came from wealthy backgrounds, many richer and better-connected than hers. The Glennallen name held no special cachet at school. The taste of normalcy had driven her to pursue music and join the Scunners. In hindsight, her life had been anything but normal.

"Iain spent some time in Glasgow after he left the service. He didn't like it. Said it was too big, and he moved back to Cairndow, on the coast, before coming to Highland."

"Iain seems nice."

Anna's hands tightened, crumpling the top of the bag. "According to the more conservative residents of Highland, Iain and I are living in sin."

Claire was having a difficult time sussing out how Anna felt about Iain and the possibility of a positive test. "Living with a bloke isn't all that unusual these days, is it?"

"I suppose not. Except when you're mayor of a small town. Living in sin is one thing; getting pregnant while unmarried is another." Anna's eyes rolled up like a panicked horse ready to bolt, and she paced the dance floor. "I don't even know if Iain wants kids. Or if I want kids, for that matter. I mean, I like them and all. I teach them. I'm a godmother, for goodness' sake. But—" She waved one of her hands around as if trying to pluck the right words from thin air.

Claire could sense the other woman's swelling panic. "It's different, because you aren't responsible for those kids twenty-four seven."

Anna snapped and pointed at Claire. "Exactly. I have a physically demanding business to run. A town to manage. I can't do that with a baby. Can I?"

It seemed as if Anna hadn't asked in a rhetorical

fashion and expected a proper answer from Claire who had a sight less experience with kiddies than Anna did.

"Sure you can. They make those pump thingies"— Claire gestured to her own chest—"and slings to carry them around in when they're wee things. You could set up a bassinet in the corner. I'll bet watching people dance would be quite stimulating for a bairn's brain."

Anna stared wide-eyed at the nonsense that had come out of Claire's mouth. Claire only knew what she'd seen on the telly. "Actually, forget everything I said. I'm useless."

"No, you're right. It's not a total disaster, is it? I mean, I love Iain and he loves me. He won't run off in the middle of the night in a panic, will he?"

"I'm sure he would never do that." Claire wasn't sure and was afraid her uncertainty telegraphed in her voice. After all, she had only met Iain Connors one time over a cuppa, but Anna was on the edge of falling apart. She needed was a friend. A friend who would lie and tell her everything would be fine. Everyone needed one of those on occasion, but Claire feared she wasn't qualified. "Do you want me to call someone? A friend? Iain? Maybe your mum?"

"My mom moved to Florida, my best friend moved to Scotland, and I don't want to tell Iain unless the test is positive." Anna looked over to a door with a unisex bathroom sign. "And if it is . . ." Possibilities roiled in the silence.

"Not knowing is worse than knowing one way or the other," Claire said as if she possessed a dram of wisdom, which she didn't. If Anna knew how difficult it was for Claire to make a decision or embrace responsibility, she wouldn't be looking to her for support or advice.

"Could you stick around for a couple of minutes?"

Anna pulled out one of the tests and stared at it. "At least five according to the box. I don't want to be alone." The last she added in a soft voice Claire couldn't deny.

"Of course. I'm not in any hurry. Go on, then, and take it."

Anna disappeared into the bathroom. Claire stared at the door for a long moment. When Anna didn't reappear, she wandered over to the ballet bar mounted on a wall lined with mirrors.

It had been months since Claire had spent more than a few seconds in front of a mirror. Thankfully, the soft white light reflecting off the wood floors was flattering.

The bike riding under the winter sun had given her face more color than usual. While her hair was choppy, it was beginning to curl at the edges, giving her a gamine appearance that wasn't as boyish as she'd feared. Her natural red sparked attractively in the light. There was nothing she could do about her clothes. The layers made her look boxy, but they were warm and comfortable.

She'd left her stage costumes behind with her bandmates and wouldn't be surprised if another woman was already wearing them in her place as lead singer. Which was fine. It's not like she had a use for tight leather pants and sequined tank tops.

Except she wouldn't have minded a few sexy pieces to wear to Holt's cabin for Saturday-night soufflé. She wanted to capture his attention and keep it. At least for as long as she was in Highland. Without her stage persona and sexy outfits, she would have to rely on her ripped jeans and sweatshirts and not-so-sparkling personality.

That nailed it. She would get in touch with him somehow—smoke signals? Morse code?—and bow out of his dinner party. The decision filled her with relief and regret.

How many minutes had ticked off? At least five. Claire rapped lightly on the bathroom door and pushed it open a crack. "Anna? Everything okay?"

"I don't know." Anna's voice came from the back corner, trembly and weak.

Claire entered and sidestepped to the second of two stalls. Anna sat on the toilet lid holding white stick in one hand and a paper covered in tiny lettering in the other.

"Did you wee on it?" Claire asked.

Anna nodded.

"Are you . . . ?"

Anna shook her head. "Afraid to look."

"Do you want me to look and tell you what it means?"

Anna held out the stick and what turned out to be the instructions. Claire had never taken a pregnancy test. She'd been scrupulously careful with her sexual partners. Her life was already complicated enough without adding a baby.

Claire held the stick up. Turns out she didn't need the instructions, as the word PREGNANT was boldly displayed in red. Anna had dropped her head in her hands, her fingers clenched in her hair, wisps of red sticking out from her braid.

Claire wasn't sure how to impart the news. Should she gently ease Anna into her new reality or give her a shove? "You're pregnant."

Anna didn't move or acknowledge the shove in any way.

"You're pregnant, Anna. I'm—" Was this a situation that demanded congratulations or commiseration? Claire wasn't sure, so she stilled her tongue and let Anna assimilate the news.

Anna's rapid breaths reverberated off the tiled floors and walls. Finally, she stood and smoothed her tutu, her fingers staying to fiddle with the hem. "That is obviously a defective test. I can't be pregnant. We've been careful. How could this happen? What am I going to do?"

Anna had pinged from denial to acceptance to panic in record-setting time.

Claire patted Anna's arm awkwardly. "Birth control fails all the time. If Iain is that bad, then you have choices, don't you?"

"Iain's not bad. He's wonderful. Amazing. Our life right now is nearly perfect. That's the problem." Anna closed her eyes and covered her mouth. "I think I'm going to be sick."

It took a few beats to realize Anna wasn't speaking metaphorically. Claire flipped the lid of the toilet open and pulled Anna's braid out of the way while she retched. Claire looked anywhere but down, feeling sympathetic queasiness herself.

After the storm had passed, Anna grabbed some tissue to wipe her mouth, flushed, then staggered to her feet and the sink. She rinsed out her mouth and splashed water on her pasty-looking face.

Not sure what to do, Claire stood close to the door and escape, thumbing over her shoulder. "Would you like to take another test for confirmation?"

Anna's bark of laughter was uncomfortably loud in the small space. "No. My gut told me I was pregnant before I even peed on the first test. Me tossing my biscuits, as Iain would say, is enough confirmation."

"If Iain is a good bloke and your life with him is perfect, then what's the problem?" Claire asked.

Anna turned and leaned against the counter. "We haven't been together very long. Just since the festival.

A baby"—she stumbled over the word—"was not in the plans. We agreed to take things slow, and now I've screwed it all up." Tears shone in her eyes.

"Unless biology has undergone a transformation, he is as responsible for the situation as you," Claire said with more tartness than she'd intended. It was infuriating that women took the brunt of responsibility and castigation in these circumstances. "Do you want to keep the baby?" she asked bluntly.

Anna's hand went to her belly as if already protecting it. "I don't know."

"That's the first thing you should decide. Talk to Iain. Will he stick by you and the baby if you choose to have it?"

"I don't have a great track record of people sticking in my life, but I think so."

"Do you want to be together baby or no baby?"

Anna didn't shy away from the question but seemed to give it due consideration. "Yeah, I do. I want him for forever no matter what."

"Then tell him that."

"Do you mean I should ask him to marry me?" Her voice rose to a near squeak of fright.

"Not necessarily. You can have a baby together without getting married." Claire shrugged. "But if you love him and want to be with him forever, then why not get married?"

"*Why not?*" Anna repeated as if Claire had suggested she jump off a cliff.

Then Anna did something that rocked Claire back on her heels, both physically and metaphorically. She threw herself into Claire for a hug. A tight one she couldn't wriggle out of without seeming rude.

It had been a long time since she'd had a real friend.

The boys in the band had been like brothers. Annoying ones, at that.

A few of the girls at boarding school had been friends. They borrowed one another's clothes and whispered about boys at night, but those relationships hadn't lasted beyond school. Once they'd gone their separate ways, promises to text and meet up were forgotten. What had happened to those girls? Had they fared better than she had? Had they made better decisions?

She stood still, her arms hanging uselessly at her sides. It took a few breaths to turn her focus outward and realize Anna was crying on her shoulder. Like a seed finding itself in rich soil, something in Claire's heart sprouted, and her arms found their way around Anna. Claire patted her on the back and murmured, "There, there. Everything will turn out fine no matter what you decide."

And Claire was confident that it would. For Anna, at least. Why couldn't Claire be as confident in her own future?

Taking a shuddery breath, Anna lifted her head but didn't break their connection. "I don't know what's wrong with me. I hardly ever cry."

"I expect it's the hormones," Claire said with more expertise than she felt.

Anna let out a gasping laugh, smiling even as tears still wet her cheeks. "I'm sure you're right. I'm sorry for turning into a blubbery mess. You must think I'm nuts. We just met."

Claire was actually thinking how nice it was to have something resembling a friend. "I don't know many people in Highland. Just the preacher, Ms. Meadows, and Holt Pierson."

Anna unrolled some toilet tissue and blew her nose. "That needs to change."

A streak of fear jolted Claire back a step toward the door. This was why she couldn't afford a friend. "Ms. Meadows keeps me busy. In fact, her buttermilk is getting warm, and I need to be getting back to cook her supper."

Anna grabbed her by the wrist. "Do you mind keeping this news to yourself? I need time to process it and decide how best to handle it."

"Of course. Your secrets are safe with me." Claire was the keeper of many secrets. One more wouldn't be a burden.

The two women exited the bathroom together.

"Thanks." Anna glanced up at a wall clock featuring a ballerina whose legs moved around the face and groaned. "I've got a class to teach in a quarter of an hour."

"It'll be a good distraction." Singing on stage had been Claire's escape until she couldn't run any longer.

"What's your number?" Anna called out when Claire was halfway out the door.

"Sorry, I don't have a mobile," Claire said with a tight smile as she slipped outside with her things. Keeping her head down, she crossed the street and retrieved her bike from the mouth of the alley.

All of a sudden, she was feeling conspicuous. It was nerve racking. Holt and Anna had turned their gazes on her and left her vulnerable. The promise of friendship dangled from Anna. Claire wasn't sure what kind of promise Holt offered, but it seemed more complicated than mere friendship.

Claire stowed the buttermilk and the audiobooks in the basket on the front of the bike and set off toward home.

Home.

The word echoed in her head. She shouldn't think of Ms. Meadows's house as her home because it wasn't. It was a temporary place to land. She couldn't get attached to Ms. Meadows or Anna or Highland—and most especially not to Holt Pierson.

Chapter Six

The sky overhead was blue for the moment, but the chilly wind whipping around her portended another storm. Claire coasted down the hill toward Ms. Meadows's house. The changeable weather reminded her of Scotland. She couldn't worry about what was going on above her, because the most dangerous section of road was upcoming. It narrowed and grew rocky at the edges. She wished for a scant few inches on the safe side of the crumbling yellow line.

A truck appeared on the rise heading in her direction, and she braced herself for the buffeting wind it would produce on its way past her in the other lane. Claire kept her head down and concentrated on keeping the bike on the straight and narrow. After Wayne's tune-up, at least the bike felt more stable.

A few minutes passed where her quickened breathing and the clank of her chain as she cycled were the only things she could hear. A roar grew louder behind her but she didn't dare glance over her shoulder. The motion might accidentally send her into the lane of traffic. A tiny puff of anticipation had her hoping it was Holt. If he offered a ride this time, she would say yes before he could finish the asking.

The pulse of bass music hit her, and she tightened her grip on her handlebars. She couldn't imagine Holt listening to rap, but people surprised her all the time, especially since she'd landed in Highland. The truck approached with the subtlety of an airplane landing, but as the bumper came into her periphery, the driver shifted over to pass her. Her shoulders relaxed slightly.

The truck's passenger window came even with her, and it slowed to pace her. She glanced over and caught a flash of white teeth in a spotted face. The teenage boy hollered something at her and the truck made a quick lurch in her direction. She reacted instinctively and jerked her bike toward the side of the road.

The driver of the truck accelerated and laughter carried over the growl of the engine. The front tire of the bike hit the crumbling gravel at the edge of the road. In slow motion, the bike skid and her center of balance shifted off the seat. She let go of the handlebars and closed her eyes, bracing for impact.

Her right hip and hand took the brunt of the fall. She came to a stop on her back, her arms thrown out to her sides, the fingers of her right hand digging into gravel and her left clutching a handful of grass.

Stunned like a bird hitting a window, she lay there, blinked up at the sky, and assessed her injuries. Her hip throbbed and her palm stung. She rotated her ankles. No excruciating pain, which meant she hadn't broken anything. She lifted her hands above her face. Her right hand was in the worst shape. Blood welled along a couple of scratches, and the rest of her palm was reddened and raw.

Besides processing the sudden shock, her brain

seemed to be working normally. She knew her name—her real one and her fake one—and what year it was. It didn't take long for anger to blossom. What a bunch of unholy gits. A string of Glaswegian curses rolled off her tongue with satisfaction. Holt had set a high bar when it came to gentlemanly behavior, and those boys hadn't had any trouble limboing under.

Sitting up, she looked around for her bike. The right handlebar had caught on the lowest string of a barbed-wire fence, which kept it from sliding down the embankment and into a puddle of mud. The buttermilk and audiobooks seemed to have survived minus a little dirt. A cow on the other side of the fence watched her and chewed its cud. She counted her blessings. Her bike was on this side of the fence, and the cow was on the other.

Gingerly, she rose and dusted herself off, wincing. Her hip would be bruised and her hand sore, but otherwise she would survive. She hauled the bike out from under the barbed wire and said a little prayer when a cursory examination showed that neither of her tubes had busted. Returning her things to the basket, she pushed the bike to the pavement.

With shaky knees, she looked up and down the road for traffic before straddling the bike and pushing off. The pedals flew around too fast. Her feet slipped off and nearly caused her to crash again. She walked the bike to the opposite side of the road and the flatter grassy verge to examine it. There was no tension in the gears because the chain was gone.

As it turned out, glares and curses didn't shame the chain into reappearing. There was nothing for it but to walk her bike back to Ms. Meadows's place. The wind whistled around her even though she wasn't riding. Dark clouds amassed on the horizon like an invading army. On her bike, she would have outrun them, but she was sure to get a soaking at a walk.

Had an evil fairy cursed her at birth or was her luck earned on the back of her bad decisions? She was going with the evil-fairy theory.

With her head down against the wind, she set off, pushing the bike. The occasional hill offered her tough going on the way up, but a break on the downward slope where she could coast while perched on the seat. Most of the country road was flat, and she plodded along, estimating she still had at least two miles to go.

The clouds began their assault and the temperature dropped along with the rain. She hesitated, then jogged with the bike across the road and continued her trudge under the cover of the trees. The bike bounced across the roots and rocks, but she was shielded from the worst of the rain.

She groaned. If Holt saw her now, she'd never hear the end of it. Even so, she glanced up and down the road, her heart dipping. All she could see in either direction were sheets of gray rain.

Holt tossed the French cookbook he'd checked out on his couch and huffed a laugh. He'd wanted a date with Claire and he'd gotten one in the most roundabout way possible. He'd have preferred taking her to the pub, but if what it took to get her alone was him navigating a complicated recipe, he would risk the possibility of food poisoning or burning his cabin to the ground.

The fever of his anticipation was alternately exciting and uncomfortable. She put him on uneven ground. He'd been stuck in a mire for so long, he'd forgotten what it felt like to not know what he was risking or how far he might fall. Their date—he hoped to goodness she considered it a date too—loomed with importance.

With the clouds gathering on the horizon, he got his chores done. While he fed the goats, he wondered if she would find their antics as amusing as he did. While he refilled water bowls for the barn cats, he thought she might like one of the kittens still suckling from its mama. And as he moved baled hay into the feeding corrals for the cows, he cursed his lack of self-restraint.

His inability to focus on anyone or anything else besides her was worrisome, but not enough to stop himself from heading to Ms. Meadows's house to see her. Anyway, he had the perfect excuse. Before heading back to his cabin to clean up, he grabbed his dad's dusty CD player and stowed it on the floorboard of his truck. He could spin the visit as merely being neighborly. He was basically Mr. Rogers.

By the time he'd showered and pulled on clean clothes, rain pattered against the windows. Nerves had him goosing the gas and kicking up gravel on the way to Ms. Meadows's place. Would he be greeted with the wrong end of a shotgun again?

He would take his chances. Cradling the CD player, he walked up the porch steps, rapped on the front door, and rocked on his feet while waiting to see how he would be received by the ladies of the house.

Ms. Meadows opened the door. His rehearsed greeting flew from his mind on seeing her serious expression. The grooves around her mouth had deepened and aged her.

A frisson of her worry arced to him, clipping his words. "What's wrong, ma'am?"

"Claire isn't home."

"You mean, she never made it back from town?"

Ms. Meadows's hands restlessly moved along the top curve of her cane, transmitting her disquiet. "I called down to the Drug and Dime, and she was there, but that was some time ago."

Best-case scenario, her errands had run long and she'd taken refuge in the Brown Cow or the library until the rain passed. Worst case, she had started home and gotten caught by the storm. He cursed himself for letting her bike the narrow road. Not that he'd had a choice. There was no *letting* Claire do anything. She was dead set on remaining independent even when common sense should have prevailed.

"I'll find her." He didn't shy away from Ms. Meadows's gaze, and considering their last interaction, she surprised him by reaching out and squeezing his hand. Hers was cool, the skin soft and fragile.

"I've become fond of the girl. I'll blame myself if something has happened." The emotion in Ms. Meadows's voice was unexpectedly raw.

"I'll find her," he repeated.

He set the CD player on a porch chair and patted her hand before ducking through the rain to his truck. His tires spun on his quick reverse up the lane. He flipped his wipers to high and drove toward town, scanning both sides of the road.

What if she'd wrecked on the slick pavement? Or what if she'd been hit and thrown into the woods or down into the field? His stomach cramped and his palms grew clammy on his steering wheel. With his imagination traversing dark roads, he almost didn't spot her in the shadows of the trees.

A curse born of relief snuck out. He slowed the truck and pulled it to the side of the road. Leaving the truck running, he hopped out and skidded down the pebbled slope toward her. While the trees had offered some protection from the onslaught, her hair was plastered to her head, her hoodie was hanging heavy and wet, and her jeans were a shade darker from the soaking.

She looked like a disgruntled cat forced to take a bath. A wave of affection overwhelmed him. He wrapped his arms around her before he had a chance to think it through.

Instead of shoving him away, she burrowed into him, her cold hands finding their way between his pullover and his T-shirt.

"You scared me," he murmured, his lips glancing over the top of her head.

"I was scared too." Her voice was muffled against him.

"What happened?"

"A truck full of arseholes ran me off the road." While anger heated her voice, she trembled in his arms. Was it fear or cold?

He tightened his hold on her. "Did they hit you?"

"No, but they went out of their way to scare me." In a smaller but no less furious voice, she said, "They must have seen me go over the handlebars, but they didn't even stop."

Holt was ready to bang some heads together. Chances were he knew them, or their parents. "Did you get a good look at the vehicle?"

"A black truck."

"Make and model? License plate number?"

She pulled away slightly and gave him a look rife with mockery. "I was a little busy trying to keep my head from cracking open."

Even though she was joking, the very real possibility she could have been seriously injured shot his knees with jelly. "How did you land?"

"Hip and hand." She held up her right hand. The

palm was covered in road rash, but the scratches weren't deep.

"You didn't hit your head?"

"Wait? Who are you again?" Did her teasing lilt make him feel better or worse?

He cupped her cold damp cheek. "You can't keep biking to town."

"You're right."

Satisfaction shot through him. He'd won.

"Not until I get the chain fixed," she added.

His satisfaction deflated, and he took her shoulders in a little shake. "Don't you give a damn about your-self?"

Her shoulders tensed. "I've taken fine care of myself for a long time before I met you."

Holt harrumphed. "Why is it so hard for you to ac-cept help?"

She opened her mouth then closed it, her gaze turn-ing unsure behind her usual brashness. They stared into each other's eyes for a long moment, and he won-dered what she saw in him. A friend? A foe?

He didn't know what to say to get through to her, so he didn't say anything at all. Instead, he did what he'd dreamed about doing, what he'd thought about doing every waking second since meeting her.

He kissed her.

Keeping his hands on her shoulders, he loosened his grip, not wanting to imprison her if she chose to escape. He let his lips linger on hers, tasting the fresh-ness of the rain. The scent of the pine needles under-foot and loamy forest surrounded them.

Her hands looped around his neck and drew him closer. With her permission given, he wrapped his arms around her, lifting her slightly off the ground and into his body. Although her stature was slight, she possessed the energy of compressed atoms ready to explode.

He mapped the delicacy of her spine and the curve of her hips with his fingers. She gasped when he gave her ass a squeeze, but wiggled closer, fitting her hips against his as if they'd been carved from the same piece of wood. It had been a long time—maybe ever—since he'd fit so well with someone.

Her tongue daubed against his lower lip, and he opened to welcome her in to play. A noise between a sigh and a moan rose from her throat. As their kiss was hitting overdrive, the blare of a horn shattered the sense of intimacy. He stepped away from her and shifted toward the road, where a truck was pulling over.

The passenger window rolled down, framing Dr. Jameson, his expression a mystery from the distance. "All right there, Holt? I got worried when I saw your truck."

Holt waved two fingers over his head and fumbled for words. "Truck's fine. We're fine, Doc. I'm . . . We're . . ."

Dr. Jameson put him out of his misery. "I'll leave you to it, then."

He rolled up the window and pulled away, leaving the sound of the rain through the trees to fill the silence.

A raindrop slid down the back of his neck into his shirt. He shivered. Claire must be a million times more uncomfortable.

"Let me get you home before Ms. Meadows calls in reinforcements. She's beside herself." He picked up her bike and hauled it up the slippery slope to put in the bed of his truck.

Claire scrambled up close behind and swung herself

into the cab before he could offer her a hand. When he joined her, he ratcheted up the heat, taking note of the way she hunched and tucked her hands under her thighs.

A mournful country song filled the ride back to Ms. Meadows. "I knew you didn't listen to rap," Claire murmured.

The truck ate up the distance in minutes. Ms. Meadows was waiting on the porch when he pulled in. If she hadn't had mobility issues, Holt had no doubt she would be pacing.

Claire hopped out and ran-walked to the cover of the porch. Ms. Meadows pulled her in for a hug, not caring that she was soaked to the bone. Holt lifted her bike from the bed and pushed it to the porch. Claire leaned into the embrace and rested her forehead on Ms. Meadows's shoulder for a moment before pulling away and wrapping her arms around herself.

She might profess her desire to stay above the fray of human frailty, but she was starved for affection and support. That need was something Holt understood.

"What happened?" Ms. Meadows asked.

"The chain on the bike snapped, and then the rains came. I was waiting it out under some trees when Holt found me." Claire cut a glance toward Holt with a clear request. She didn't want Ms. Meadows to know she'd taken a tumble.

It was difficult to remain silent when confronted by Ms. Meadows's sharp gaze. "Come in and warm up, Holt."

He hesitated at the bottom of the steps, not sure if Claire wanted him there. Their kiss had left behind a discordant undertone. She didn't meet his eyes, and he waffled, worried if he let her stew on the kiss she would talk herself out of dinner Saturday night.

A smile erased the earlier worry and took a decade off Ms. Meadows's face. Holt could imagine she'd been quite a catch back in the day. "Are you scared of a little old lady?" she asked.

The shot of humor and unexpected welcome drew him forward. "In case you're interested, I left my last will and testament on my kitchen table so the police could find it."

"I promise not to touch my gun." Ms. Meadows barked a laugh and led the way through the screen door. "You go take a hot shower, girl, while Holt and I have a drink."

"Yes, ma'am." The deference in Claire's voice surprised him, although anyone with eyes could see her relationship with Ms. Meadows went beyond caregiver and client. In fact, it wasn't clear who was caring for who.

Holt followed Ms. Meadows and only caught a glimpse of an old-fashioned wooden dresser and colorful quilt before Claire disappeared inside her room with a last inscrutable look aimed in his direction.

Ms. Meadows led him into the heart of the house—the kitchen. She sat heavily at a wooden table with a scarred top. He hesitated at the door, remembering what had brought him to the house to begin with.

"Hang on, I left something on the porch for you," he said. "Did you notice?"

Ms. Meadows's brows rose over the top of her glasses. "I didn't pay it any mind. Too preoccupied."

Holt retrieved the CD player from the chair on the porch. His feet slowed in front of Claire's door. The shower was running. Forcing all thoughts of Claire naked under the hot water out of his head, he returned to the kitchen and set the player on the table in front of Ms. Meadows like an offering.

"I hope you can get some use out of it. It's been collecting dust in the office," he said.

"I appreciate the thought, but what's it for?"

"Uh-oh, I ruined Claire's surprise. She checked out a couple of audiobooks for you."

"That was mighty sweet of her." Ms. Meadows's smile was shadowed. "I didn't want help around here, but after my fall in the spring, Preacher Hopkins insisted. Claire has been an unexpected blessing."

Holt cursed himself for not knowing she'd had a fall. He was her nearest neighbor, and he'd failed. "Did you hurt yourself badly?"

"Nothing broken, thank the Lord, but I was bruised. Body and ego. I feel forty up here"—she tapped her temple—"but my body reflects every year."

Holt couldn't think of anything comforting to say. No one could outrun the march of time. Ms. Meadows cleared her throat and jabbed her cane toward the counter. "Why don't you make yourself useful?"

"What do you need me to do?"

"First off, there's a bottle of whisky in the top cabinet. Pour two glasses."

That was an order he would happily fulfill. He gave her a mocking salute. "Yes, ma'am. I'd taken you for a teetotaler."

The half-full bottle had a fine layer of dust. He retrieved two heavy tumblers and poured them each two generous fingers. He set one in front of Ms. Meadows.

"Samuel, my late husband, and I enjoyed an evening tipple while we snuggled in front of the TV."

He hesitated with the glass halfway to his mouth. He'd known she was a widow, of course, but the affectionate mention of her husband made him curious. Instead of asking questions he had no right to, he threw his whisky back in one go. The warmth banished some of the chill spreading through him from his rain-dampened clothes. He poured himself another tot while Ms. Meadows sipped.

"Do you know how to make corn bread?" she asked.

"Erm . . . no." A bag of cornmeal and a carton of eggs were on the counter. A cast-iron skillet was oiled on the stove.

"What is the world coming to? I seem to remember your mama was a fine cook. She always brought a tasty casserole to the church potlucks." A grudging respect was in Ms. Meadows's tone, but she ruined it by tsking and adding, "Now I question her parenting choices for not teaching you to make corn bread."

Holt let the jab go considering he deserved worse. He was pleased not to be making his first corn bread at gunpoint. "Are you willing to make up for the deficiency?"

She harrumphed and banged her cane on the floor once. "I suppose I must if we want corn bread to go along with our soup beans."

She walked him through the process. It was a simple recipe, and the skillet was in the oven in a few minutes. He joined her at the table and nursed his remaining whisky.

"Of course, there's a spicy version with peppers and cheese and a sweet version with sugar, but I like the plain, old-fashioned kind." She barked a laugh. "That about sums me up too. Not spicy or sweet, but plain and old-fashioned."

"I ran across Jessie Joe and Jessie Mac in town. They send their regards. You were one of their favorite teachers. What grade did you teach?" he asked.

"High school biology. I only taught a few years." Her good humor dimmed, and Holt regretted his attempt at small talk. It seemed Ms. Meadows's past was littered with conversational mines.

Claire shuffled into the kitchen wearing black yoga pants and a bulky red Highland sweatshirt. Only the tips of her fingers were visible from the sleeves. Her hair was wet and tucked behind her ears, and her face was makeup-free and rosy from the hot shower.

"Holt made the corn bread," Ms. Meadows said. "As soon as it's ready, we can eat."

Holt tried to demur, but Ms. Meadows patted his hand. "It's the least I can offer for returning Claire home in one piece."

"It was less a rescue and more a mission of mercy," Claire interjected with more humor than heat. "That was a cold rain."

"Would you like a glass of whisky?" Holt half rose to retrieve another glass, but Claire waved him back down.

"I don't actually like whisky if you can believe it." She laughed and shook her head. He felt as if he were missing out on a joke.

"Don't mention that in front of Dr. Jameson. He's a fanatic," Holt said.

She merely hummed and glanced toward the oven. "Holt checked out a cookbook at the library today. French gourmet. Does he have a chance of pulling off a soufflé?"

Ms. Meadows looked at him with a pointed interest that made him squirm like she really was a teacher, and he was a student who had put tacks on her chair. "From not even knowing how to cook corn bread to a soufflé . . . That's quite a leap."

"I like a challenge." He tried to infuse his nonchalance with confidence and not incompetence.

"Who are you threatening with this experiment?" Ms. Meadows asked.

Holt leaned back in his chair with a slow smile. "Claire. I invited her over Saturday night. If it's okay with you, of course, Ms. Meadows."

"I don't have to go if you need me here." Claire worried her bottom lip. Was she recalling their kiss?

"I've lived for years on my own. I can handle one evening by myself, girl. You should go and have fun." Ms. Meadows thumped her fist on the table like a judge's gavel. "That's settled then. Holt, you will make Claire dinner Saturday evening."

"But what about— "

"I'll cozy up in bed with one of these fancy audio-books you checked out for me." Ms. Meadows tapped the CD player. "I don't suppose I can see what you chose."

"I'm such a numpty. I forgot all about them. And the buttermilk. I left them in the bike basket." Claire disappeared.

The oven beeped, and Ms. Meadows directed Holt. He was doling out the soup beans and corn bread in bowls when Claire returned.

"They're none the worse for my adventure." Claire handed the audiobooks to Ms. Meadows.

The delight with which the older woman examined the cases made him glance toward Claire. They locked eyes, exchanging a smile. It was the first time she'd really looked at him since their kiss. The tension across his shoulders loosened enough for him to enjoy the simple meal.

In fact, the last meal he'd enjoyed this much had been with his parents. He wasn't sure whether it was the food or the company that was so satisfying. Taking the cookbook had been a shot of providence. Cooking for himself was depressing; cooking for someone else was exciting.

The conversation meandered safe subjects including the upcoming Burns Night street festival.

"I'm not sure I would even recognize Main Street," Ms. Meadows said wistfully. "I haven't been able to drive in years, and the church van goes the back way."

"It's as pretty as ever and especially so this Christmas. Anna is going all-out on decorations. Why don't you allow me to escort you both to the festival?" Holt asked.

Claire glanced toward Ms. Meadows to take the lead in answering. "It's hard for me to get around. I'm not sure it's feasible."

"I'm sure I can borrow a wheelchair or a walker to make things easier," Holt said.

"I don't know . . ." Ms. Meadows's voice trailed off. "But regardless of what I decide, you should certainly go, girl."

"It depends." Claire's answer was vague. Probably deliberately so. He decided not to push her. There was time to win her over.

"Think on it. You can let me know later." Holt scraped up the last of his soup beans with corn bread, then sat back and patted his belly. "That was amazing. Can I help clean?"

Claire popped out of her chair as if a fire ant had bitten her bottom. "That's not necessary, I can—"

"What a fine idea." Ms. Meadows patted Claire's hand. "A word of wisdom. Never turn down a man's offer to clean. Now if you two will excuse me, I'm going to figure out how to work this thing."

Ms. Meadows tucked the CD player and the books

under her arm and hobbled out of the kitchen, more spry than usual, her excitement palpable.

Holt wasn't sure if Ms. Meadows was playing matchmaker or not, but he was grateful she had ske-daddled. Claire had gone back to not looking at him. The awkwardness that sprang up between them would steal the oxygen needed to turn their spark into a fire if he let it

"Was I that bad?" Holt propped his hip against the counter and leaned over to see her face.

"Bad?" She tucked her hair behind her ears before turning the water on, plugging the sink, and adding a squirt of dish soap.

"Bad at kissing. I reckon it's been a while, but I've never had any complaints."

The pink wave making its way up her neck and into her cheeks was fascinating to watch. "I didn't complain."

"No, but you're acting like I have cooties now."

He won a speculative glance from her. "What are cooties?"

"Sticky, gross boy germs."

"You aren't sticky or gross." Her lips quirked. "Or a boy."

"Ah, we're making progress. I'm not sticky or gross and you had no complaints on my technique. Is it my breath? Do I smell of livestock?"

Like the mound of bubbles outgrowing the sink, Claire couldn't contain a giggle. "You don't smell bad."

"Then what's the problem?" His hands tightened on the counter as he prepared for her answer to knock him sideways.

"I'm . . . It's . . . *complicated.*" The plates clattered

together on their way into the water. "I'll be moving on soon enough."

The news wasn't a surprise. She was used to wandering the world. Highland's charms wouldn't keep her satisfied for long. Knowing that didn't stop the crimp of disappointment in his chest somewhere around his heart.

"No reason we can't hang out and have fun until then, though." His light tone belied his internal turmoil.

"True." She drew the word out as if the pros of his argument barely outweighed the cons. "As long as you understand that's all it can ever be. A bit of fun."

"Trust me, the last thing I want is to settle down." When had he become such an adept liar? Next time Mr. Timmerman invited him to play poker, he would make a fortune bluffing the table.

"Me either. I'm allergic to staying in one place." Her fierceness had a grim edge.

"So we're agreed. We'll hang out, have some laughs, share a soufflé, and then no hard feelings."

She handed him a clean, dripping plate and a towel. "Agreed. Now make yourself useful and dry."

While he wouldn't call the atmosphere between them relaxed, it had lost its awkwardness. Now it held a tension that reflected the inevitability of an ending, but was also charged with an expectation that veered distinctly sexual.

While earlier, she avoided looking at him, now her gaze clashed with his every few seconds. Their hands brushed, hers slick and soapy against his. So preoccupied had they become with each other, he barely saved Ms. Meadows's cast-iron skillet from a soapy death.

"Do you want to get shot by Ms. Meadows?" At her quizzical expression, he said, "Even I know not to use hot water and soap on a seasoned skillet. It's blasphemous."

"As in, the Lord will strike me down?"

"You joke, but Thou Shalt Not Wash Your Iron Skillet with Soap barely missed the cut for the Ten Commandments." Holt took a scrub brush and cleaned the skillet, setting it back on the stove top. "And some would add in Thou Shalt Support the Georgia Bulldogs as a solid number twelve."

Claire submerged the soup pot in the water. "I didn't realize the state had an attachment to a certain breed of dog."

"It's not a dog, it's a football team. Their mascot is a bulldog."

"I didn't realize football was popular in the States."

It took a few blinks for Holt to cotton on to her confusion. "American football with the big pads and the quarterback throwing the ball. Although your style of football—it's called soccer around here—is getting traction too."

"And do you support the Bulldogs?" she asked.

"I watch every Saturday, even though I didn't go to college." Part of him regretted not going off to school like so many of his friends, but it would have been a waste of money. He'd known the farm was his future. Still, he wondered if he'd missed out on an important life experience.

"My parents expected me to go to university, but I . . . didn't." A story lived within her pause. Something along the lines of *War and Peace*.

"School isn't for everyone," he said simply even though he wanted to know more. He wanted to know everything, but she was as skittish as a polecat, and he would bide his time. After all, they had a date on the books.

Claire handed the rinsed pot over and Holt dried it, setting it to the side of the sink. The kitchen was clean and there was no reason to hang around unless she offered one. He wouldn't mind sneaking out to the porch to continue having "fun."

"I should go?" His voice wavered between a statement and question.

"You need to spend some quality time studying that soufflé recipe." She wiped the bubbles off her arms with the dishtowel. The hot water had inflamed her palm and had him pulling her hand toward him.

"Ah, Claire. That must hurt." He stroked her wrist with the pad of his thumb.

"It could have been worse." She pulled her hand back and lowered the sleeve, gesturing him toward the door. She didn't speak again until they were on the porch. "By the way, thanks for not telling Ms. Meadows what happened. I don't want her to worry next time I go to town."

Holt clamped his teeth together. He wanted to put his foot down and forbid her to ride the bike into town. He had to content himself with saying, "The road is too narrow and dangerous."

"What choice do I have?"

"I would be happy to take you to town."

"You're offering to be at my beck and call as a personal chauffeur?"

"I'd be happy to be your Jeeves," he said.

A smile flitted across her face, banishing the shadows that seemed to hover around her. "You surprise me."

"Better than being a bore."

The soft ping of the rain falling on the tin roof was hypnotic and soothing. He dreaded leaving the comfort and company to return to his empty cabin.

"I would appreciate a lift back to Wayne's some-time this week so he can fix my chain."

"My pleasure." It was the polite thing to say, but also the truth.

"I'll walk up to your place on Saturday. It's not far, is it?"

He wanted to argue with her, but decided to cede the field. "Less than a mile. Once you're about halfway to the barn, you'll see my cabin off to your left."

"I'm looking forward to it." Her shy smile did funny things to his inside.

He ducked into the misty rain and splashed through muddy puddles to his truck before he did something inadvisable like kiss her again. The headlights illuminated Claire, still standing on the porch. He hesitated with his foot on the gas. Saturday night couldn't come soon enough.

Chapter Seven

Holt was a car-chasing dog who had no clue what to do now that he'd caught the bumper. He'd lured Claire with the promise of fancy French cuisine, when what he should have done was eat his pride, go back to the library, and find a cookbook featuring recipes with less ingredients or geared toward idiots.

He read the recipe again. He'd thought he'd followed it to the letter. This wasn't even supposed to be the difficult one. The grand idea to make bread to go with the artisanal cheese he'd bought at the farmer's market as an appetizer had seemed like a great idea. Peasants in the Middle Ages had figured out how to make bread. The gooey blob of dough he was kneading looked nothing like the accompanying picture.

Worst-case scenario, he'd pull out the frozen chicken wings and fry them up to accompany the soufflé. Southern hot chicken meets French haute cuisine. The shot of humor settled him down. He plopped the dough in a bowl and covered it with plastic wrap. Now he was supposed to let the dough prove. What was it supposed to prove? Hopefully, that Holt wasn't courting disaster.

The soufflé recipe was intimidating. The ingredient list had looked doable, but the instructions were shoving him to the edge of a panic attack. They involved whisking eggs until they had stiff but not dry peaks. It was in English, yet he didn't understand.

He paced back and forth, then peeked at the bread dough, which hadn't proved anything. While he might need a cooking for idiots book, he wasn't an actual idiot. He knew when he was in over his head. He grabbed his phone and called for reinforcements.

Anna Maitland didn't answer her phone. He left a message and then called Iain Connors.

"What's up, mate?" The Scotsman hadn't lost any of his burr since moving to Highland.

"Please tell me you know how to cook."

"I could tell you that, but it would be a lie." Iain's rumbling laugh did not improve Holt's mood.

"Is Anna around?"

"She's working."

"On the Burns Night celebration?"

"I suppose." Iain's non-answer held seeds of worry.

"Everything okay with you two?"

"She's been acting odd the last couple of weeks."

"What'd you do?"

Iain grunted. "Why do you assume it's my fault?"

Holt let Iain stew on the question in silence.

Finally, Iain groaned. "I have no idea what I did."

"Listen, I will be happy to play Doctor Phil if you'll come over and help me. I'm in a pickle." Holt checked the time. He was behind schedule.

"I'll be there in a tick." Iain disconnected, and Holt breathed a sigh of relief. Any sort of backup would be appreciated.

Holt read through the recipe one more time, pulling

out all the ingredients he'd need for the soufflé. The number of eggs and egg whites called for was crazy.

Iain knocked on the front door and let himself in as Holt was making a mess separating whites from yolks. He picked a piece of shell out and said, "I'm a useless idiot. What was I thinking?"

Iain stood at the threshold of the small kitchen and surveyed the mess. "What in the devil are you doing?"

"Attempting to impress a woman. What else would cause such chaos?" An egg escaped and rolled toward the edge. Holt made a grab to save it and failed. It landed with a splat on his shoe. He wiggled his foot and the egg hit the door of the lower cabinet and slid to the floor, leaving behind a slimy trail.

Iain ran a hand down his beard, not bothering to disguise his amusement. "And what woman would this be?"

"Claire. The one you met at the Brown Cow the other morning."

"Ah, what's her story?" Iain joined him at the counter and tilted the cookbook so he could skim the recipe. The page was dotted with flour and egg white. Holt was sure to get an earful from the librarians when he returned the book.

"Claire Smythe is a mystery."

"Have you tried searching for information on the internet?"

Holt grimaced slightly and nodded. "Only mentions of a Claire Smythe are in reference to the Scunners. It's like she sprang into existence when she joined the band."

"Smythe could be a married name."

The possibility hadn't even occurred to Holt. Was her insistence they not get serious because she had a husband in Scotland? Was she running away from him? Had he been a member of the band? He tried to remember the other band members' names, but couldn't. Surely he would have noticed if she'd shared a last name with one of them.

Iain, unaware of how shaken Holt was from his suggestion, asked, "Why did you pick such a complicated dish? I could help you with a hearty beef stew or a steamed pudding. I'm a dab hand at scones as well, but this"—he waved his hand at the page—"is quite ridiculous."

"I picked this because it seemed like a good idea at the time." Dinner with Claire *had* seemed like a fine idea. "How do I get stiff peaks?"

"That sounds like a problem for your doctor."

"Har-har."

"Looks like you have more eggs to separate." Iain gestured at the eggs on the counter.

"Thank you, Julia Child." Holt got back to work on the eggs. Even though it was clear Iain wasn't going to be much use, Holt's nerves settled into something manageable.

"Anna is a much better cook than I am." An uncharacteristic uncertainty emanated from Iain.

"All right, what's going on in Loveland?"

Iain let his head fall back as if the secret code to understanding women had been carved across the wood beams by Holt's ancestors. If history had taught Holt anything, it was that the males in his lineage had been as ignorant as him and Iain.

"I don't know. Everything was amazing until it wasn't. All of a sudden Anna's distracted and emotional. She asked me if I wanted to adopt a dog together. I told her we had just gotten settled in the house, and she had a lot going on with the studio and the Burns

Night festival. I told we should wait until spring to see if things calmed down."

"Seems reasonable."

"That's what I thought. She burst into tears, ran into the bathroom, and slammed the door in my face. It was a good thirty minutes before I coaxed her out."

Holt frowned while he picked eggshells out of the bowl. "That doesn't sound like Anna at all. She's a ball-buster."

"Exactly." Iain paced the length of the galley-style kitchen. "Do you think she regrets asking me to come back to Highland with her? I thought things were going well, but . . ."

Iain didn't need to put his fears into words. Holt understood well enough.

"Have you asked her what's wrong?"

"Of course. She smiled—but not a real smile, her *bless your heart* smile—and told me nothing is wrong, everything is fine."

"Yikes. Something is for sure wrong if she gave you her *bless your heart* smile." Holt pointed toward a drawer at the end of the kitchen. "I think there's a whisky thingie in there."

"Excellent. I could use a drink."

"Not whisky, you lout. A whisk. For my stiff-peak problem."

Iain riffled through the drawer and handed over a whisk. "I've racked my brain, but I can't think of anything I did wrong."

"Maybe it's something you didn't do right."

"Her birthday isn't until spring. We're not married, so I couldn't forget an anniversary. What else could it be?"

Holt began to whisk the egg whites, leaning over to read the instructions again. Peaked but not dry. What the eff did that mean? After a few of minutes of vigorous whisking, the eggs were frothy, and his wrist was tired.

He opened and closed his hand to stretch the muscles. "I don't have the stamina to do this by hand."

Iain snickered. "I would think living alone would have built up your stamina."

Holt couldn't quite stop a grin from breaking out, but turned serious with his next question. "Has she kicked you out of bed?"

Iain's smile flipped into a grim frown. "We're sharing the bed."

"That's good news."

"We haven't done anything but sleep in it for almost two weeks."

"Ouch. Maybe I should give you a go with the whisk."

Iain glanced in the bowl and made a not-very-encouraging sound. "Mrs. Mac has an electric mixer she uses for macaroons and such."

"Would she let us borrow it?"

"I'm sure she would, but she's the cook at Cairndow, so that wouldn't be very convenient, I'm afraid."

Holt dropped the whisk in the bowl. "Do you have anything useful to suggest?"

"I suggest you pick an easier recipe." Iain took the cookbook and flipped through. "Didn't the library have a less posh cookbook?"

"I promised Claire a soufflé."

"Sometimes we do the best we can do and hope it's enough." Iain wasn't any older than Holt, but in that moment he sounded years wiser.

Holt snapped his fingers. "What am I thinking? My mom has cookbooks up at the house. Wait here."

Holt retrieved a dog-eared cookbook from a shelf

in the kitchen of his parents' house. He stood in the
entry to his childhood home for a moment, the silence
broken only by the ticking of a clock. It was a lonely
sound. One he'd lived with for too long. But tonight,
at least, he would have Claire with him and no matter
what they ate, they would have fun.

By the time he stepped back in the front door of
the cabin, Iain had the counters cleared and the dishes
in the sink. Together they picked a casserole recipe
with enough beef and cheese to qualify as a heart
attack risk. He could use the cheese he'd bought for
the soufflé, and he had ground beef in the freezer he
could defrost. Getting creative, he opened four boxes
of macaroni and cheese to scavenge the elbow pasta. It
would have to do.

Holt checked the bread dough. He should have taken
before-and-after pictures of it. He had no idea if it had
proved itself worthy or not. After dumping it into a loaf
pan, Holt said a little prayer and slipped it into the oven
to bake.

Between him and Iain, they muddled through the
steps of the recipe. The cheese on top disguised any
flaws. It might even turn out edible.

A knock came on the front door. A moment of
panic had Holt brushing flour off his shirt and smooth-
ing his hair.

Pasting on a warm smile, he opened the door. Anna
stood there, dark circles under her eyes, her hair sticking out of its braid.

"Oh, it's you," he said, gesturing her inside.

"Gee, don't set me on fire with your warm welcome.
I got your message, but it smells like you and Iain have
things under control." She stepped inside, craning her
neck to glance around the cabin. "Where is he?"

"Bathroom. What's going on with you two?"

The look she sent his direction was hunted. "Why? What did he say?"

"That you're acting super weird." Holt gestured from her head to her toes like she was Exhibit A. "Which you totally are."

Iain came out of the bathroom but stuttered to a stop upon seeing Anna standing there. "Hullo," he said cautiously.

"It was nice of you to help Holt out." The formality in her voice was odd.

Holt glanced between the two of them. It was becoming obvious Anna and Iain needed to sit down for a heart-to-heart. Holt didn't have that kind of time. He had to salvage his and Claire's hopefully edible, possibly romantic dinner.

"It's been great to see you guys. I really appreciate the help, Iain. The next beer at the pub is on me." Holt sidled around Anna to the door, throwing out as many verbal and physical hints as possible without actually telling them to skedaddle.

"What in bloody hell is wrong, love? Why won't you talk to me?" Iain took a step toward Anna with his hand out.

Before she could take it, a knock sounded on the door and made all of them jump. Holt muffled a curse and opened the door.

Claire stood on his porch, shifting in her boots and tucking her hair behind an ear. She was dressed in jeans with artful fraying around the knees and thighs exposing slivers of skin and a black T-shirt with a faded Lynyrd Skynyrd emblem on the front under a too-big windbreaker.

The sunset streaked orange and deep purple across the sky, fooling the eye into thinking it was warmer than it actually was. Holt bit his lip to stop from lecturing her about why she should have let him pick her up. The evening had already headed toward destinations unknown. Getting her hackles up would only send it careening off the rails.

"Come on in." He gestured and with a moment's hesitation, she took a step inside. "Let me take your jacket."

She slipped it off, and he hung it on a hook next to the door.

The tension between Iain and Anna was palpable. Falling back into Southern customs, Holt drew Claire forward with a light touch at the small of her back. "Claire, you remember Iain from the Brown Cow. You probably know Anna Maitland from the festival. She's Highland's mayor now and the owner of Maitland Dance Studio."

Anna shot Claire a guarded look full of secrets. "We've actually crossed paths recently."

"How are you?" The question from Claire took on greater weight than what was usually a polite afterthought.

"I'm—" Anna let her head fall back with a huge sigh. A tear trickled out of the corner of her eye. "—exhausted all the time. Stressed out. Scared."

Iain closed the distance between them and took her hands. "Are you having regrets? Do you want me to go back to Scotland? I only want you to be happy. Tell me how to make you happy again." His desperation was heartrending.

Anna's huffing laugh was tear-soaked. "You might be the one who wants to run back to Scotland. Something happened."

"Something bad?" Dread drew Iain's mouth into a tight line.

Holt was getting more and more uncomfortable with the direction of the conversation. Were Anna and

Iain going to break up during his first date with Claire? That was fate throwing serious shade.

"Do you guys maybe want to be alone?" Holt interjected.

It was Claire who shushed him. Her gaze was stuck on the couple, but a small smile curved her lips. Was she taking delight in watching the unfolding destruction?

"I don't know how to tell you this." Anna looked over at Claire with a helpless expression.

"Spit it out," Claire said with a marked encouragement. "The bloke obviously loves you."

Iain appeared as confused and left out as Holt felt.

"Okay, here's the deal, Highlander." Anna took a deep breath. "I'm pregnant."

Iain rocked back a step as if the news was a physical slap. "How . . . When . . . *What?*"

Anna tightened her grip on Iain so he couldn't escape. "I know it's a shock. Believe me, no one was more shocked than I was. I have a doctor's appointment tomorrow. I decided I'm keeping the baby no matter what. You can stay or go."

"Wow." It wasn't clear from Iain's tone if he was excited or panicked or both.

"If you want to go to the doctor with me, that'd be great. Or if you don't, then—"

"Of course I want to go." A slow smile spread over Iain's face.

"You're not upset?" Anna asked.

"I'm upset you think I'd be upset. Did you assume I would leave you?" Iain shook his head at her shrug. "Don't answer that."

"What now?" Anna asked.

"We take things day by day."

"Everything is going to change."

"Change is inevitable and doesn't have to be a bad thing."

Anna collapsed into his arms. Iain didn't flinch at her weight. Her voice was muffled against his shirt. "I'm sorry we're ruining your date, Holt."

What could Holt do except chuckle? He shot a side-eyed glance toward Claire. "My dates aren't usually this exciting. It's setting a standard I can't live up to."

"Is this a date?" Claire's eyes widened like a spooked horse's. "I thought I was merely a test subject."

"It's not *not* a date." Holt tried on his most charming smile.

The cloud of awkwardness had shifted from Anna and Iain to him and Claire. To cover his discomfiture, he asked, "How did you girls meet?"

Anna smiled and rolled her eyes toward Claire. "I made Claire buy a ridiculous number of pregnancy tests at the Drug and Dime for me. I was too embarrassed. Then she stayed with me for moral support while I peed on the stick."

Holt studied Claire slyly. For a woman who claimed to be a loner and who didn't need friends, she was becoming entwined with Highland and its residents at breakneck speed.

Iain sniffed. "Speaking of ruining your date, something is burning."

Holt made a run for the kitchen, jumping over the back of the couch. He opened the oven and actual flames licked out. He flipped the sink faucet on, grabbed the water hose, and pulled the trigger, aiming as best he could at the fire. Unfortunately, the hose only extended so far and water went all over the floor. Enough hit the burning food to send a cloud of gray smoke into the kitchen and trigger the smoke alarm.

Pulling the bread and the casserole out of the oven,

he surveyed the damage. The bread had been a lost cause from the beginning, but now it had turned into a briquette. The cheesy top layer of the casserole was black in places.

Holt threw the oven mitts aside. "This is what happens when I attempt to impress a woman. Fire and destruction."

Claire sidled up next to him, her hand over her mouth.

"Are you horrified or amused?" Holt asked.

She dropped her hand and burst into laughter. "This is the most drama-filled date I've ever been on, and it's only been ten minutes."

Over the obnoxious beeping of the alarm, he leaned in to ask, "So you're saying it is a date?"

Her laugh morphed into a cough.

"Head to the porch while I clear this out of the cabin." Holt jerked his head toward the door.

Iain had opened the front windows and was using the door as a giant fan to move the smoke out. Holt took the bread and the casserole and dumped them at the edge of the woods. A less discriminating raccoon or possum would surely appreciate his effort.

By the time he'd returned, the alarms had quieted and the smoke had dissipated. His cabin would smell like scorched bread for the foreseeable future, though.

Claire sat on the top step of the porch, enjoying the waning sunset. Iain and Anna stood next to the rail, their arms around each other, harmony restored. "We'll head out and let the two of you get on with things, mate," Iain said sheepishly.

"Gee thanks." Holt shook his head but exchanged a brotherly half hug with Iain. Holt put an arm around Anna for a quick squeeze. "Congrats, you two. Sounds like you're going to have to refurbish a room for a nursery."

Panic like a fox set out ahead of a pack of dogs had Iain blinking dumbly.

"You two have a lot to hash out. Like what you're going to name the little tyke. I'm thinking Holt if it's a boy." Holt winked.

"What if it's a lass?" asked Claire.

"I don't know. Holt?" He waved Anna and Iain down the porch steps to their respective vehicles. "Have fun figuring things out, y'all!"

Holt had no doubt that Iain and Anna would work things out. The two of them were made for each other.

Holt felt only happiness for his friends when he turned to Claire and raised an eyebrow. "Dinner is ruined. Are you up for an adventure?"

Chapter Eight

An adventure? Once upon a time, she would never have been able to turn down an offer like that. Especially coming from a man as handsome as Holt. She would have jumped without hesitation, without looking, without worrying about the consequences.

"Come on, Claire. I burned dinner and unless you want to split a frozen pizza, we're going to have to go out and grab something. This will be a real authentic Southern experience. Trust me?" Holt's lopsided smile made her feel like kicking her defenses aside. At least for an evening.

"Sounds like I don't have a choice." She tempered the grudging words by returning his smile. "I am starving."

"Let's go, then." He grabbed her hand as if it were the most natural thing in the world, led her to the passenger side of his truck, and opened the door for her.

After they were on the road, he tossed several glances in her direction. "What do you think about Iain and Anna?"

"I hope they'll be happy together."

"I'd put money on them getting hitched by New Year's. What about you?"

"Sure. I guess that's a possibility." She didn't know either one of them well enough to predict the outcome.

"Have you ever been married?"

It was the sort of personal question that set her on edge. "Why do you want to know?"

"We did agree this was a date, right?" He didn't take his gaze off the windscreen. "In case you're curious, no wives hidden in the storm cellar. What about you? Any husbands in the attic?"

"I'm not a female version of the dastardly Rochester from *Jane Eyre*." Her weak attempt at a joke garnered a twitch of his lips. It felt good to make him smile. She cataloged the risks of answering him, but she couldn't see the harm. "I've never been married. Never even come close. My lifestyle with the Scunners was too transient for anything long-term to develop."

"I've seen enough behind-the-music documentaries to know dating band members is a given." While it wasn't a question, his curiosity was obvious.

But he was curious because he wanted to get to know her, not because he suspected she was hiding something. Was there any danger of cracking the door just a little? "That's the truth of it. I dated the pipes player for a bit."

"Did it end badly? Is that why you left the band and stayed in Highland?"

Claire's mind whirred. It wasn't the reason. Jamie was a dolt, but an easygoing one who had taken his dumping with a sangfroid she'd attributed to laziness rather than emotional maturity. Claire had been convenient, but he hadn't loved her. And if she were honest, she hadn't loved him either.

On the other hand, a bad breakup was as good an

excuse as any to explain why she had quit the band
and stayed behind. "Yes, it ended badly. I couldn't stay
with the band any longer. But I don't want to talk about
it."

"Of course you don't. I don't blame you." It was
only when Holt's posture changed that Claire realized
how tense he'd been. The impish grin he shot in her
direction set the atmosphere in the cab at ease. "How
do you feel about bingo and barbecue?"

"I can't say as I have strong feelings about either."

"You will after tonight. The best barbecue in town
is Big Eddie's food truck. He's usually only open for
lunch, but it's bingo night, which means he'll be set up
in the American Legion parking lot."

"We're going to eat in a parking lot?"

"Of course not! We'll go inside and play a couple
of cards while we eat. A percentage of the money goes
toward a fundraiser for a countywide literacy program." Holt drove past Main Street on a road Claire
had never traveled.

It was disconcerting to realize how small her world
had become since moving in with Ms. Meadows. Uneasiness had her looking around her with suspicion,
but nothing unusual dotted the landscape. Fields gave
way to a string of two-story middle-class houses, then
shops. On the corner of the next intersection stood a
large concrete building with an AMERICAN LEGION
sign out front.

Cars and trucks filled the lot and spilled out to line
the street in all directions. Holt crossed the intersection and pulled into a half-full gravel lot on the other
side of the street. Had the entire town turned out?

Holt helped her out of the truck, and as they made
their way across the street to the parking lot, she
tucked the T-shirt she'd bought at the thrift store into

her ripped jeans, feeling self-conscious. Despite the cooling evening, knots of people stood around eating off plates piled with food. Woodsmoke laced with delicious scents ringed the air, and her mouth watered.

Holt put a hand on the small of her back and guided her toward a food truck in the far corner, nodding and exchanging greetings, but not stopping for introductions. She was grateful Holt didn't offer any fodder to the curious looks.

A large black smoker pumped out the most delicious smells Claire had ever experienced. A dark-skinned black man in a white apron came around from the back of the truck. "Holt Pierson! You son of a—"

"Eddie!" an older black woman taking orders called out sharply.

Eddie grinned "—biscuit. How you been?"

Holt clapped Eddie on the shoulder. Big Eddie was tall and broad and round. He would have been formidable if he hadn't had twinkling eyes and an infectious smile.

"The farm keeps me busy. I tried to make Claire here dinner and nearly burned the cabin down. I'm hoping to make it up to her with a pulled pork sandwich."

Big Eddie stripped off one of his gloves, wiped a hand down the front of his apron, and offered it for a shake. "Nice to meet you, Claire. I'm Eddie. I was Holt's center in high school."

"The center of his what?" Claire asked.

Eddie's eyes widened before his deep, chesty laugh rolled over her. "I forget sometimes the rest of the world isn't as football-obsessed as the South."

"Claire is from Scotland."

"Like Iain and Gareth, eh?" Eddie asked.

She got the impression he was asking more to be

polite than from any pointed interest in her background. "Indeed. It seems Highland calls to us."

Eddie pulled on his glove and went back to chopping a steaming pile of meat. "Hey, Ma! Pass down two plates, would you?" To Holt, he said, "Are y'all going to play some cards?"

"That was the plan."

"You'd best watch your back. These ladies are ferocious competitors." Eddie grinned as he put a portion of meat on each plate and held them out.

When Holt went to pull out his wallet, Eddie waved him off. "On the house."

"Thanks, man."

"Have fun," Eddie called out as he turned back to his work.

"That was nice of him." Claire had never considered herself particularly carnivorous, but her stomach disagreed. She couldn't wait to dig into the food.

"He's the best. We've been friends since kindergarten."

"How long have you known Anna?"

"Since before I can remember. We were in Sunday School together at church from before we could walk." He nodded at a dapper-looking gentleman who opened the door for them.

The room was lined with tables, and almost every chair was filled. The hum of conversation undercut the occasional yell of a bingo number. Sticking close to Holt, Claire followed him to a table along the back wall and two seats on the end. He set their plates down.

"Beer or tea?" He thumbed over his shoulder toward a bar that ran the length of the opposite wall.

A little liquid courage wouldn't go amiss. "Beer, please."

"I'll be right back. Go ahead and get started before it gets cold."

She slid onto the folding chair. Holt weaved his way through the people, a smile on his face as he exchanged greetings and handshakes along the way. Everyone seemed to know him. Not only know him, but like him. Holt was part of the fabric of Highland, woven so tightly he would never unravel.

An odd wistfulness came over her. The closest she'd ever become to belonging was with the Scunners, and even then she'd not revealed her true self to them. Who knew her? Who liked her? Certainly not her parents on either count. She was a single thread.

"You shouldn't let Eddie's hard work go to waste." A bony finger poked Claire in the arm.

Sitting next to Claire, a woman with a tight gray Afro and beautiful dark skin peered at Claire through thick bifocal glasses. She was one of those women whose age was indeterminate from her face, but her sloped posture and knobby knuckles put her past seventy.

"I was going to wait for Holt to tuck in, but I am famished." Claire pulled the plate closer and picked up the pork sandwich to take a bite. The smoky tender meat was heavenly, and she closed her eyes and hummed in appreciation.

When she looked over, the woman was smiling. "Eddie has a gift, doesn't he? He's my grandson."

"The food is amazing."

She beamed at Claire, in full approval for her opinion. "Did Holt bring you here on a date?"

The conversation turn unbalanced Claire, and she hemmed around an answer for too long. "I suppose?"

"You suppose? Are you interested in Holt or not?" The woman took a bite of a tall whipped-cream-topped piece of pie, but never took her magnified eyes off Claire.

"Things are . . . complicated. I'm not from Highland, you see."

"Obviously not, but that's a good thing to my mind. Someone like you would do Holt a world of good."

Before Claire could probe for specifics like why her and what sort of good could she do, Holt returned with two bottles of beer and bingo cards tucked under his arm. He stooped to give the old woman a buss on the cheek. "How're you doing, Ms. Frannie?"

"Fine, Holt, just fine. Your young lady seems nice, but I must say, you could have picked a more romantic place than the Legion for a date." Her scolding tone was good-natured.

"I'm not like Eddie. I tried to cook Claire dinner and ended up setting off the smoke alarm. We had to leave for a while to let the cabin air out."

Ms. Frannie laughed and patted Holt's arm, but aimed her comments toward Claire. "You should hang on to this one." The woman rose and shuffled away, leaving Claire and Holt as alone as they could be in the room.

"Everyone sure does like you around here." She hadn't meant her assessment to come out dripping with such accusation.

"Yeah, I can't explain it either." He devoured his sandwich and the sides of slaw and macaroni and cheese, finishing before her even though she'd had a head start. "Ms. Frannie's wise, though. You should do what she says and hang on to me."

She coughed when the sip of beer she was taking went down the wrong pipe. The sexual undertones in his voice were unmistakable. The air crackled around them like a lightning storm. After their kiss in the rain, she could sense the inevitable approaching like a force of nature, and she knew he sensed it too.

"I bought us a couple of bingo cards, but . . ." He let the possibilities dangle. She should take Ms. Frannie's advice and hang on to what she wanted.

"But we could give them to someone else and head back to your cabin. I don't care if it still smells like smoke." They didn't have all the time in the world. Not tonight—she would need to return to Ms. Meadows's— and not in the future either. She wanted to be alone with him.

He stood and held out a hand. "Let's go."

He handed the cards to a couple entering the hall, and they were on the road in record time. She expected him to put the moves on her as soon as they walked in his cabin, but he didn't. No, he wasn't going to fumble with her like a boy. He was a man.

"Can I get you a drink?"

"A glass of wine?" Claire waited on the back porch of the cabin and stared over the field to the line of trees.

For once, she wasn't afraid of the endless darkness, because she wasn't alone. Were the answers she sought hidden in the deep, fathomless forest? The autumnal scents of crushed leaves and a bonfire stirred in the air. She'd always considered herself a city girl, but comfort lurked around her.

Holt joined her with her requested glass of wine while he sipped from a bottle of American beer.

Her parents had only ever served Glennallen Whisky in their house. Had she hated the taste because of her childhood or her palate? The light, uncompli-cated wine banished her worries and she focused on Holt. "Is all this land yours?"

"As far as the eye can see." A self-deprecating laugh

accompanied his shrug. "Well, not technically mine. The deed is in my dad's name."

"But as an only child, you're due to inherit." She looked at him under her lashes.

"I suppose so, but I don't want that to happen anytime soon."

He tipped his bottle up, and Claire followed the line of his tanned throat as he drank deeply. When he finished, he set the bottle on the porch rail and took a seat on the top step. He looked up and gestured her over with a nod of his head.

She did as he bade, stretching her legs out down the steps. "It's amazing to think the laws of primogeniture are alive and well in America."

"The laws of whats-it?"

"It used to be in Britain the eldest male would inherit lands and titles. Even if he was tetched in the head or an absolute dolt." She hid her slight smile by taking a sip of the wine.

"I'll have you know, I'm not a dolt. Jury is still out on whether or not I'm tetched." The voice he adopted reminded her of the dried-up priggish teachers at her boarding school.

The laugh that burst out of her surprised her to the point she covered her mouth to muffle the sound. He grabbed her wrist and pulled her hand away, which only made her giggle more.

"Are you drunk after a beer with dinner and a glass of wine?" Holt's smile was a little lopsided. The crinkled lines at the edges of his eyes only emphasized their twinkle.

Claire was a lightweight when it came to alcohol. Her boarding school roommates had smuggled in half-full bottles of gin and vodka and wine all the time. One girl had even managed a mostly full bottle of tequila once. That had been a fun night, but a bad morning. They had begged her to bring back bottles of Glennallen Whisky but she never did.

Alcohol and drugs were in constant circulation when she'd been on the road with the Scunners. Being fuzzy-headed around a bunch of blokes she didn't know and didn't particularly care for wasn't an option. As much as she had rebelled against expectations, she had a firm sense of self and safety.

"I'm hardly drunk," she said with more vehemence than she'd intended. His smile wasn't defensive or judgmental.

"It's okay if you are. I'll take care of you." Holt transferred his attention to the sky, where stars twinkled. "And don't worry, not in a creepy way."

His words reverberated and echoed in the vast emptiness that had been part of her life for so long, she'd almost forgotten about its existence. Until Holt had reminded her.

She didn't need anyone to take care of her. She'd been standing on her own since she had left school. Yet for the first time in forever, she felt like she could close her eyes and fall backward and know there would be someone to catch her. A trust fall.

She hadn't trusted anyone in a long time. Now, all of a sudden, she had Holt. And Anna. And Ms. Meadows. They were all worthy of her trust, and she was a first-class rotter for withholding it.

She scooted closer and angled her torso toward him, draping her arms around his shoulders. She brushed her lips across his cheek in a prelude. He didn't move except to turn his head to make kissing him easier. Their lips met with an aching gentleness that undid all her carefully wrought defenses.

Holt was always trying to make things easier for

her. He had helped her with her bike. He made her feel attractive and worthy. He had cleared the way for her to confide in him even though she was still resisting. In short, he made it easy—too easy—to fall for him.

He would also make it easy to leave. He wouldn't pile on recriminations or guilt. He would be happy with what she could give him, which didn't feel like enough. He deserved more.

She broke away and buried her face in the crook of his neck, needing to be as truthful as she could be. "I can't stay in Highland in forever."

"I know." He raised a hand to brush the hair off her forehead. "I'll take whatever you're comfortable giving me."

She raised her head and stared into his eyes. "Nothing good will come of us getting involved."

"Nothing good? Darlin', you haven't even given me a chance to show you what I can do." His slow, sexy smile matched his honeyed drawl.

A blush lit her like she was experiencing spontaneous combustion. Traveling the world had left her jaded when it came to men, but Holt had reset her expectations. More accurately, he had raised them. She was usually so careful, so reserved, so protective.

A little voice urging her to surrender grew louder and more insistent. Her body tipped into his before her head came to the same decision. The sound he made was a throaty growl of satisfaction. He wrapped his arms around her and lay flat on the porch, drawing her down until she lay half on top of him, her chest pressed tight against his.

One of his hands cupped the back of her head, and he speared his fingers through her hair. She let him take control. While she might not be ready to trust him with the truth or any piece of her Franken-heart, she did trust him with her body, which was no small thing.

His fingers edged under her shirt and skimmed across the skin of her back, inciting pleasurable shivers. He sat up without taking his arms from around her—which made her wonder at the state of his abs—and pulled her into his lap. His meandering hands were heating her up in ways she'd forgotten existed.

"How about we move this party inside?" It was a question that most men might not wait for an answer to, but Holt didn't move, his patience awing her.

"That's a fine idea." Her Scottish lilt had grown more pronounced with her arousal, as if letting Holt get a foothold behind her defenses put him closer to the true heart of her.

He rose to his feet, bringing her with him until she stood on the top step and he stood on the one below, their faces level. His dark-blue eyes were nearly black and unreadable in the shadows. A shot of trepidation had her mind whirring to life. Was she making a mistake?

The question fragmented into meaningless letters the moment he kissed her, his teeth nipping at her bottom lip before his tongue teased hers out to play. Urgency sharpened his earlier tenderness into something less comfortable, but more exciting. Before she could react, he scooped her into his arms and walked toward the cabin door.

He grappled with the handle, his lips curving against hers. "Done in by a door when I was trying to be suave. Could you help me out?"

Her laugh was breathless both from his kiss and the situation. She blindly reached below her hip, grasped the handle, and pushed the door open. The scent of singed food lingered, but it only made the welcome of the cabin warmer. The place bore Holt's fingerprint in the most delightful ways.

The furniture was a combination of heavy wood pieces that qualified as antiques and more modern oversized couches and chairs that looked inviting. Tartan throws in various plaids were tossed around the room as an invitation to cuddle. Holt bypassed the living room and carried her down a short hall toward what could only be his bedroom.

Butterflies began to waltz in her stomach. She was nervous and excited for what was to come. *To come*. Thankful the darkness gave refuge, she buried her hot face in his neck. The pulse of his blood registered hard and brisk against her lips. Hers galloped along even faster.

A rustic king-sized bed made of roughhewn logs took up most of the room. A simple green quilted cover and white pillows were the only decoration. The rest of the room was utilitarian and uncluttered.

Holt set her down on the long edge of the bed, cupped her face with both hands, and proceeded to kiss her until the laws of time and space fractured. She was floating through the universe, her only tether to reality his touch.

Her hands went to the edge of his shirt. It was half tucked in, and she remedied the situation by yanking it up and over his head. Then she was touching his skin—smooth and hot—and scored her fingernails down his back. His intake of breath was gratifying and gave her a sense of control.

That control lasted less than a millisecond. Holt's hands grasped her shirt and lifted. She grabbed his wrists and clamped her arms down to stop the rise of cotton. A shot of something resembling modesty overtook her. The number of stage changes she performed in front of her male bandmates had driven her self-consciousness to nil.

But if she allowed this to continue, he would strip away more than her clothes. Vulnerability was not a welcome state.

"What's wrong?" His gruff voice didn't hold its usual lightness and charm. Did she really know him?

"My bra and knickers aren't terribly sexy." It was an accurate if not entirely truthful answer to his question.

The flash of his teeth in a smile reassured her. "I don't mind. Anyway, you won't be wearing them for long."

"But what if you're disappointed after you actually see them?" She swallowed past a rising lump of emotion that included both confidence and shame. She was complicated and so was her life. She had been living in a limbo that was coming to an end. Why was she dragging a nice bloke like Holt, whose life was serene and perfect, into the maelstrom with her?

His smile disappeared and the shadows masked his expression. He twisted one of his hands around to break her hold and link their fingers. "I do see you, and I'm not disappointed."

The lump grew until she was afraid if she spoke, the truth of her would spill out. Instead, she raised her arms. He took the cue to lift her shirt over her head and make quick work of her plain white bra. Gently, but inexorably, he pushed her flat on the bed with the hard heat of his chest, his hips driving her knees apart.

She was trapped. It was scary and thrilling. She'd always had an out. An escape route. She had run away from complications more times than she could count, starting with her parents. She squirmed against him, the friction of his hair-covered chest against her bare breasts distilling her thoughts over escape and truth and guilt into an intense need.

She fisted her hands in his hair and drew his mouth to hers. There was nothing sweet or innocent or gentle about the kiss. He didn't protest, but met her intensity with a bruising sexual need of his own. She grappled with the waistband of his jeans.

He lifted off her to rip at the button and zipper with one hand and reach toward the chest of drawers by the bed with the other. He clamped a condom packet between his teeth while continuing to work on the fastenings of his jeans.

She took the opportunity to shimmy out of her jeans and knickers, tossing them over his shoulder and grabbing his biceps to pull him back to her. His jeans and underwear had only made it as far as his thighs, but she didn't care. The part of him she needed was ready and available.

She plucked the condom from between his teeth, ripped it open, and rolled it onto him. Her fingers lingered on the hard length, and she bit her bottom lip to keep from crying out in thanks. She didn't deserve him in any way, but she wasn't going to be all noble and walk away now.

"Tell me what you want." The growl in his voice made her even more aware of her emptiness.

Never had she told a man what she actually wanted. The question was too complex, so she simplified it. "I want you."

Had she said the wrong thing? She only had a millisecond before the worry poofed into nothingness. No, not nothingness. He entered her in one swift stroke, his hips flush against her. Her back arched and her fingernails dug into his back muscles. She was filled and surrounded by him. He'd given her what she wanted.

Her body convulsed around him. Had anything felt as good as he did inside of her, on top of her? She didn't have time to ruminate, because he began to move. Not too fast or too slow, but hard enough to move her across the bed. He was just right for her.

She slid her hands down his back, glorying in the shift of muscles, to grab hold of his bare buttocks. Her eyes closed. The oblivion of pleasure was nigh. Uncomplicated pleasure was what she needed, but was that all she wanted?

Her hands tightened on his flesh and his thrusts slowed. He shifted over her, propping himself on his elbows and threading his fingers through her hair. "Look at me."

Danger pulsed through her, pacing her pleasure. She should keep her eyes closed and spur him back into rhythm. She opened her eyes and met his gaze. The rising moon sent diffused light through the open curtains. It was painfully romantic.

Her heart throbbed in concert with her body. One fact crystallized in her head. She *did* want him, but not just for sex. She wanted to cuddle next to him in bed and tell him about her childhood, the push–pull of her family's expectations, her life since running away. She wanted to slip on one of his T-shirts and wallow in his scent. She wanted to make him laugh.

She tried to save herself and look away, but he wouldn't allow her to. Their gazes remained locked as his strokes slowed and gentled. Her climax came over her with the suddenness of a fall. But he was there to catch her.

She floated through the blissful feeling until she tumbled back to earth. He rode her until her body slackened and then held still over her, a fine sheen of sweat breaking over his shoulders.

Still, he didn't allow her to escape. He kissed her with a tenderness that drew tears to her eyes. One slipped out and trailed toward his hand. This time when she squirmed, he rolled off her. He discarded the condom and pulled his underwear and jeans back up, but left the front gaping.

Her nakedness sent a fiery blush over her entire body. She was raw, her nerves exposed by pleasure, and shocked by the vulnerability he'd demanded and she'd surrendered.

What now? Would he expect to lie in bed and have a heart-to-heart? If she stayed, she might reveal more than she was comfortable with. Rising, she slid off the bed and searched for her clothes. Her shirt had been flung in one direction and her knickers the other. She didn't bother with her bra. Lynyrd Skynyrd didn't seem the type of band to mind. She pulled her knickers and jeans on.

"What are you doing?" No anger or frustration could be detected in his question, but she tensed anyway.

"I've been gone too long and need to check on Ms. Meadows. It's my job." She stuffed her arms into her jacket and zipped it all the way up to her neck.

He regarded her long enough to send shards of panic whizzing through her. She was at an impasse. Or was she? She would simply walk home. The moon had risen and it wasn't far even without a bike. She turned away from him, stuffed her feet into her trainers, and made her way outside.

The darkness gave her a moment's pause. She didn't relish running off into the night. Her imagination was active enough to picture threats only seen on the pages of fairy tales.

"Hang on. I'll drive you." Holt walked out of his

cabin barefoot, pulling on a T-shirt with his jeans un-buttoned, his white underwear visible.

She weighed the ignominy in accepting a ride of shame versus getting eaten by a wolf and scrambled into his truck. They didn't speak on the short trip, but he grabbed her wrist to stop her from bolting to the safety of the house.

"Did I do something wrong?" The interior lights threw his face into harsh relief.

What he'd done wrong was be *too* nice and car-ing and sexy. Which made him sound perfect and her crazy. She was the one who'd screwed up. She shouldn't have let Holt charm his way past her defenses. "I'm the one who did something wrong."

His eyes narrowed in disbelief at the *it's not you, it's me* line, but even the most trite excuse could reflect a patina of truth.

She slipped away and barely kept herself from sprinting to the house. When she was inside, she al-lowed herself the weakness of looking back. Only the outline of the man was visible on his reverse up the lane. If it had only been great sex, then the night would have lived on as a warm fuzzy memory to recall when she was old. It had been more than great sex. The way he'd looked at her and made her look at him had trans-formed the experience into something both terrible and beautiful.

"How was your date?" Ms. Meadows's voice came from her bedroom.

Claire pushed the bedroom door open and peered inside. Ms. Meadows was tucked into her bed with the CD player next to her and a pair of old-fashioned head-phones around her neck.

Claire wanted to deny it was a date, but with the scent of him clinging to her skin, she didn't even try.

"He burned dinner, so we ended up at a bingo hall eating barbecue."

Ms. Meadows raised a brow. "At least he can think on his feet. Did you enjoy yourself?"

She had enjoyed herself immensely minus the excavation of her soul. "It was fine."

Ms. Meadows's sharp gaze did its own digging. Already feeling off-kilter, Claire looked away. "I'm beat. If you're settled in for the night, I'm going to go to bed."

She and Ms. Meadows exchanged good nights, and Claire shut herself in her room and crawled under the covers still in her clothes. For one night, she would wallow in his scent and the memories before the morning brought a reckoning. It was time to make difficult decisions.

Chapter Nine

The next morning, with Ms. Meadows settled into her favorite chair, Claire paced in her room. Or tried to pace anyhow. It was a half dozen mincing steps from wall to wall along the edge of her bed. Her childhood bedroom in Glasgow had been huge with the walk-in closet and attached bath. She didn't miss the designer curtains and linens and echoing silence. Her room at Ms. Meadows's house was cozy and comfortable.

A decision loomed in tandem with her approaching birthday. What was she going to do? She had responsibilities and had made promises. Lachlan expected her to return to Glasgow and become his partner. Her parents expected her to return as well and offer them her allegiance. She had been avoiding hard conversations for years, partly because she didn't know what she wanted. But mostly because she was a coward.

How much of a coward was now becoming clear as she grew older and more mature. Although, given her flight from Holt's bed the previous night, *more* mature didn't count for much.

Humiliation flared like sticking her head into a kiln, and she had to force herself to not replay her ride of shame home. Holt unsettled her. Not because she was scared or intimidated by him, but the opposite. She was comfortable with him. So comfortable she could feel herself wanting to tell him everything. But they weren't in a relationship.

Her future awaited in Scotland. For the first time, she was ready to face the consequences of her birth and her choices. Had she been unfair to her parents? Weren't most teenagers unfair to their parents?

As loath as she was to admit it, her parents had been right about one thing. Music hadn't brought her fame or fortune. It had been a fun detour, but she'd not found true happiness onstage. Was happiness worth chasing when it was fleeting anyway? Maybe given time, helping run Glennallen Whisky would make her happy. Or at least leave her satisfied.

Needing a distraction from her life's conundrum, she pulled the tarnished silver box from under her bed and took it to the kitchen. While Ms. Meadows napped, Claire would polish the box and surprise her with it. It deserved pride of place.

A wooden crate with shoe and silver polish was stashed in the hall closet. It took a fair amount of work to uncover the beauty of the silver, but it was even prettier than she'd expected. A metaphor lurked but she ignored the niggling sense of irony.

The clack of Ms. Meadows's cane on the wood floor came as Claire was finishing the last side. Ms. Meadows entered the kitchen with a smile, but it vanished when she spotted the silver box on the table.

"What are you doing?" Grooves carved by time and travails emphasized Ms. Meadows's age.

"It's the silver box from the shed. Isn't it lovely?"

"I told you to leave it alone."

"Yes, but I thought—"

"You thought you'd stick your nose where it didn't belong, eh?" Ms. Meadows snatched the box from the table and clopped back down the hall toward her room. Each strike of her cane transmitted her anger.

Claire rocked back in the seat, still holding the polishing cloth. While she felt fully chastened by a favorite teacher, Ms. Meadows's reaction had also stoked her curiosity to new heights. What could provoke such a reaction?

Claire waited for something else to happen. Nothing did. Finally, when lunchtime came and went without Ms. Meadows making an appearance in the kitchen, Claire fixed a sandwich with crisps, poured a glass of tea, and knocked on Ms. Meadows's door. There was no answer.

Worry coalesced into an uncomfortable spiky ball in Claire's stomach. She didn't want to invade Ms. Meadows's privacy, but what if she had collapsed and needed medical attention?

With her heart fluttering like a trapped bird, Claire turned the knob and pushed the door open enough to see inside. Half expecting to see Ms. Meadows sprawled on the floor, Claire let out a long breath when she saw Ms. Meadows sitting on the bed with her hands in her lap and the silver box at her hip.

"I brought you lunch if you're hungry?" Claire remained in the doorway. She'd already intruded by taking the silver box from the shed.

Ms. Meadows gestured her in then let her hand fall back to her lap as if it were unbearably heavy. Claire took small steps inside and set the tray on the nightstand. When Ms. Meadows didn't speak, she backed toward the door.

"No. Stay. I should apologize," Ms. Meadows said.

"It's I who should ask for your pardon. I over-stepped and I apologize. I didn't realize—" Claire's gaze bounced to the silver box. She cleared her throat. "I wanted to do something nice for you."

Ms. Meadows's gaze rose from her lap to meet Claire's eyes. "Will you come and sit with me?"

The only place to sit was on the end of the bed. Claire perched on the mattress and tucked her hands under her legs, intensely aware of the polished silver box between them.

"It's been twenty years or more since I last opened it." Ms. Meadows lay a hand over the top. "I decided to leave my ghosts behind, but seeing it again . . ."

"Can I help?" Claire wasn't certain if Ms. Meadows needed help of the physical or emotional kind. When Ms. Meadows didn't answer right away, she asked tentatively, "What's inside?"

Ms. Meadows didn't break eye contact with the silver box. "Mementos."

"From your husband?"

Ms. Meadows shook her head slightly. "My son."

Claire straightened at the offering of new information, fighting a spark of anger at the unknown man. Why hadn't he called or visited his mother? "I didn't realize you have a son."

"Had a son. He's passed on."

Claire darted her tongue along her dry lips before whispering, "I'm sorry."

"It happened a long time ago." Ms. Meadows pursed her lips in what resembled a small smile, but nothing about her countenance lightened. "Sometimes, though, the years seem like days, and I wake up hoping it was all a bad dream."

Curiosity overwhelmed Claire, yet she couldn't bring herself to add to the grief already shrouding Ms.

Meadows. A platitude seemed as out of place as prying questions. Claire simply touched the back of Ms. Meadows's hand as an offering of sympathy.

Ms. Meadows accepted, clasping Claire's hand in a grip that was stronger than expected. Her hand was warm and papery soft. They sat in silence, side by side on the bed, their hands resting on top of the smooth, cold silver box that put Claire in mind of a dug-up coffin.

Claire's Glennallen grandmother had not liked hugs, jammy hands, rambunctiousness, or loud singing. In short, she had not liked Claire. Although, to be fair, Claire had not liked her much either.

Ms. Meadows was different. It seemed a shame she hadn't had a house full of children and grandchildren to bake for. Kids who would have loved to explore the woods and play hide-and-seek and build tree houses. She wouldn't have minded a mess. After all, she hadn't minded Claire's messes.

"My son died in a car accident right before he graduated high school. He was only eighteen." A waver in Ms. Meadows's voice had Claire holding on even tighter to her hand as if she could somehow shore up the faltering tower of Ms. Meadows's emotions.

It was an irony not lost on Claire that she had cut off her parents around the same age. While Claire hadn't died, had her parents grieved her loss? Had Claire been selfish?

The box obviously held pain, but also a great deal of love. "Do you want me to put it back in the shed? Or leave you to look inside?" Claire asked.

Ms. Meadows took in a deep breath and let it shudder out. "No. Stay. I don't want to be alone."

The words echoed over and over in Claire's heart. She didn't want to be alone either. Not anymore. Trouble was, she wasn't sure if returning to the Glennallen fold would alleviate her loneliness or exacerbate it.

Ms. Meadows pulled the box into her lap and retrieved a tiny key from the drawer of the nightstand. Her hand shook, making it difficult to fit the key into the lock, but Claire didn't offer to help. This was something Ms. Meadows needed to do on her own. Finally, the key slid home. Ms. Meadows hesitated, then flipped the box open quickly as if acting before she could change her mind.

A posed picture of a smiling young man wearing a tuxedo stared back at them. Ms. Meadows returned the boy's grin as she picked the photo up. "His senior picture. He was handsome. Girls called the house all the time."

Claire took the picture when Ms. Meadows held it out to her and studied his face. He had the same broad forehead and blue eyes of Ms. Meadows. His dark wavy hair was worn shaggy in a style that had been popular decades earlier. Optimism and good humor shone from the picture.

If he'd lived, he would be old enough to be her father. He would have experienced love and loss, joys and hardships. Instead, he was forever locked in the ignorance and innocence of youth. Knowing the future that awaited the boy in the picture made her heart constrict.

"Kevin missed his curfew. He was always one to push the boundaries. Samuel and I were angry with him. We were going to give him what-for when he got home. Grounded for two weeks, Samuel said." Ms. Meadows touched her son's face with a finger, her eyes watery. "The sheriff showed up instead and I knew. As soon as I saw his face, I knew."

"I'm sorry." It was a useless thing to say, but Claire had nothing else to offer. While she had faced hardships, she never been burdened with such a loss.

"Lost control of his car on a curve and hit a tree. Thankfully, he'd dropped his date off already and was headed home alone. Speeding, of course. Probably doing his best to beat his curfew." Blame tainted Ms. Meadows's voice.

"It's not your fault."

Ms. Meadows waved off the words like a gnat. "I've had nearly forty years to come to terms with it. Samuel and I tried to be good parents. Most of the time, I think we were, but I'll always wonder."

Tears Ms. Meadows wouldn't appreciate her shedding stung Claire's eyes. "Anyone would be lucky to have you as a mother."

Her declaration came out with an embarrassing amount of vehemence, but she couldn't walk back the sentiment, because it was true. Ms. Meadows transferred her regard from her own pain to Claire.

"What about your mother and daddy, girl? Do they wonder where you are? Do they worry?"

There was no doubt her parents did wonder, but was it because they missed her or because of the business? For the first time, she wondered whether she should give them a chance to show her.

"Won't they be missing you this Christmas?" Ms. Meadows asked when it was clear Claire wasn't going to answer.

The pang she felt was something new. Regret perhaps? She forced a tease into her voice. "Are you trying to get rid of me, Ms. Meadows?"

Ms. Meadows tilted her head as if putting real thought into the question. "I've been alone a long time.

I didn't think I'd like having someone all up in my business twenty-four seven. But I like you, girl, and no, I don't want you to leave."

Claire's spine curved with the relief of her answer.

"*However...*" The word hung between them, and Ms. Meadows peered over her glasses at Claire. "You are a young woman, and you have holed yourself up with me to avoid something. Or someone. That's all well and good for now, but you need to face up to your life soon."

Claire didn't even try to deflect. Ms. Meadows would only parry and drive her point home. "You're right, and I will. I'm not quite ready yet, though. Is that okay?"

"Of course it's okay. You are welcome to stay here as long as you need." Ms. Meadows closed the silver box and hugged it to her waist. "I'd like to lie down with my memories now if you don't mind."

Claire closed the bedroom door behind her and retreated to make herself a cup of tea. She sat and stared at the scarred top of the table for a long while. The silence of the house held a new quality. It was expectant. It wasn't wolves or bobcats in the dark woods she needed to fear, but change. The inevitable force of change stalked closer.

After assuring herself Ms. Meadows was settled for the afternoon, Claire walked to the main road and set out toward the Pierson farm. The raging waters of her emotions from the night before had settled if not into a placid lake at least into a navigable river. She would focus on living in the moment. And the moment required she offer Holt an explanation, even an apology.

It was another unusually lovely day, and she enjoyed the walk. When she got to the drive leading to Holt's family farm, she stopped to pull her jumper off and tie it around her waist. Holt's truck wasn't at his cabin, but parked next to the red barn straight out of a children's book.

Now that the moment was upon her, nerves had her slowing. There was still time to turn around, return to her room, and hide under the covers. A man emerged from the shadow of the barn to root around in the bed of the truck. His broad shoulders and baseball cap were becoming a not just familiar, but welcome stomach-tumbling sight. A zip of energy got her feet moving forward as her heart pounded faster.

Her body's reaction took on a syncopated feel. *Thump. Thump. Shuffle. Shuffle.* It was a dance set to music her body recognized. The last time she'd felt this way was onstage while holding a crowd in the palm of her hand.

Holt looked up, his gaze plugging into her like another energy source. He didn't move to meet her halfway. What did that mean?

She stopped on the other side of the lowered gate of his truck. Explanations lodged in her throat, too big and too many to parse, and she wasn't sure if he even wanted to hear them.

"Howdy." Not a hint of what he was feeling or thinking transmitted in the word.

"Hullo. I . . ." She swallowed. "I'm terribly sorry, Holt."

"Could be I need to apologize. I didn't mean to . . ." Now he was the one who seemed to lose his ability to speak.

"You did nothing wrong. Nothing. I was scared."

"I scared you?" His hands tightened on the frame of the truck.

"Not physically." A nervous half laugh escaped. "I mean, you are a fine specimen of a man. Brawny. *Big*."

Her gaze dipped of its own accord to between his legs as if she had suddenly developed X-ray vision. Or wished she had anyhow. Rolling her eyes to the side, she forced her attention toward something more innocuous, like the goats frolicking in their pen. She squinted.

"Is that goat . . . Bloody hell, two of your goats are fornicating. Right there in the open. Right there in front of the other goats." She shielded her eyes as if the goats might be offended by her presence during their intimate moment. "Is that normal?"

"I consider sex a normal healthy aspect of life, so yes, totally normal. And kind of fun too, if done correctly," Holt said so blandly she dropped her hand and looked him in the eyes. They were sparkling with humor. "I'm pretty sure you had fun last night, didn't you?"

"Of course I had fun." She huffed a little in surprise. "You're not angry with me?"

"Angry? No. Confused as all get-out? Yes." He moved to the end of the truck and half sat on the tailgate, crossing his feet at the ankles and curling his hands around the edge. His worn jeans did good things for his lower body, and the black T-shirt with the Highland slogan across the pocket did wonders for his chest.

"How are you single?" The question that had been niggling at her since they'd met popped out.

His eyebrows shot up. "How are you single?"

She pointed at her chest. "Me? I think that much is obvious."

"It's not obvious to me. You're gorgeous and funny and have the sexiest accent on the planet."

She made a scoffing sound as she tucked her hair behind her ear, knowing a blush spread like a rash along her cheeks and neck. "Please. You're the one with the sexy accent with your drawls and howdys and aw shuckses. I'm a complete mess."

"Are you?" Holt cocked his head.

"Look at me." She gestured up and down at her ill-fitting clothes from the thrift shop. Of course she'd picked them on purpose. Her tight, sexy tour clothes would have torpedoed her plan to live incognito in Highland.

"I'll admit you're aren't exactly cotillion material, but underneath the baggy clothes is a body I'll not soon forget. Every time I close my eyes I see you in my bed without a stich of clothes on."

If possible, she grew even hotter and splotchier. She pushed the sleeves of her shirt up her forearms. "I know that's not true."

Holt tipped his head back and closed his eyes, his mouth taking on a decidedly roguish twist.

She stepped forward and slapped his arm. "Stop that nonsense right now. I'm being serious."

As fast as an adder, he took her hand and laid it over his heart as if he were offering it to her. "I'm being serious too. Last night was special. If I did something wrong or if we moved too fast, I'll back off. You say the word."

She searched his eyes but saw only sincerity. The last thing she wanted was for him to back off, but was that being fair to him?

"My life is complicated. My parents—" She pulled her hand free and shook her head, not ready to speak of them so soon after Ms. Meadows's interrogation. Her feelings were raw where her past was concerned. "I've been running away from things since I was a teenager. It's all I know."

"Running from what things exactly?"

"Responsibility mostly. A life I wasn't sure I fit into.

Or at least, I didn't fit into it then. Maybe I will now. I don't know."

"No plans to go back on the road with your band?"

The question surprised her, because she had let go of the Scunners months earlier without regrets. Already, the boys felt like summer camp friends whom she was fond of but wouldn't keep in contact with. "No. I'm done with touring."

"Really? Because you seemed like you loved singing onstage."

"I did, but I got tired of that life. When I quit, I think everyone was relieved. They'll find a new lead singer or maybe they won't. A couple of the boys have girls back in Scotland. I won't be surprised to hear they've settled down."

"Why did you stick around Highland after the festival?"

"Because I decided I could get lost here."

"Who's trying to find you?" His questions probed for the truth like it was a splinter and they were uncomfortable. "An ex?"

"No." None of her relationships had inspired that kind of devotion.

"Family then?"

"Yes, family." Her parents and Lachlan were wanting to find her, no doubt.

"When you say you've been running since you were a teenager, did you run away from home?" His questions were boring too close to the truth.

No Glennallen came into their inheritance until they were twenty-five. It was expected, if not encouraged, that young Glennallens would sow some wild oats before returning to the fold, sober and wise and ready to take up the mantle. Lachlan's big adventure was a semester abroad during university in Switzerland delving into the banking system. Not exactly a rebellion. Claire, on the other hand, had taken her temporary freedom to extremes. "I was legally an adult when I left. It was less running and more shirking my duty."

"Have you spoken to your parents since then?"

"I check in every so often," she said defensively, not adding it was through the occasional stilted email or a brief call with her family's solicitor.

Donnison had been like a kindly, albeit distant, uncle her entire life. She trusted him, although even he had tried talking her into coming home sooner rather than later. She hadn't spoken to him since leaving the Scunners and doubted he was savvy enough to track her down, but he'd always been full of surprises. Like the candied lemons he'd slipped her every time he visited the house.

"That kind of distance would break my parents' hearts," Holt said.

Had he meant that to sound judgy? She squared off with him and propped her hands on her hips. "Believe or not, we don't all have bloody perfect parents like you apparently do. I'll wager you've never spent the Christmas holidays alone because, *of course*, my parents would rather go skiing in Austria than pretend their little girl had been good enough for Saint Nick to visit."

Her words had come fast and furious and she was breathing hard by the end of her diatribe.

"Your parents left you alone for Christmas to go skiing in Austria?" His eyes had widened.

Hell and damnation. She'd given him too many clues in her emotional response. Trying to remedy her mistake, she tried on a smile. "I mean, not *alone* alone. I wasn't the star of a classic Christmas comedy gamely foiling inept robbers or anything."

His slow exhale didn't signal the start of a smile. He looked unusually serious. "This Christmas will be different."

"Why is that?"

"Because you have me."

Her heart inflated with a puff of helium and rose into her throat.

Holt added, "And Ms. Meadows and Anna and Iain. You have friends in Highland whether you want them or not."

Was he putting himself into the friend group despite the previous evening's activities? Her fledging courage stood on the edge of a cliff. Did she dare leap? "Is that what we are? Friends?"

Holt uncrossed his ankles and braced his legs apart. Hooking his fingers through the belt loops of her jeans, he tugged her forward until she was framed between his thighs. He slipped his hands under her tied jumper to her hips, the warmth sending a tingle through her body.

"I hope we're friends, but that doesn't mean I don't want more. As long as you give me the green light."

"Do I need to steal one of the traffic lights in town?" She looped her arms around his shoulders.

"They are bigger than they look from the ground, as I found out in high school. And way more expensive than you might think." He lay a kiss on the tip of her nose. The sweetness of the gesture made her ache.

"And what if I'm not ready to give you the green light?" Her body was more than ready to flash a giant neon right-this-way arrow, but her head was urging caution.

"Then I'll woo you until you are. Believe or not, I can be charming when I put my mind to it." His smile was slightly lopsided.

"I believe it all right." Claire hadn't counted on getting involved with a man during her time in limbo. "So we're clear, I'm leaving Highland. I can't stay forever. Speaking of my parents, they'll need me home soon." Too soon.

"As you've informed me several times now." Holt seemed unworried by the news, which should have been a relief but wasn't.

"You don't mind?"

"I didn't say that, but I understand. As long as both of us know going into this what will happen, no one will get hurt."

"Right. No one will get hurt." She had the urge to shake on it.

Instead, she leaned into him and lay her head on his shoulder. Holt had a strength that went beyond the physical. He was like a tree that weathered storms and remained standing, tall and proud, offering its shade and protection freely.

"Speaking of parents abandoning their children for Christmas . . ." he said leadingly.

"Are yours skiing?"

His laugh vibrated from his chest through her pleasantly. "The closest my parents would get to the slopes is in a chalet by a roaring fire with a good book and whisky. No, as of this morning, they're parked in Florida, enjoying the warm winter down there."

She lifted her head. "Down there? It's warm here too compared with Scotland."

"Wait a day and the weather will change. Today's sixties could drop to the twenties tomorrow."

"Better than the fog and drizzle of Glasgow."

"Do you get homesick?" he asked.

"Not really." It was the truth, yet the truth was much more complicated.

She missed the harsh beauty of the real Highlands. She missed following the cobblestone paths her ancestors had tread. There were times when she even missed her parents. Or at least, the security of her family name, but if she were being honest, she mostly missed what had never existed—a normal childhood.

"Do you miss your parents?" she asked.

"Terribly. We video-call every week, but it's not the same. I thought I'd like the independence—after all, I've lived on the farm all my life—but independence means I have to make tough decisions about the farm by myself. It means I can't walk up to the house to have dinner with my parents. I guess I didn't appreciate them like I should have until they were gone."

Did her parents feel that way about her? They hadn't given her any clues in their emails, but then again, the Glennallens were expected to project confidence and equanimity. She had missed out on those particular traits. Could she get a stiff upper lip surgically implanted?

A noise drew her attention back to the animal pens. "They're at it again."

Holt lightly slapped her bottom and shifted out of her hold. "Speaking of getting at it again, I have chores to finish."

"Do you need help?"

"I can always use an extra pair of hands. You good with animals?"

"We-e-l-l-l . . . I don't have a huge amount of experience." Or any experience at all.

"There's nothing to be afraid of." He strolled toward the fornicating goats. "Unless you spook an animal from behind; then they might kick you. Or if you spook an animal from the front, they might bite you."

She followed a safe distance behind him even

though the goats were fenced. Holt stood on the bottom rail of the fence, leaned over, and flapped his cap at the goats to separate them. His shirt rose enough for her to get a glimpse of taut skin above his low-riding jeans. His thick blond hair was damp with sweat and curled at his nape. She quit paying any attention to the animals.

"Get off him, Rufus. You're embarrassing the lady."

"Wait a tick. Are they both boys?"

He ran a hand through his thick blond hair and put his cap back on. "Yep. They must be bored without Mom here. The goats are her pet project. She wanted to try yoga with them."

A dark-brown-and-white-spotted sheep trotted over from the corner of the next pen they approached. Holt picked a carrot from the bucket sitting at the post and held it out to Claire.

"No, thanks. I'm not hungry." She deserved a bigger eye roll than he gave her. "Oh, it's for the sheep. Of course."

She took the carrot by the top and dangled it within reach of the brown-and-white sheep. "Here, sheepie, sheepie," she said in her best singsong, *don't bite my hand off if you please* voice.

The sheep raised its head and opened its mouth, exposing an intimidating set of teeth. She let out a little gasp and dropped the carrot. The sheep munched happily, not minding eating off the ground.

She rubbed her hand down the front of her jeans. "Obviously, 'Scotland the Brave' was not written with me in mind."

Holt poured the contents of the bucket into a trough, and the other sheep lined up like schoolchildren. "Seems like it fits pretty well, if you ask me. You set out on your own and conquered the world."

She let out an inelegant snort. "Conquered? More like survived. So far, anyway."

He lay his arms over the top rail and watched the sheep. "I'm kind of jealous."

"Of what?"

"You've traveled. Experienced and seen things I've only read about in books." He tossed her a glance. "I'd like to explore London. Go see the White Cliffs of Dover and the actual Highlands. Maybe even travel to Europe."

She had been to all of those places. She'd seen most of the UK, Western Europe, and even driven up and down the East Coast of the US playing festivals the previous two summers. While Holt was envious of her, she was just as envious of him.

He had a family. He had a place to call home. A place calling him home. No matter where he went, he belonged in Highland. He belonged *to* Highland.

She had never belonged anywhere. No one had ever claimed her. "Seeing all those places was amazing, and it was fun but—" She bit her lip and stubbed her toe against a weed struggling to survive.

"But what? You got to fly wherever whenever you wanted."

"What I really wanted was somewhere to land."

The animal snuffling and crunching didn't make the silence that fell between them any more comfortable. Finally, he whispered, "I'm an idiot."

Her laugh was shaky with poorly repressed tears. She hadn't cried in front of anyone in years, and now Holt had seen her in such a state twice. "No, you aren't, but I'm not sure you realize how great you have it here. Anyway, there's nothing stopping you from traveling. You can see a lot in a week or two."

He nodded then nudged his chin in the direction of

the red barn. "Speaking of sightseeing, want to gaze at some cows?"

The veer away from weighty emotional topics was appreciated. "Is it true the brown cows give chocolate milk?"

"Har-har."

As they strolled, Claire cast glances at him from the corners of her eyes. They were exploring new territory, and she was filled with the same fear and trepidation and excitement of any explorer.

"Most of the cows are grazing or in the milking house. The gals in here need a little TLC," he explained as he herded her through the door.

The cow in the first enclosure had big brown eyes with feathery lashes to make any supermodel jealous. Claire remained on the non-kicking side of the stall while Holt replaced a bandage on the animal's injured foreleg. He was gentle yet firm in his ministrations.

"What's her name?" she asked.

"This is a working farm. We don't name the animals." He didn't look up.

Movement at the far end of the barn drew her gaze. A tabby cat squeezed through a narrow gap of a stall and sauntered to the middle of the barn, stopping to give its privates a good tongue lashing. "Not even the cat?"

Holt finished with the cow and joined her outside the stall, wiping his hands on a work towel. "That nightmare of a cat does have a name. A well-earned one at that. Meet Vlad the Impaler. A more blood-thirsty brute you've never met. He believes in leaving rodent sacrifices where his humans can properly appreciate them."

She didn't have to fake a shudder. "Charming."

Holt checked his phone. "A couple of the boys will

be here shortly to help with the milking. Then I'll need to clean up, but how about I pick you up and take you out tonight?"

"More bingo?"

"No bingo tonight. I thought we'd head downtown."

"Highland has a nightlife?"

"At least until they roll up the sidewalks around ten. It's actually kilt night at the pub. How about it?"

"What does that even mean?"

"A free whisky shot for men wearing kilts." He waggled his eyebrows.

"Are you going to wear a kilt?" The pitter-patter made her wonder if she needed to book herself an EKG before she actually saw Holt up close in a kilt. Her obsession with him during the summer games had taken place at a safe distance.

"Of course I am. I don't get a chance to wear one often enough."

"All right." She croaked her agreement out.

"I'll pick you up around six." He leaned over and kissed her on the cheek. "Can I give you a ride back to Ms. Meadows's?"

"No. I'll walk." Hopefully, by the time she got to Ms. Meadows's house, her imagination would calm and she would cool off.

"If you're feeling brave, you could cut through the woods behind the cabin. It's a straight shot over the stream to Ms. Meadows's house versus going around on the road. A road with no shoulder."

From here, the woods were a long dark monolith, and the thought of entering them made her feel jittery. "I'll take my chances on the road. See you tonight."

He didn't protest even though she could see it was killing him to let her go.

A white pickup with splattered mud turned onto the

graveled drive, and she moved over into the grass by the fence. Two men around her age eyed her on the way by. She ignored them and continued on.

Could she sleep with Holt and not become emotionally involved? The question was moot. It was too late. She was attracted to him, but even more she liked him. A lot. If she had a single cautious, logical bone in her body, she would have refused him and put distance between them.

Unfortunately, based on her past decisions, she'd been born without caution and was bereft of logic. She wanted Holt and she would have him for however long she could.

Chapter Ten

Holt shuffled a hand through his damp hair and pulled on a pair of lace-up brown boots to go with his green-and-blue-tartan kilt and forest-colored Henley. He didn't have a sporran or the fancy dress shoes he'd seen Dr. Jameson wear with his kilts.

A frisson of anticipation had him heading to his truck early. He wanted to butter up Ms. Meadows. Her opinion mattered a great deal to Claire. While he'd managed to get his foot in the door without getting shot and they'd broken cornbread together, he'd like to gain her enthusiastic blessing.

But another reason niggled at him. After Claire was gone from Highland, Ms. Meadows would need looking after until she could find another live-in helper. Guilt at the way his father had treated Ms. Meadows made him want to settle the feud and be a good neighbor.

Claire gone. The two words stifled his excitement at their step forward. He couldn't fault her for being honest with him. At least about the duration of their relationship. He wasn't as confident she had been as honest about other things.

So what? He would live in the present instead of spending his energy attempting to excavate her past for the pieces of the puzzle she didn't want him putting together. He could do that. Right?

He made the turn down the narrow lane to Ms. Meadows's house and was at the door in record time. Claire answered his knock, and for a moment he stuttered for words.

She wore a version of a kilt herself, except shorter and much sexier than his. It was a traditional Christmassy green-and-red tartan shot through with gold. Dark-green tights encased her lithe legs. He tried—and failed—not to think about them wrapped around his hips. Her long-sleeved black T-shirt wasn't fancy but hugged her lean curves. Her auburn hair was semitamed into attractive waves around her face.

He was acquainted with her amazing body, but she held him rapt because of something less tangible. Her magnetism onstage had made her the center of attention with the Scunners. She'd done her best to hide under the ripped jeans and layers of shirts the last several months, but now she'd unleashed it, and he had a feeling every eye would be on her tonight.

"You're early. Come on in." Her gaze trailed down his body, lingering on his kilt and legs with what he hoped was an appreciative gleam. She gestured him into the kitchen. "Keep Ms. Meadows company while I finish getting ready."

Ms. Meadows was eating a beef stew with a wedge of still-steaming corn bread. She blew on a spoonful while regarding Holt with a tranquility he didn't feel. "Heard you burned dinner."

"You heard right. It was a total disaster."

Ms. Meadows smiled before blowing on another spoonful of stew. "Didn't sound like she minded, and here you are again to take her out. You two getting serious?"

Had Claire talked to Ms. Meadows about her plans to leave Highland? If not, he didn't want to be the one to deliver the news. "No. Just having fun over the holidays."

Ms. Meadows made a disbelieving harrumphing noise before taking a bite of stew and corn bread. "I thought you young'uns broke up to avoid being stuck with someone through Christmas. There's all sorts of pressure to buy a present."

A present. He hadn't even thought about that. Another thought bolted through him. What if she left before Christmas? What if he didn't even have a chance to ponder a gift? "I wouldn't know what the young'uns are up to. I spend my days with goats and cows and a murderous tomcat."

Ms. Meadows took another dual bite and nodded. "You're lonely."

"That's not what I said." The denial came out with a vehemence that insinuated the opposite. Did the old woman have the sight? "I mean, sure, I miss my parents."

She made another throaty sound, this time with more disgust. "Don't know why you'd miss your father. The rascally whippersnapper."

Hearing his sixty-something deacon of a father called a whippersnapper tickled his funny bone. A laugh rumbled out of him, and Ms. Meadows's lips quirked into an answering smile.

Feeling more comfortable, he launched his own probe. "Will you have family coming by for a visit during the holidays?"

"No." Her smile turned upside down, and she focused on her beans.

Jessie Joe and Jessie Mac had said she'd left teaching after getting married. Holt searched his memory banks for tidbits of gossip about Ms. Meadows's family, but all he recalled was that she had been a widow for as long as he could remember.

"My parents are planning to spend Christmas in Florida this year. I haven't talked to Claire, but the three of us should spend Christmas together. What do you think?"

"I think . . ." Ms. Meadows stirred her stew with an unnecessary vigor, and Holt prepared himself for a resounding rejection. "I think that would be very nice."

"What would be very nice?" Claire's voice from the kitchen door made him pop up like a jack-in-the-box.

She leaned in the doorway wearing her usual black combat-style boots with the kilt. Her brown eyes were rimmed in a smudgy black liner that emphasized their caramel notes. The hard edge of her makeup and boots with the traditional kilt matched her personality. She was gorgeous when she was natural and windblown, but he couldn't deny her sultry side was sexy as hell.

"You look—" His voice cracked like he was a teenager on his first date. He cleared his throat and dropped into a husky baritone. "You look amazing."

"Thanks." Worry flickered over Claire's face and she leaned over the back of Ms. Meadows's chair. "Are you sure you'll be all right?"

"I've lived on my own for longer than you've been alive, girl. I'll survive another evening," Ms. Meadows said between bites. "I'm going to finish eating and take myself to bed to listen to my books."

"You leave the dishes for me to wash up later," Claire said.

The irritation in Ms. Meadows's narrowed eyes

was ruined by the start of a smile. "Yes, ma'am. You young'uns skedaddle and have fun."

Claire hovered as if she was tempted to give the old lady a hug, but in the end she merely nodded and said her good nights, leading Holt back outside.

As Holt opened the truck door and handed her into the passenger seat, he said, "Are you worried about anything in particular?"

"Not really, but sometimes she seems frail and unsteady. It's only age, I suppose." Claire snapped her seat belt home then glanced over at him. "There's nothing to worry about, is there?"

"Absolutely nothing." He closed her door and circled the truck to swing himself behind the wheel.

"She was having a hard time when she advertised for help." Claire continued to pick at her uneasiness like a scab. "Apparently, she took a tumble last summer."

"You leave her to go into town. Hell, you walked up to the farm this afternoon." He cranked the truck engine but kept it in idle.

"You're right. It doesn't make sense but . . . everything seems scarier at night."

He shifted into reverse and maneuvered to the main road. "Even if Bigfoot wandered out of the woods hungry, he wouldn't eat Ms. Meadows. She's a tough old bird."

Claire let out a small laugh. "I'm not worried about monsters in the dark. I'm worried about ones closer to home. What if she falls again? What if she breaks a hip?"

He wasn't sure what assurances he could offer. "Have you told her yet?"

"Told her what?"

"That you're leaving Highland."

She turned her face toward the window, but her green-tinged reflection from the truck instrumentation was pensive. "She knows I have to leave eventually, but we haven't agreed to a date yet. I thought I would talk to Preacher Hopkins to see if he can find a replacement."

"By the way, how did he find you?"

She squirmed a little. "It was fortuitous. I had just told the blokes I was done. They left me in the parking lot, and I had a mini-meltdown because I had nowhere to go. He offered me a ride, and we got to talking. Next thing I knew, I was meeting Ms. Meadows."

"He's a good man." What were the ethics of pumping a preacher for information?

"Honestly, it would be better for her to have someone who can drive anyway."

"I don't know that she would agree. She seems fond of you."

"I'm fond of her too." The shock in her admission made Holt shoot her a smile.

"You're surprised?" he asked.

"I'm dumbfounded. I never meant to get attached. To *anyone*."

Ouch. Her dig hit him somewhere in his chest, dangerously close to his heart. "You can't help who you care for. It's natural to want to belong."

She shifted toward him. "You mean like in a family?"

He half shrugged. "Sure."

"There is nothing natural about my family. We are a strange bunch, and I'm the strangest of all."

It was difficult to suss out her relationship with her family. Sometimes it sounded like she resented them, and other times she obviously shouldered regrets. "Families can be weird. Sometimes on the farm, a mother will reject her calf for no reason at all."

"Does it die from neglect?"

"No. Another cow might step in, especially if she has recently lost a calf. Or we'll bottle-feed the calf until it's old enough to survive on its own. If your parents were off skiing all the time, who took care of you?"

She was silent for so long, he wondered if she hadn't heard the question. "They weren't gone all the time, but when they were, Demilson looked out for me. He was a . . . friend of the family."

"What about friends from school?" The kids he'd gone to school with like Anna and Izzy and Big Eddie had known him practically since birth and formed a safety net of connections he'd relied on through the years.

"I have a feeling our school experiences were different."

"Are kids different in Scotland? Were you picked on or something?"

Her regard was blistering in the small space of the cab. He was being weighed and judged in her eyes. Would he prove worthy of her trust? With a sigh, she seemed to come to a decision. "I attended a boarding school."

Boarding schools were so out of the realm of his experience, he could only pull on movies and books for perspective. One thing they had in common was rich people. What sort of life had Claire run away from and why? Instead of asking her what he really wanted to know, he stayed with a less aggressive line of questioning. "Was the school harsh or fun?"

"Both on occasion, but it was mostly fun. It was all girls. You can imagine the self-inflicted drama."

"Did you have lots of friends?"

"I thought I did, but none stuck."

"Why is that?"

She made a pensive humming sound and stared out the windshield. "The same social hierarchy that ruled our parents' world extended to us in microcosm. It was a game I was never willing to play. Most of them went off to university and I didn't. Our lives diverged."

Speaking of games, he wondered if he'd already lost with her. Claire had spent her entire life not letting herself care too much about anyone and moved on before it became a possibility. He wasn't likely to change her mind, much less her heart.

And yet . . . Ms. Meadows had wormed her way behind Claire's defenses, and she'd insinuated he had too. Was there hope?

"You followed your dream. That's something to be proud of," he said.

"Yeah, that's what people keep telling me, but I wasn't being brave. I was—*am*—a coward. A bloody coward."

Holt swallowed, unable to find a reassuring platitude. He'd chosen the safe path and stayed home on the farm. It hadn't been easy, but he loved the work and couldn't imagine doing anything else. Did that make him brave or cowardly? He didn't have anything reassuring to tell himself either.

Instead, he took her hand in his and linked their fingers. They might not build a lasting connection, but they could connect here and now. He half expected her to pull away, but she clutched his hand as if he offered a lifeline.

They made the turn onto Main Street and Claire gasped, sitting forward on the seat. "It doesn't even look like the same street at night."

Holt was used to the over-the-top decorations, but through Claire, he appreciated them through a fresh perspective. Every streetlight was wound with twin-kling lights, and Santa or Rudolph or Frosty outlined in lights hung from the tops.

Most of the businesses had strung icicle lights across the awnings and outlined their windows in tin-sel. Red-and-green-tartan bows decorated the wreaths scattered through town, and the life-sized blowup Santa in a kilt playing the bagpipes had started in plenty of tourist selfies.

The tree in the center of Main Street took up the alcove, its branches extending into the sidewalk. Jessie Joe and Jessie Mac had done a spectacular job on the decorations. While it wasn't anything compared with the Rockefeller Center tree in New York City, it had become the focal point of Highland's downtown dur-ing the holiday season.

"Highland is a wacky little town, but I love it," Holt said.

"It stands to reason I would pick the wackiest town to lie low in." Her grin eased the tension pulsing from her.

He found a parking spot toward the end of the street. The mild clear day had turned into a chilly clear night. Without jackets on, they walked briskly down the sidewalk toward the pub.

Claire took his hand and tugged him to a stop in front of the tree. A tartan ribbon and bows glowed in the string of lights winding around it. The star at the top was heavy enough to bend the branch. The imper-fection only added to its charm.

"My parents had professionals decorate our house for Christmas," she said softly. "It could have been a magazine spread."

Her small admissions were slowly filling in the por-trait of her childhood. She had grown up with plenty of money and not enough attention. He gave her hand a squeeze. "I assume you didn't bake Christmas cookies with your mom either."

"The only time I ever saw her in the kitchen was to give the cook a menu request." Claire got them walking again, but slower now.

"A cook? Boarding school? Professional decorators? Ski vacations? How rich is your family?" He regretted the questions when she tensed, her arm strung taut against his. "You don't have to answer that."

"I don't usually talk about the way I grew up. People can get weird."

"Like they try to get close to you for your money?"

"To be clear, I don't have any money. I refused to take handouts once I left." Her laugh was tinged with self-mockery. "That makes me sound way more self-righteous than I am. I almost crawled back before the Scunners took off. I mean, the band never got rich or famous, but we started booking paying gigs at festivals. It was enough to live on, and that's all I cared about back then."

The door to the pub opened and even from the distance, music and laughter poured out along with a half dozen twenty-somethings he didn't recognize. Once he and Claire went inside, any meaningful conversation would be impossible.

He couldn't let this moment pass. Drawing her under the awning for the antiques store, he faced her. Her gaze remained on the middle of his chest. "You're not a kid anymore. You're a grown woman. You don't have to hide from your family. They can't make you go back to Scotland. Can they?"

She ruffled her hair and tipped her face up to meet his eyes. "Did you ever consider bailing on the farm and doing something completely different with your life?"

"Of course it crossed my mind."

"But you didn't bail. Why not?"

He opened his mouth and then closed it. If he wanted her truths, then he needed to give up his own. "It would have broken my dad's heart."

"But would they have let you go if you had wanted to be a doctor or lawyer or something else?"

"Of course they would have." In his heart was the confidence of a child with endlessly supportive parents.

"Because you love them, and they love you."

"Of course."

"Not every kid has parents like yours." Even though he had a few years on her, she was older and wiser than him by a country mile. "Mine have expectations. And not just my parents. I have obligations that I can't walk away from. But I'm here now. With you."

His heart squeezed. He would have to be content with whatever she could offer him, and he wasn't one to let opportunities pass him by.

Christmas lights twinkled all around them. The romantic vibe penetrated even his practical nature. He lowered his head as she rose on her toes. Their teeth clashed. She let out a little yelp and covered her mouth, laughing.

He ran his tongue over his teeth and smiled. "Is the mood deader than one of Vlad the cat's offerings?"

Chapter Eleven

Holt had a way of putting her at ease even in her most awkward moments. His smile warmed her despite the chill sneaking under the hem of her skirt. She snaked her arms back around his shoulders. "Not dead. In need of mouth-to-mouth."

His eyebrows waggled as he lowered his head. She kept still this time and let her eyes drift closed as his lips touched hers. From the outside looking in, the kiss probably appeared chaste. His lips toyed with hers until she was breathless and ready to beg for more. He didn't give it to her, merely sucked her bottom lip between his and gently nipped it before pulling away.

She lay the side of her face against his chest. Was that his heart or hers pumping as if recovering from a sprint? He stroked a hand over her hair and down her back.

"You ready to have some fun?" he asked.

She was more than ready for some very adult fun that involved his huge bed and less clothes. He put his arm around her shoulders and guided her to the pub's door. A drink and music would have to do.

After the intimacy outside, the noise and warmth

and scent of the pub were jarring. But the atmosphere also held a welcome she had missed. She had played countless pubs, and the rhythm was the same anywhere in the world. She took a deep breath and felt instantly at home.

Holt's name reverberated from patrons scattered in different groups around the pub. Of course he was well known and equally well liked wherever he roamed. With his hand on her lower back, Holt weaved through the crowd, exchanging handshakes and pleasantries and making introductions. Her cheeks were growing sore from smiling.

From the far corner of the pub, Iain Connors snagged her attention. He stood half a head taller than most men, talking to someone much shorter with a sliver of red hair visible. Holt had been drawn into a debate about the state of the dairy market. She caught Holt's gaze and pointed toward the corner.

"I'll join you in a sec," he said.

Claire made her way toward Iain and Anna, forcing herself not to look back at Holt even though her neck grew hot. Maybe she was afraid he wouldn't actually be looking.

Iain spotted her first, giving her a spare lift of his chin in greeting, although he didn't take his eyes off her when he whispered something in Anna's ear. The petite redhead turned with a wide smile and closed the distance between them, looping her arm through Claire's and steering her toward the seclusion of a back table.

Various musical instruments sat on chairs or leaned against walls, and a pang like homesickness reverberated like a dissonant note in her chest. The most she'd done since her last performance with the Scunners was sing in the shower.

Turning her attention to Anna, Claire was struck by the difference a few days had made. In their previous meetings, anxiety and worry had drawn circles under her eyes and stolen her smile, but the storms had cleared and left behind a glowing serenity.

"I assume you and Iain have everything worked out?" Claire asked.

Anna and Claire settled into a niche behind a table strewn with empty beer bottles. The hum of conversation cast a net of privacy.

The light that came into Anna's eyes was brilliant. "I'm having the baby. Marriage wasn't on my radar, but we both knew it was going to happen eventually anyway. It makes sense for us to go ahead and get married. It will make Iain's immigration easier anyway. Lots of pros."

Claire's sharp intake of air was from surprise and happiness and the tiniest hint of jealousy. Claire didn't begrudge Anna her happily ever after. She had earned it.

Claire feared not only hadn't she earned one, but she didn't deserve her own happily ever after. Any relationship with Holt would be growing on top of a fault line of half-truths. It would only be a matter of time before it crumbled.

Claire's smile grew tremulous. She was thankful Anna was so caught up in her own delight, she didn't notice. "When is the big day?"

"I'm not sure when we'll get married, but probably before the baby comes. That would make Mom happier. She's old-fashioned."

"Do you want a big wedding?" Claire asked.

Anna rolled her eyes with a shake of her head. "I've never wanted a fancy church wedding. Even if lightning didn't strike us down at the altar, I'm not sure I could look Preacher Hopkins in the eyes while I repeat my vows if I'm visibly pregnant. The man taught me in Sunday school when I was eight."

"If you do it soon, no one would even know you're pregnant." Claire glanced down at Anna's flat stomach.

"Even if I wasn't pregnant, I wouldn't want a big wedding. I wasn't that girl who dreamed of getting married and having kids. In fact, before Iain, I thought it would never happen, and I was totally fine with that. My students are my kids. You know what I mean?"

Claire did understand. She had no desire to be a mother only to screw up her kid. Not to mention the fact she'd never been truly honest with a man. "I've never liked a bloke enough to even consider the L-word, much less marriage and bairns."

Anna's gaze shifted somewhere over Claire's shoulder before returning. "Not even Holt?"

Holt had snuck closer to the true heart of her than anyone, and she was tempted to invite him in and tell him everything. But if it was going to end anyway, wouldn't it be easier if neither one of them were fully invested?

"I barely know Holt. Anyway, he deserves a woman who can be his partner in every way. What we're doing is merely a fun distraction. I can't stay in Highland."

"Why not?"

Claire sputtered for an answer before landing on a childish, lame, "*Because*."

A sharp curiosity tinged with laughter flitted across Anna's face. "Your fun distraction is headed this way," she murmured.

Claire shifted to watch Holt. A thrill zipped through her as if her heart had plugged into an energy source. His kilt swung around his knees, his movements full of power and grace. He possessed a singular masculinity the kilt only emphasized. The universal question popped into her head. What was Holt wearing under his kilt and would she get an answer tonight?

Holt slid an arm around her shoulders. "Sorry about that."

"No worries. I'm not needy and requiring all of your attention." Claire battled an unusual vulnerability.

"You may not require my undivided attention but you certainly command it." His focus was so intense it might have been only the two of them in the crowded pub.

Claire's hand found its way to his shirt, and she grabbed a handful and drew him closer to continue what they'd started outside by the Christmas tree. The staticky whine of electronics scythed through the pretense of intimacy.

Claire leaned away from Holt. A flurry of activity was taking place in their corner. Five men took up various instruments and made their way to the semicircle of a dais in the opposite corner, including Iain, who cradled a guitar.

The man tapped the microphone and said too loudly into it, "Ladies and gentleman, the Highland Jacobites!"

She faced the stage and Holt slipped behind her, his arm around her waist. Her weight shifted backward into him. His heat and strength exerted their own gravitational pull. It was too easy to lean on him—physically and metaphorically.

The Jacobites arranged themselves in a semicircle. The hum of conversation had picked up in intensity while the musicians took some tuning chords, then fell silent as the band launched into an upbeat Scottish reel.

Claire's toe tapped without conscious thought. The beat infected her like a virus. Or was it an antidote? She closed her eyes and let her head rest against Holt's shoulder.

"Why don't you join them for a song? Iain and the boys would be happy to have a professional." The heat of his breath in her ear made a shiver skate down her back.

Only then did she realize she'd been humming along, the lyrics scrolling through her head. "I can't."

"Why not?"

"Because I left the Scunners." It sounded lame even to herself. She had left her band, not lost her voice or stopped loving music.

The chesty sound he made landed between confusion and amusement. "Singing one song in a small-town pub doesn't count as a betrayal of your old band. Why are you punishing yourself?"

She half turned in his arms to see his face. "I'm not."

Or was she? Returning to the family fold would mean shutting the door on music.

Holt didn't argue, only held her in place with his steady blue eyes. It took a physical effort to force her gaze away. When she did, she noticed Anna watching them intently. The other woman shifted the direction of her stare from them to the band. The vibes coming from Anna were a mixture of protective and calculating.

"What the story with you and Anna?" Claire asked before she could stop herself. She had zero right to get upset by anything in his past. "Did you two ever date?"

His laugh was devilish. "Never in a million years could I imagine dating Anna. She's like a sister. I've known her since before I could walk. I'd pull her pigtails and call her carrot. She'd yank my shorts down during recess. You know, we were friends."

"That's quite a shared history." The ache in her chest felt a lot like jealousy. Not of his past with Anna but of a future Claire could picture in vivid, painful detail. Holt would watch Anna and Iain's child grow and be part of its life as an almost-uncle. Anna would attend Holt's wedding and be godmother to his first child. A daughter with dark-blond hair like him.

Claire put the brakes on her runaway imagination. If she was going to leave Highland with her heart intact, she had to live in the moment and not regret what could never be. Closing her eyes, she took a deep breath and tried to appreciate where she was. The here and now was Holt's solidness at her back and music she loved in her ears.

The first set of music faded and the swell of conversation took its place. The band leader announced a break. Iain weaved his way back to their corner, stopping to chat with Anna before pinning Claire with his gaze.

Claire fought the urge to make a run for it, although she wasn't sure why. Iain hadn't recognized her. Not that she looked like the young redheaded whisky heiress from the papers so many years ago. Still she tensed, waiting for the question she dreaded.

"Will you join us for a song in the next set, Claire?" Iain asked.

Although she should have expected the request, she was surprised. And relieved. Relieved enough to nod with the enthusiasm of hearing a not-guilty verdict. She tempered her answer. "One song. I'm out of practice."

"We'll take what we can get." Iain backed away and whispered something in the ear of one of his bandmates.

The man raised his beer in Claire's direction with a grin.

She already harbored regrets at her agreement.

"Why the dread at singing?" Holt asked.

"No dread." She forced her lips to move but wasn't sure it was into a smile or a grimace.

"You are an amazing singer, but a terrible actress."

She let her facade drop. "It's silly, but I don't want to be reminded of how much I miss singing."

Holt's lips pursed a moment. "That pipes player must have really pulled a number on you."

For a few blinks, Claire was confused. Then she remembered using Jamie as an excuse. "Not really. No one's heart was broken. At least, mine wasn't."

"Sounds like you're hard on hearts. Should I beware?" Though his tone was light, his gaze was heavy.

Was he insinuating his heart was involved even marginally in what they were doing? The way her heart answered the question made her wonder about the state of her vital organ. Before she had to formulate a response, the Highland Jacobites were called back to the stage for their second set and Iain gestured her over.

"You know 'Caledonia,' don't you?" Iain asked on their way to the dais.

Claire's already off-kilter heart stumbled. It was a song about missing one's home. Every Scottish singer worth anything knew the song. She didn't want to sing it, but before she could suggest another song like "Big Country," she was in front of the microphone and one of the boys behind her was counting off.

While it wasn't the biggest stage she'd been on, she stared out at the packed bar with a rising panic. Stage fright had never infected her. Until now.

Her gaze darted from face to face until she found

the one she was looking for. Holt had stepped out of the corner shadows and stood in the sea of people, his arms crossed over his chest. Solid and dependable.

She'd never been lucky enough to have someone in her life like him. Or maybe she'd never given anyone a chance to be solid and dependable. It was a question she couldn't ponder when her cue in the music was approaching.

She took a deep breath and sang the melancholy song not to Scotland, not to her parents, but to Holt. She already knew that she would miss Holt when she left Highland. Her Scottish lilt thickened and sweetened.

The bar noise receded, and now the sea of faces all watching her filled her with satisfaction. She held the audience in her hand. It was addictive, and she'd missed the power.

When the last plaintive note died away, applause cut by whistles had her grinning at the crowd. Phones were in the air recording her performance and snapping pictures for social media. Dread stole into her and left a lump in her stomach and throat.

The sandy-haired band leader leaned to speak in her ear. "How about one more?"

After months of being scrupulously careful to stay off her family's radar, she'd gone and effed it up. Tilting her face away, she shook her head and hopped off the dais. She ignored the compliments and requests for a selfie and pushed through the crowd to find Holt. His smile anchored her and made her feel safer in the chaos.

"Will you take me home?" The desperation she couldn't keep out of her voice erased his smile. "Now?"

"'Course I will." Holt slipped an arm around her shoulders and led her through the crowd to the door, brushing off attempts to engage them in conversation in a way that didn't offend anyone.

As soon as she hit the sidewalk, she didn't stop until her back was against the brick wall in the alcove next to the sparkling Christmas tree, seeking safety in the shadows. She never should have gone to the pub with Holt. She'd known better and yet she couldn't resist wanting to do regular couple-y things with him even though they weren't a couple.

Holt leaned his shoulder against the wall next to her. The wall of his body blocked the chilly breeze and added a layer of protection her psyche needed.

"What—or who—are you afraid of, Claire?"

"I'm not—"

"Don't lie to me. Smythe isn't your real name, is it? I could help you if you'd trust me. Do you want to try to answer my question again?"

There was no anger or impatience in his expression, only disappointment. An emotion she was keenly familiar with. She'd been a disappointment all her life. She wouldn't lie to him, but neither would she invite him to judge all her past decisions and heartaches.

"I want you to take me home," she said hoarsely. "Or else I'll walk."

"Claire, would you please just—"

"No!" She turned away from him and started toward the road to Ms. Meadows's.

He fell into step next to her. "Come on, I'll drive you home."

While her pride was screaming at her to keep walking all the way back to Ms. Meadows's house, common sense won out. "Fine."

"Fine."

Their combined maturity level was in a free fall. She resented having to take his hand to climb into the truck. Why did the bloody behemoth have to be so far off the ground?

He joined her, closing his door a little too hard, and cranked the engine. She shivered in the cool air blowing out of the vents and scrunched herself as small as possible, staring out the passenger window, grateful for the darkness pressing in on all sides.

Even if someone happened to post her picture or a video on their social media, the possibility of her parents or Lachlan finding it was low. But not impossible. Lachlan would be on the first plane out to drag her home. Her parents might send Dennison, or maybe they would wait her out in Scotland. She fingered the hair at her nape. They might not even recognize her.

The farther down the dark, deserted road she traveled, the safer she felt. That was part of the problem: Holt made her feel safe. Too safe. She needed to keep her guard up, and she couldn't around him.

As he turned down the narrow lane to Ms. Meadows's house, she shifted slightly to look out the front windscreen, but as she took a deep breath to tell him they shouldn't see each other again, he cleared his throat.

"Look. It's not in my programing to half-ass things even if this is supposed to be a fling or whatever. I can't help but care and worry about you. When you're ready to trust me, come find me. Otherwise, don't bother." His voice was gravelly and cut her deeper than she expected considering she had been ready to deliver the same message.

"Understood." And she did understand him. She wanted more than anything to slice her heart open and excise the pain. He would know how to stitch it up and make it all better. But she couldn't take the risk.

She pushed her door open and in the harsh light of

the cab, she stole one last look at him. He remained in profile even though she was sure he could sense her regard. Finally, she hopped out, shut the door behind her, and quickstepped to the porch.

Only when she was inside did she give in to temptation and peek through the curtains. The truck hadn't moved. Her heart paced faster, wondering if he would stride to the front door, apologize, and offer to take whatever she could give. He reversed out of the lane and disappeared.

And still she stared out of the window hoping for a different outcome. It wasn't relief but a profound loss that filled her. One shaky breath followed another until they had evened out and she had control of her emotions. Their one night in bed together had rocked her foundations. A second time might blast them into rubble. It was for the best.

"What's the matter, girl?" Ms. Meadows's sharp voice made her start and spin around. Ms. Meadows was in her dressing gown and standing like a sentinel in the hallway, her hands resting on top of her cane.

While Claire wasn't a good liar, she was excellent at deflection. Which is exactly the skill she needed to employ at the moment. Slapping on a brittle-feeling smile, Claire took a breath and promptly burst into tears.

Chapter Twelve

Claire came awake not with a start, but slowly with her memory expanding like ripples on placid loch water. Her stomach was a mess of nerves and knots, her head throbbed from her crying jag the night before, and her eyes were still swollen.

She couldn't even say that she and Holt had broken up. Two dates and one roll in the sheets didn't constitute a relationship. She felt like she'd loaded her heart in a tiny trebuchet and aimed it at the side of a cliff. Is that why it was called a fling?

She lay back and rubbed her eyes with the heels of her hands. A knock on the door had her bolting upright. Ms. Meadows didn't wait for her to say anything but toed the door open and shuffled inside the room.

Ms. Meadows had let Claire cry on her knobby shoulder, fixed her hot chocolate, and tucked her into bed without asking her any questions. She'd only shushed and *there, there*'d until Claire had fallen asleep.

Exhibiting the same kindness from the night before, Ms. Meadows plopped a glass of water on the bedside table, a few droplets sloshing out, pulled out a bottle of aspirin from the pocket of her flowered dress, and gestured at the side of the bed. Claire scooched over to give room for Ms. Meadows to sit at her hip.

"You look like the devil gnawed on you and spit you out, girl. Take the medicine." Ms. Meadows waited until Claire had taken two aspirin and drunk all the water.

"I'm sorry," Claire said softly.

"For what? Being human?"

Claire huffed a small almost-laugh and fiddled with the edge of the thermal blanket. "I'm supposed to be taking care of you. Not the other way around."

Ms. Meadows patted Claire's busy hands and squeezed slightly. "It feels good to take care of someone else for a change. Now tell me: Do I need to load the shotgun and give Holt Pierson what-for?"

Her almost-laugh turned into a real giggle at the image she painted. "Holt didn't do anything except ask me for something I can't give him."

"And what's that?"

"The truth."

"Ah, yes. I've been wondering about that too, but I vowed not to push you. I understand more than most wanting to keep pain close." Neither of them spoke for a moment, then Ms. Meadows added, "Will you allow an old woman to give you some advice?"

"I would love some," Claire said.

"There are good people in the world. Ones who want only the best for you. Life can be a long, hard road. Having someone to share your burdens with makes the going easier."

Her words burrowed deep. Claire had been traveling alone for so long, she couldn't remember what it was like to have a companion. Truths overwhelmed Claire until she couldn't keep them contained any longer.

"My name isn't Claire Smythe. It's Claire Glennallen." Claire collapsed back against the pillows and waited to see whether Ms. Meadows recognized her name.

Ms. Meadows tilted her head. "Are you kin to the folks who make the whisky?"

Claire nodded. "My family started the distillery a hundred years ago."

"I see." It felt like Ms. Meadows could see through the crack in Claire's defenses to everything else she'd kept hidden. "I assumed you were hiding from a boyfriend, but you're not, are you?"

"If only it was so simple. It's my family I'm hiding from."

"Why?"

A simple question with an answer that had grown more complicated over the years. "I don't know. Because I'm a coward? I'm not close with my parents, but there are expectations that I'll enter the family business. To complicate matters further, I have a cousin whom I made promises to a long time ago. He's counting on me too."

"You're here to figure out where your loyalties lie?" Ms. Meadows asked.

"Yes, I believe I am." Claire nodded once, finally able to acknowledge what she hadn't been able to articulate even to herself. "I can't keep burying my head in the sand, but I promise I won't leave until we find a replacement for me."

Ms. Meadows smiled, but there was a sadness in her eyes. "I've been figuring things out too, and I've come to a decision."

"What's that?" A sudden fear of being thrown out on her bum tensed her muscles.

"I'm going to move into an assisted living facility

after the New Year and sell this place to the Piersons."
A waver in her voice brought Claire to sitting once
more to take Ms. Meadows's hands.

"But this is your home."

Ms. Meadows looked around the small bedroom.
"This was my son's room. I didn't touch it until years
after Samuel died. He came in here sometimes and
grieved. I don't think he realized I could hear him. Our
sadness colored the walls, but the foundation was always love and happiness. I couldn't imagine leaving. I
thought I'd die here."

Tears stung Claire's eyes. How could she have any
left after last night? Maybe grief was like love. People
had an endless supply of both. "I can't imagine you
anywhere else than here. Why leave now?"

"I'd forgotten how to care about someone else until
you came along. I miss the connections." She looked
to the posters still tacked to the walls of bands and
basketball players, the edges curled with age. "I still
have some living to do. Several old friends of mine
are in a nice facility at the edge of town. They play
bridge and take buses to shows in Atlanta. I think I'd
like to see more than these walls before I kick the
bucket."

"That sounds absolutely brilliant, ma'am." Claire
smiled her first real smile.

"Will you help me sort through the house before
you skedaddle off to solve your own problems?"

"Of course. When do you want to start?"

"Now I've made the decision, an urgency to get it
done is like an itch I need to scratch. What do you say
to a little breakfast and then we'll get to work?"

The next three days passed in a flurry of activity
that was a welcome distraction from mooning over
Holt. Unfortunately, she couldn't keep him from ran-

sacking her dreams, and she woke every morning with a hollowed-out, empty feeling.

On the third day, a storm front rolled in after the temperature had risen into springlike sixties. Ms. Meadows stood on the porch and stared up at the darkening sky. Although it was only late afternoon, the sky was like dusk.

Ms. Meadows's worry transmitted to Claire. "What's wrong?"

Ms. Meadows squinted harder at the sky. "Don't like the feel in the air. Let's see what the weatherman has to say."

On the telly, a woman gesticulated in front of a radar with lots of green and red and yellow. Talk of the possibility of tornadoes being spawned by the moving front had Claire's stomach clutching. Tornadoes belonged in *The Wizard of Oz* during the summer, and not in the foothills of the Blue Ridge Mountains right before Christmas.

"Oh, dear," Ms. Meadows said as she sank into her arm chair.

"How terrified should I be?" Claire asked.

"We'll be fine here in the hollow. A few trees might get blown over in the woods, but the house has survived worse. Much worse. We might lose power, though."

The two of them stayed in front of the telly and watched the front creep closer to Highland. Rain pelted the windows and roof, and the wind gusted against the house and sent shudders through the walls. The lights flickered once and then the electricity cut out with a snap, leaving only the noise of the storm to fill the unnatural silence.

"What now?" Claire asked.

"The power won't be back on until morning at the

earliest. I'm going to bed." Ms. Meadows rose, leaning heavily onto her cane, her breathing heavy for so little exertion.

Claire popped up from the sofa to take her arm. "Are you feeling okay?"

Ms. Meadows offered a wan smile. "I'm tired is all. We've been working hard."

Ms. Meadows shuffled into her room and shut the door. Claire put the niggle of worry down to the storm. The wind rattled the windows and sent the chimes hanging on the front porch into a fugue.

Claire rocked and waited for something momentous to happen, but the house stood strong against the storm, and Claire found that as the tension ebbed, fatigue crept into its place.

She was physically and emotionally exhausted. The restlessness of her nights combined with the work of organizing the house caught up with her. Instead of crawling into her bed, she stretched out on the sofa, still feeling the need to maintain a vigil. Weather in Scotland could be unpredictable, but it was not usually violent.

A sound woke her. Her heart thundered and she bolted uptight, attempting to pinpoint the threat. Full darkness had fallen, but it could be anywhere between early evening and right before sunrise. The soft patter of rain fell, but the wind no longer buffeted the house. For all she knew, she'd open the front door and find them transported to a different land.

The noise came again and this time, it registered as distinctly human. Clumsy and disoriented from sleep, Claire scrambled off the couch and ran toward Ms. Meadows's room, banging her shoulder against the doorframe.

She skipped the etiquette of knocking and entered. "What's wrong?"

Ms. Meadows was a dark shape under the covers, and Claire flipped the light switch. Nothing happened. The power remained out. "Bloody hell and damnation," she muttered.

"That's no language for a young lady to be using." Ms. Meadows's voice came out as a breathy laugh that morphed into a cough.

Claire scooted her feet along the floor to avoid tripping or stubbing a toe. "I thought I heard you call out."

"I'm having trouble getting my breath." Her words came haltingly. "And my chest is tight."

Panic seized Claire's body. She needed to stay by Ms. Meadows's side. No, she needed to call for help. "Who should I call?"

"No one. I'll be fine. Could you get me a glass of water?" Ms. Meadows pushed up against the pillows.

The darkness shrouded Ms. Meadows's face, which in turn made it difficult for Claire to determine how ill she was. She decided not to argue until her adrenaline faded, and she could have a good think on what to do. With her eyes adjusting to the darkened house, she made her way to the kitchen, filled a glass, and returned, only bumping her knee once and her big toe twice.

She handed the glass to Ms. Meadows. The old woman's hands shook, and she used both to bring the glass to her lips for a sip.

"That does it. Something could be seriously wrong, ma'am. I'm calling nine-nine-nine."

"You dial nine-one-one here."

Claire noticed Ms. Meadows didn't argue with her. It took some fumbling for her to make her way into the den and locate the cordless phone. Instead of a comforting backlight to the numbers, it was dark. She hit buttons but nothing happened. The cordless phone wouldn't work until the power came back on. She didn't have a mobile phone and neither did Ms. Meadows. She could bike for help. Except her chain was still broken.

What were her options? She could stay with Ms. Meadows and hope she didn't worsen until the power came back on, when she could call for help. Or she could head to Holt's farm. But would he help her considering their last parting?

Ashamed, she dismissed the slight punch of doubt. He was a good man. A trustworthy one.

She returned to Ms. Meadows. "How are you feeling? Better, worse, or the same?"

"Uncomfortable, but no worse."

"How long have you felt sick?"

"I was dizzy earlier, but I woke up with the tightness in my chest."

"The cordless phone isn't working with the power out, and my bike chain is still broken. It's going to take me awhile to get to Holt's cabin."

"It's closer to cut through the woods."

The fact Ms. Meadows wasn't arguing ratcheted up Claire's anxiety. Holt had pointed to the woods from his back porch and said Ms. Meadows's house was only a short distance as the crow flies. But could she do it in the dark without pooping her pants in terror?

"How far it is?"

"Ten minutes or less on foot. Look for the path behind the shed. Once you cross the creek, turn slightly west."

"West?" Would she wander the wilds of Georgia until she turned feral?

A breathless chuckle had Ms. Meadows launch into a cough. "Veer to the right once you cross the creek. You can't miss the cabin."

She would save precious minutes by facing her fears—one of them at least—and trekking through the woods. "I'll go as fast as I can. Holt will know what to do."

Claire hesitated, loath to leave her employer. No, her *friend*. The emotions roiling through her were impossible to put into words. "Ms. Meadows . . ."

Ms. Meadows grappled for her hand in the dim light and gave it a squeeze. "I'm not going to give up the ghost, girl. Now, get on with you."

Claire stumbled out the back door and took a deep breath of rain-washed air. The passing front had left behind cooler temperatures. Droplets still spit out of the sky in bursts, but the clouds had broken up and the flash of the moon provided an unexpected comfort.

She slipped behind the shed and scanned the uneven growth of trees, spotting two narrow openings in the dark-green branches twenty feet apart. Which one was the trail to Holt? Aware time was ticking away, she chose the one on the right, because . . . why not?

The going was slower than she would've liked. Roots and rocks and brambles caught her unawares. She went down on her hands and knees once, the wet seeping into her jeans. Water rained down on her every time the wind shook the trees.

She stepped through a spiderweb and let out a yell that would have done her Scottish ancestors proud in pitch if not in courage. Linear time ceased to exist for her. It might have been minutes or hours. Just as she was imagining how long it would take for a bear to eat her, she stepped out of the thick trees onto the narrow bank of a stream.

Sidling to the edge and squinting at the flowing water, Claire assessed the depth and breadth, but it was impossible to estimate. The moon had scurried behind more clouds. Logic decreed the stream would be swollen after the deluge, but was it dangerous?

Broken branches lined the bank, and she tested the water with one. The current grabbed hold and tugged it out of her hand. She tried again with a different branch, this time holding it in both hands. The water was somewhere between calf-and knee-deep close to the bank, but less than a dozen feet across.

The spot she stared at seemed as narrow and shallow as any other. Who knew what pitfalls were hidden along its path? At this point, she couldn't retreat and go around by the road. Seconds accumulated into minutes the longer she dallied. She had no choice but to cross.

She inched toward the edge of the bank with the intention to lower herself into the water. Before she could enter gracefully, the sodden earth gave way under her boots. The current pulled her feet out from under her before she could gain traction. She scrabbled and grabbed for anything stable, finding a thick root in her hand.

She was able to right herself and push to standing. The water swirled around her knees. It was swift, but now that she was in it, the far side of the stream appeared tantalizingly close.

One good leap would put her in the shallows on the other side. The water was dark and she tried (and failed) not to imagine what could be lurking underneath. Leeches? Snakes? She shuddered from fear and cold. Her sodden jeans were clammy and plastered to her legs, and her boots were cement blocks weighing her down.

What if Ms. Meadows had worsened? She was counting on Claire, and it had been a long time since anyone had counted on her for anything. She couldn't run away from this. Even more telling, she didn't want to.

Gathering in a huge breath in case she went under and was swept downstream, she stabilized her footing, bent at her knees, and pushed off. It was inglorious and clumsy and she flailed widely, but she made it to the opposite shallows and was able to gain traction on a submerged log.

She ended up on her knees, the water rushing around her hips but not swift enough to drag her in farther. She staggered to her feet and clamored up the other side, breathing hard and thanking whatever deity was watching over her.

Trees lined the other side and threw off her bearings. All she could do was follow Ms. Meadows's directions and veer toward the right, which was hopefully west and would bring her to the clearing leading to Holt's cabin.

Not bothering to scope for a trail, she ducked under a low pine bough. The woods weren't as dense on this side of the stream, and a clearing was visible after only a few feet. She burst out of the tree line and scanned ahead of her for cabin. A sob escaped when all she could see was rolling hills. Time was slipping away and with it, her hope.

Then she saw a darker shadow in the night. Holt's cabin. She ran toward it, stumbling over her own feet before righting herself. The going was easier in the meadow. She sluiced through calf-high brown grass. A small herd of cows was gathered under a lone tree in the middle. She gave them a wide berth.

No lights shone from the cabin. A sudden fear that Holt wasn't home assailed her before the gears of logic turned. The power outage would have affected the farm as well. A battery of emotions marched through her. Worry at her reception, fear for Ms. Meadows, but mostly relief knowing no matter what, Holt would help her, and she didn't have to handle the situation alone anymore.

She took the stairs up to his back porch in two leaps and banged on the door with a fist. "Holt! Are you here? Please be home." After yelling his name, she said the last in a smaller, more desperate voice and put her ear against the door, trying to contain a spate of tears.

Footsteps sounded on the other side and before she could pull back, the door jerked open, leaving her to pitch forward into Holt. Without thinking about propriety or the uneven footing of their friendship, she wrapped her arms around him.

He was shirtless. And hot. In both temperature and the percent of muscle exposed. She couldn't stop herself from burrowing against him. The hair across his chest tickled her cheek, and his heart thumped a steady albeit quickened rhythm. The cold water had seeped into her bones and left her shivering.

"What's the matter?" He sounded as if her earlier panic had diffused to him.

"Ms. Meadows is sick and her phone isn't working with the power outage. Can you call an ambulance to her house with your mobile?" Urgency had her words tripping over themselves, but it seemed he got the gist of her message.

He lifted her away from him, spun on his heels, and strode through the kitchen. She stepped inside but didn't stray off the tile onto the carpet. She had already messed things up between them. No need to include soiling his carpet with her squelchy boots.

Once he'd hung up the phone, he returned to stand in front of her. The shadows hid his expression, and she became aware of the fact that he hadn't invited her inside.

"I need to get back to Ms. Meadows." Her chatter-ing teeth made the words stutter out of her.

"You need to get dry clothes on."

"N-no time. She's all alone, Holt. Would you please give me a ride? I don't think I can make it back over the stream." Now that she was safe and the ambulance had been called, exhaustion crept onto her shoulders like a giant hand pressing her down.

"Of course. Hang on a second." He disappeared, and she remained where she was, wrapping her arms around herself for warmth. She closed her eyes and rocked back and forth to try to generate heat.

A soft blanket enfolded her in an embrace. She popped her eyes open and fisted the blanket tighter around her. His return had been silent. Or had she dozed off standing up? If animals could do it, people probably could too. She touched her mouth to make sure she hadn't drooled.

He had dressed in a half-tucked T-shirt and jeans. "Come on out to the truck. We might even beat the ambulance to the house."

She relinquished control to him and did his bidding, climbing into the truck and wilting in the seat. The artificial interior lights were a shock after the darkness of the last few hours.

Neither of them spoke on the drive to Ms. Mead-ows's house. Holt dodged around downed limbs. A fallen tree across the road halted them, but only for a moment. He engaged four-wheel drive and swerved off the road onto the muddy verge. The tires spun and the back end of the truck drifted down the embankment before finding a grip and bumping over the rough ter-rain and back onto the road.

Claire white-knuckled the edge of the seat, her heart pounding. "Can an ambulance navigate this?"

Holt's mouth tightened, but his non-answer was answer enough.

The bushes on either side of the lane to Ms. Meadows's house were broken and bent, obscuring the view. Her mailbox had been knocked down. The ambulance could easily pass it by in the darkness.

Holt pulled up and Claire had the door open before he'd come to a complete stop. She dropped the blanket as she ran toward the front door. How long had she been gone? It felt like the sun should be rising, but darkness still had a solid grip on the world.

She clattered through the front door and called Ms. Meadows's name. Claire stopped in the bedroom doorway, afraid to venture further. What if she was too late?

"Hello, girl." Ms. Meadows's voice was a mere whisper.

"Oh, thank the stars." Claire sagged against the doorjamb before gathering herself and moving to the side of the bed. "An ambulance is on the way. I took forever, didn't I?"

"Not so long. Twenty minutes maybe. I'm glad you didn't get lost." The strain in her voice was telling.

"It was a near thing."

Footsteps sounded down the hall and the dark form of Holt appeared. "Hanging in there, Ms. Meadows?"

"By my fingertips."

"Burt down at county dispatch called and said a tree on the main highway was blocking the ambulance. They're having to take an alternative route, but it shouldn't be much longer."

"Thank you, Holt. You've proven yourself to be a fine young man." Her ragged breaths were coming in near pants. "If I'd known it would only take hiring a pretty girl to get you Piersons to come around, I would have done it years ago."

"It shouldn't have taken a pretty girl to get me to check on you. I apologize for that. But now we're truly neighbors again, I won't make that mistake again."

Am I the mistake? Claire tensed, but his expression was a mystery in blackout.

"If you want to ride to the hospital with Ms. Meadows, you should change into dry clothes, Claire," Holt said.

"What happened?" Ms. Meadows asked.

"The stream was rain-swollen and deeper than I expected. I got a soaking."

Ms. Meadows reached out a pale hand, and Claire took it. Her hand was thin, but her grip was gratifyingly strong. A siren cut through the silence, growing louder. Flashing lights reflected through the open front door and down the hall.

Holt guided the emergency personnel inside and to Ms. Meadows's room. Space was scarce, so Claire made her way to her small bedroom to change clothes. Another wave of relief almost drowned her. Ms. Meadows was in the hands of the professionals. Everything would be okay. Wouldn't it?

Her wet jeans were shrink-wrapped to her legs, and they fought her every inch as she stripped them off. Grit and leaf litter were stuck to her clammy skin. She did her best to brush herself clean. What she needed was a hot shower to banish the chill she couldn't shake, but there was no time for niceties. Fumbling for clothes, she pulled on whatever her hands landed on first.

Bumps and squeaks and the murmur of conversation increased her urgency. She needed to be ready to leave with the ambulance. The noise in the hallway increased in volume. She eased her door open.

Ms. Meadows was half reclined and strapped on a gurney. A woman pushed from the head and a man pulled at the foot of the contraption. They both had radios strapped to their belts with a mouthpiece lashed close to their shoulders.

Claire grabbed clean socks and her still-wet boots to pull on as she followed them outside. Holt stood out of the way at the bottom of the porch stairs. "They'll take good care of you, ma'am."

Claire hopped as she pulled on her socks and stuck her feet in her boots, leaving the ties flopping. Water from the soles and sodden leather seeped through her socks. "Wait! I need to go with Ms. Meadows."

Holt grabbed her wrist and halted her rush forward. "Let them have the room to work. I'll give you a ride to the hospital."

The flashing red and white lights of the ambulance gave his expression a sinister cast. She swallowed and said, "I've already asked too much of you."

He gave a slight shake of his head. "Maybe I asked too much of you."

The cryptic retort left her nonplussed.

"We'll follow you, Jennifer," Holt called out.

The EMT shot a grin at Holt. "Good luck keeping up."

Either the situation wasn't as dire as Claire feared or the EMT was into gallows humor. Claire acquiesced and climbed into Holt's truck. The seat was damp and chilly from her earlier ride.

Holt followed the ambulance, which had its lights flashing but had not turned the siren on. Claire kept her gaze fixed on the lights. Several minutes passed before she worked up the courage to ask, "What did you mean back there?"

She half expected Holt to play dumb, but he didn't. "I meant, maybe I was asking for more than you're able to give. Maybe I don't deserve your truth."

The words were like a hammer to her heart, cracking it wide open. He deserved so much more than what she could offer him.

The bright lights of the hospital drew her insides as tight as a bowstring, and part of her welcomed the worries about Ms. Meadows. It made her own fears seem insignificant.

The ambulance pulled up to two glassed automatic double doors. The EMTs had Ms. Meadows out and were entering the emergency area by the time Holt had parked the truck in the main lot.

They trailed the gurney inside, and Claire didn't have time to whisper words of encouragement to Ms. Meadows before they rolled her out of sight for evaluation. Her eyes were closed and her hands crossed at her waist in the standard funeral positioning. An oxygen mask obscured most of her face, but her chest rose and fell in a now steady, unlabored rhythm.

With tears springing into her eyes, Claire teetered on her feet. Big warm hands cupped her shoulders from behind, and any strength deserted her in the face of such temptation. She leaned into Holt.

Claire couldn't help Ms. Meadows, and Holt couldn't help Claire. What was the point of having friends if they only brought heartache? She'd been part of the Scunners, yet apart from them at the same time. It had been easier that way and yet . . .

Maybe the point wasn't to help Ms. Meadows or to expect Holt to help her. The point was to have a hand to hold through the rough spots.

"My family should have been better neighbors to Ms. Meadows. When Dad comes home, I'm going to sit him down and give him a good talking-to," Holt said.

The parental tone he took made her smile through

her worry. Holt would make a good father. She stiffened against him even though she hadn't voiced her opinion aloud. Holt could never be more than her friend, and even that had an expiration date.

His arm snaked around her chest to pull her even closer to him. His body felt heavenly against hers. She fit against him like she was the lost puzzle piece finding its match. "You're an ice cube. Can I warm you up?" His breath tickled her ear and sent a different sort of shiver through her.

Okay, maybe they could manage friends with benefits.

The notion was forgotten when a black woman in a white coat came into the waiting room with a brisk efficiency that left Claire half intimidated and half in awe. Without stopping, she scanned the room and changed course on spotting them. Claire stepped out of Holt's sphere toward the doctor.

With a smile, the doctor held out a hand, shaking first Claire's then Holt's hand. A smile was a good sign. No one smiled politely before delivering tragic news, right? Except they were in the South, where, according to Ms. Meadows, *bless your heart* wasn't a Christian blessing at all.

"Good to see you, Holt. How're your parents?" The doctor's accent was honeyed Southern but crisp like the comb. DR. MARILEE IVEY was embroidered across the pocket.

"Fine. Dad semi-retired and is taking Mom on a sojourn around the country in an RV. They're down in Florida basking like lizards for Christmas." Holt and the doctor were obviously friends of long standing.

"How's Ms. Meadows?" Claire interjected impatiently.

Dr. Ivey tapped the e-tablet she held. "You must be Claire, Ms. Meadows's caregiver."

"Is she going to be all right?" Claire was seconds away from stomping her foot.

"With the right treatment, she's going to be fine." Finally, Dr. Ivey looked up and met Claire's eyes with an earnest transparency that set most of Claire's anxiety at ease.

"What treatment? What is wrong with her?"

"Ms. Meadows's heart went into atrial fibrillation."

"That sounds serious," Holt said.

"Left untreated it can lead to stroke, but you did the right thing in bringing her to thc hospital. We are going to try to get her heart back in rhythm using drugs, and if that doesn't work, then we'll use a small electrical shock."

"And that's it? She'll be as good as new afterward?" Claire asked.

"Well . . ." The drawn-out qualifier from the doctor threw a match on Claire's worry, making it flare once more. "She'll have to take blood thinners for some time to avoid clots, and it seems her blood pressure isn't well controlled at the moment. But, yes, she'll be as good as new after some tweaks."

Claire drew in a shuddery breath. "How long will you keep her in the hospital?"

"At least overnight. The cardiologist will see her tomorrow to decide the next steps."

"Can I see her?" Claire asked.

The doctor shook her head. "We'll start pushing the anti-arrhythmics through her IV shortly, and she'll need continuous monitoring. I'm afraid you'll be in the way. She told me to tell you to head home and to get some sleep." Dr. Ivey's smile was kindly.

Claire voiced her worst fear in a whisper. "She's not going to die?"

Dr. Ivey reached out and squeezed Claire's hand. "Not on my watch. I'll call in the morning with an update. What's your number?"

Claire glanced over at Holt helplessly. Holt cleared his throat and rattled off his number. Dr. Ivey nodded and strode through the automatic double doors. The doors shut with a clack.

Holt's voice was firm and ready to repel her arguments. "You are coming home with me."

Strangely, she didn't want to argue. "I hate to keep asking for favors, but that sounds great."

She almost smiled at his shocked glance toward her. "You must be exhausted. Let's go. You can get cleaned up at my place. With luck, the power will be back on."

Claire hoped her relief wasn't as palpable as it felt in the sterile waiting room. "Only one night, though. I don't want to impose."

His blue eyes scrunched at the corners as if he was suppressing a smile. "We'll see. Hospitality is what we Southerners are known for, after all."

His drawl dripped with innuendo. Or was that her imagination? Or more likely, wishful thinking. He turned and rocked toward the exit, his brows raised in an unasked invitation to follow.

Resistance was futile. Her body was already moving alongside his before her brain had the chance to consider the implication. Exhaustion rose up in the silence that blanketed them in the cab of his truck. She sank into the buttery leather of his seat and let her eyes drift shut.

The truck's engine spooled down, and the lack of movement made Claire jerk to consciousness. Disoriented, she looked around but didn't see the comfort of lights coming from Holt's cabin.

"The power is still out, then?" She rubbed her eyes.

"Looks that way. I have a gas water heater, though, if you don't mind showering in the dark."

"A shower would be amazing." Sandy grit made her scalp and clothes itch.

The darkness inside the cabin was dense and even though she followed Holt closely, she stubbed the toe of her boots against the edge of a couch and the leg of a side table.

"Do you have a torch?" she asked.

"A torch? No, I'm not a caveman. I do have candles and I might be able to dig up a flashlight."

A slight laugh whispered past her lips. "A torch *is* a flashlight."

"Ah. Scottish speak." He walked with more confidence than she felt in the unknown layout. "Hang on, let me find some matches."

Claire waited.

A few curses punctuated the sound of Holt rummaging through drawers. "Remind me not to store the matches with the scissors."

The flare of a match broke the blackness and illuminated his face. A candle sputtered to life. Holt lit a second candle with the match and offered one of the jars to her.

"You know where the bathroom is. I'll grab you a T-shirt and shorts to change into. Once the power is back, we'll do a load of laundry." He disappeared into his bedroom, one poster of his bed visible through the crack in the door.

Nerves in her stomach sizzled like sparklers. Their night together had left an indelible memory, but she needed to put his bed out of her head and focus on the couch. That's where she should sleep tonight.

He returned holding a bundle. She took the clothes and hugged them to her chest. Their scent was fresh and masculine. She should have gone back to Ms. Meadows's house because if she was ready to bury her nose in a T-shirt he wasn't even wearing, what was she likely to do to him?

She accepted the truth. She wanted Holt. She wanted to trust him. She wanted to share everything with him. She wanted to take his hand and lead him to his four-poster bed.

Instead, she backed into the bathroom and shut the door.

Chapter Thirteen

Claire sped through her shower, not sure when the hot water would give out. Washing away the dirt and grit was heavenly. Being surrounded by the smells of his shampoo and soap was strangely comforting. Or perhaps not so strange when she really wanted to be surrounded by the actual man.

She dried off and slipped the shirt and shorts on sans knickers or bra. Not surprisingly, Holt's clothes were too big. The neck of the shirt slipped toward one shoulder, and she had to roll the waistband of the shorts to keep them up. Even so, they hung low on her hips. Using his comb, she cleared the snarls in her hair. Between the weak candlelight and the fogged mirror, she could do little else in terms of her appearance.

She balled up her clothes for the washer and cracked open the bathroom door to assess the situation. Cooler air streamed over her and made her shiver. Candles lit the room in a soft glow from the coffee table. Holt was on his haunches, blowing on the beginnings of a flame in the stone fireplace.

She allowed herself a moment to admire the curve of his muscled thighs in his jeans. He was barefoot and had changed into a soft-looking long-sleeved T-shirt, although he'd shoved the sleeves up his muscled forearms. His back moved with his efforts to start the fire. He was one giant, beautiful muscle.

The rich scent of food made her stomach growl. A faint hint of steam wavered in the candlelight from two large mugs. The promise of hot food swept away any self-consciousness, and she stepped out of the bathroom and toward the couch. It appeared to be some sort of soup or stew in the mugs.

"How did you manage to heat up food?" Her fingers itched to take up one of the mugs and start shoveling the soup in a manner unbefitting her birth.

Holt turned, still squatting, and smiled at her. "Gas stove. Having hot water and hot food makes our plight a bit less torturous, doesn't it?"

"It's not tortuous at all. It's—" She almost bit her tongue to stem the word *romantic*. It was dangerous to think that way.

The silence between them wasn't quiet in the least. It was filled with words unspoken and feelings unnamed. Finally, Holt rose and gestured toward the mugs.

"Give me your clothes and then eat before it gets cold." His voice was rough, as if the words had tried to claw their way out.

She sank onto the couch and wrapped both hands around the nearest mug. The aroma of beef and vegetables tickled her nose. After putting her clothes in the wash for later, Holt returned and set a bottle of Glennallen Whisky on the table along with two glasses.

He dropped into the nearest armchair, his knee close enough for her to reach out and touch, and picked up the other mug of stew.

Doing her best to ignore the bottle of whisky mocking her from the table, she stared into the mug and tucked in. After the last spoonful, she set the mug back down and scooted into the corner of the couch, searching for warmth.

"Has it turned colder or am I a wimp?" She aimed for jovial and landed somewhere near a whine.

"There's a blanket behind you. You definitely don't qualify as a wimp after your adventure tonight. The temperature dropped fast after the front moved through. We'll be in the thirties by the time the sun rises." As if on cue, the wind whistled down the chimney and made the flames dance and crackle.

"And when will that be? Ten minutes?" Claire had lost all sense of time since waking with Ms. Meadows. The night had felt interminable. She was exhausted, yet wired at the same time.

"A few hours yet. It's not quite two AM."

"You haven't heard from the doctor?" The fleece of the blanket was soft and warm against her bare legs.

"I doubt we'll hear anything before shift change in the morning, but Marilee is one of the best. She'll take good care of Ms. Meadows." His confidence did little to soothe her worry. He lifted the whisky bottle and she tensed, half expecting him to present it to her as Exhibit A of her trial. Instead, he raised his brows. "Interested in a glass?"

"No." The words came out with a virulence that would be difficult to explain. She tempered her voice and returned to her own line of questioning. "You and Dr. Ivey seem to know each other well."

"When you grow up in a small town, you tend to know everyone well. Sometimes too well." Regret and amusement warred in his voice.

Claire straightened on the couch, getting more than she'd expected with the simple observation. "Were you and the doctor a . . . a thing?"

Of course Holt had dated other women. She had no right to feel territorial considering she had been the one to push Holt away. He would be better off with a woman like Dr. Ivey. She was smart, capable, and not hiding any secrets.

Holt's eyebrows quirked. "We saw each other a few times. It was years ago and fizzled out. Our schedules never meshed."

"Oh, good." As soon it was out of her mouth, she realized how petty it sounded. "I mean, not good that it didn't work out. That's too bad. You should really go back after her."

"I should?"

Of course he shouldn't. What drivel was coming out of her mouth? The last thing she wanted was to push Holt into the lovely, capable doctor's arms for comfort.

"No, you shouldn't."

Holt knocked back the last of the whisky in his glass, stretched his legs out in front of him, and linked his hands over his stomach. "You are the most frustrating, confusing, *fascinating* woman I've ever met."

A laugh-sob rose up and escaped from her throat. The prickle of tears was as unwelcome as it was unexpected. The amber whisky reflected her guilt in the candlelight. "I know. I'm a terrible person."

"That's not what I said at all." He sat forward, his forearms braced on his knees as if he wanted to touch her, but was unsure of his welcome.

She stared at his hands, strong and capable. Even as she told herself she didn't deserve him, she longed for him to lay those hands on her—in comfort or desire, she wasn't picky.

With a muttered curse, he hauled himself up, sat next to her, and pulled the blanket over his legs. The heat of his body and the familiar scent of whisky on his breath blasted away her rickety defenses.

"You're right. My name isn't Smythe. It's Glennallen. Claire Glennallen." Her long exhale was one of relief. She'd told the truth.

Hadn't she? The long silence that followed made her question her sanity.

"Glennallen," Holt said softly. "Like the whisky?"

"Exactly like the whisky. As in that's my family. I'm due to inherit a percentage of the company in a few weeks."

"Ah. Hence your comments about complicated families and responsibilities." The crackling fire filled the quiet. "Do your parents want you to come home?"

Home had been an unfamiliar construct most of her life. It was only since coming to Highland that she understood what a home should feel like. Warm and welcoming and somewhere she could be herself.

But Holt wasn't asking her to wax philosophical. "My parents need me home."

"That's not the same thing."

"It isn't, but I don't know what my parents want. We're not close. We never have been."

"Why?" The simple question was difficult to answer. How long had it taken Newton to determine why the apple had fallen on his head?

"I wasn't what they expected. I showed no special talents. I didn't stand out amongst their friends' children. I was a disappointment."

"Is that what they told you?"

"Not in so many words, but it's how I felt."

"Did you leave in order to rebel?" There was no judgment in his voice. His arm snaked around her shoulders, and she notched herself into his warmth and laid her cheek against his chest.

"Maybe? I really did love music though." She hesitated and dug deeper for the truth. "I'll admit I took great satisfaction in telling my parents I wasn't going to university. My father almost had an apoplectic fit. My mother cried."

"They were shocked and probably worried about what would happen."

Claire closed her eyes. Was he right? Maybe, but at the time she'd only seen anger and disappointment. "I was probably being unfair, but they didn't make it easy to reconcile. It's like they were waiting for and wanting me to fail. Father expected me to fall into line like my cousin Lachlan."

"What's your cousin like? Are the two of you close?"

"We used to be fairly close. He loves the distillery. It's his passion. Whereas I could pick up that bottle and smash it against your stone hearth with not a moment's remorse." She huffed something resembling a laugh. "Except for the broken glass."

"I would imagine there's quite a bit of money involved in your inheritance."

Normally, she never discussed the pounds and pence of her inheritance, but with Holt, she was comfortable, knowing he wasn't a money-grubber like some of the boys who'd come sniffing around before she'd joined the Scunners and assumed a different name. "Which is why no Glennallen comes into their inheritance before they turn twenty-five. It's supposed to give us time to mature and finish university."

"It's not too late. You could still go to university," he said.

"Ugh. I'm terrible at maths."

His laugh rumbled at her. "I skipped college too."

She rolled her head back on his shoulder in order

to see his shadowy profile. "You didn't need to go, did you? You knew you were going to manage the farm."

"Yeah, but it was hard to see all my friends go off to college and come home with stories about parties and tailgating when nothing had changed for me."

She wrapped an arm around his chest and gave him a hug. "Do you wish things had turned out differently?"

He ran a hand up and down her arm, causing a shiver to pass through her that had nothing to do with cold. He seemed to be seriously considering her question. "No. This is what I'm meant to be doing. I'm a good manager. A great farmer. I understand animals. Working the farm was my destiny, and most days I love it. What about you?"

She pulled her hand back into her lap. "What about me?"

"Is Glennallen your destiny?"

"Does it matter? It's my reality. My great-great-grandfather founded Glennallen Whisky, and I'm expected to take up the mantle." The truth was bitter on her tongue.

"But is that what you want?"

"What choice do I have?" She couldn't live in Highland forever, especially not with Ms. Meadows choosing to move to an assisted living facility. Neither did she have any desire to go back on the road and tour. She had no skills to survive a regular life.

"Surely there are options."

Impatience with herself shortened her words. "I've spent the last five years selfishly chasing something I could never have—my freedom. I made a promise to Lachlan, and I won't let him down."

Holt made a chesty sound of acknowledgment. Of course he understood duty. Claire sagged against him, relieved. While she had strived to be opaque, he had always been transparent. The relief at stripping away her secrets had left her with a lightness of spirit that she hadn't experienced in so long, she had forgotten what it felt like.

"What would have been your second choice of career?" she asked.

"I've thought I'd make a good veterinarian like Doctor Jameson. Or even a lawyer."

An image of Holt as a British barrister in the traditional black robes and white wig made her giggle. "I have no doubt you'd succeed at any profession you tackled. Do you ever regret taking over the farm?"

His pause was pregnant with futures that would never be, but in his voice she could only hear his certainty. "I don't. What about you? What would you be if you weren't on the hook with the distillery? What do you love?"

She stared into the glowing orange embers in the fireplace and pondered his question. She had spent so long running from something, she had never considered a destination. Maybe because she knew anything other than working at Glennallen Whisky was an impossibility.

What did she love? Music. She loved music. While algebraic equations had seemed unnecessary to her life, music had been like water or air. Necessary to her survival. "I love music. I wrote a few songs for the Scunners. They were good, but there's not a huge market for Scottish rock music, believe it or not."

"I can imagine there's not." His laugh tickled her heart. "What about teaching music?"

"Teaching? Like kids?"

"Or adults. The community college offers adult

education classes. Fun stuff like dancing and photography and music."

She picked over the implication. Was he saying he wanted her to stay in Highland? But no, it was impossible. They barely knew each other. It was too complicated. "I couldn't teach. I'm not—"

"Stop it right there. You are smart and strong and talented and anyone who says you aren't can stuff it where the sun don't shine."

Leave it to Holt to get her laughing through her stifling insecurities. He was sorely wrong about one thing: She wasn't strong. She wasn't strong enough to walk away, and neither was she strong enough to tell him what she really wanted.

But she could show him. She scrambled into his lap, settling astride him, and took his face between her hands. The stubble on his cheeks rasped against her raw hands. It only made her feel more alive.

His kiss was more intoxicating than any whisky ever made.

He threaded his hand through her hair and tugged her head back. With his lips on her throat, he murmured, "What happened to being just friends?"

"Dash that."

Her borrowed shirt ended up over the whisky bottle, the shorts on the floor. Holt's clothing was tossed at the end of the couch. Either the fire had warmed the room, or they kindled their own heat. She ended up back in his lap, riding him. It had the ingredients for quick and dirty sex. Instead, it was slow and sexy.

Claire let her lips travel over Holt's cheeks, eyelids, jawline before settling on his mouth. With the lies stripped away, Claire could love him the way she'd wanted to for a long time. This time, she met his gaze as she orgasmed and didn't hide the tear that trickled down her cheek.

He wiped it away with the pad of his thumb and joined her in a pleasure so intense, it left them gasping and limp. The chill eventually returned and instead of covering them with the blanket at his hip, Holt picked her up and carried her to the four-poster bed in his room and tucked them under the covers.

Her last thought before drifting into an exhausted sleep was she felt like she was home. Finally.

Chapter Fourteen

Holt jerked out of the black nothingness of sleep, blinked, and attempted to place himself in the universe. His bed. Snug under the covers. A woman curled into his side. Naked.

He turned his head. Claire Smythe—no, Claire Glennallen—lay next to him, her hand curled under her chin and all the worry of the weeks before erased from her face. She was beautiful in her innocence, but he preferred the sarcastic light in her eyes and the wry twist of her mouth. She was complicated, and he liked that.

Yes, she'd lied to him, but he'd known she'd been hiding something. He hadn't come close to guessing she was a whisky heiress, though. Glennallen Whisky was his favorite and had worldwide recognition. And she didn't even like the stuff. He grinned.

His insides rearranged themselves the more he dwelled on Glennallen Whisky. It sounded as if she were resigned to accepting her inheritance. Who was he to argue? Hadn't he done the same?

She had family in Scotland, and no matter the state of their relationship at the moment, he hadn't missed the note of longing in her voice when she spoke of them. Her inheritance would bring her wealth and security. There was no reason for her to stay in Highland.

What did he have to offer? Nothing to compete with what waited for her in Scotland.

Sunlight filtered through clouds diffused through the room, lifting the darkness of their blackout. He glanced over. His bedside clock blinked. The power was back on.

His phone chirped with a message. He muttered a curse and grabbed it. The voicemail was from Marilee and gave no information, only a request to return her call. Holt hit the number and waited through three rings before Marilee answered with a clipped, "Hello, Holt."

"How is Ms. Meadows?" Holt kept his voice low, but it woke Claire anyway.

She bolted upright, the sheet clutched nearly to her chin. He regretted being the one to force reality back on her. She swung around and stared at him with wide eyes, waiting for the answer.

"Her heart has returned to a regular sinus rhythm." It sounded like Marilee was only half invested in the conversation. Beeps and the sound of voices were in the background.

Holt lifted the phone from his ear and hit the SPEAKER button. "I assume regular sinus rhythm is good news?"

"Yes. The drugs worked, and she converted around five AM. She'll be on blood thinners and needs to see the cardiologist to determine next steps."

"When will she be released?" Claire asked.

If Claire's presence was a shock for Marilee, no surprise filtered through the phone. "Probably tomorrow. I've ordered more tests to make sure we aren't missing an underlying problem. Visiting hours don't start until ten, but I'm sure she'll be happy to see you both then. Keep in mind, though, that she's had a long night."

"We'll be there. Thanks for everything, Marilee."

"It's my job, but I'm glad I was on duty. My shift is ending, but I'll check in later this evening when I'm back." Marilee hung up.

Holt dropped back into the pillows and wished he could pull the covers over their heads for a little longer, but duty called.

"I've got to see to my chores before I can run you up to the hospital for a visit." He slipped out of bed and stretched.

"Blimey! Put some clothes on before you have to take *me* to the hospital for heart failure." Her words were muffled, but when he turned, she had only pulled the comforter over her nose, leaving her eyes peeping over.

"Are you telling me you're feeling shy after last night?" Heedless of the embarrassment his nakedness was causing her, he put a knee on the mattress and leaned over to kiss her forehead.

"It was dark and stressful. The blackout. Ms. Meadows." She sighed and leaned closer, dropping the comforter down enough so he could transfer his lips to hers for a brief kiss. "Last night was . . ."

He tensed as he waited for her verdict. A mistake or magical?

"Weird."

"I'm hoping weird means something different in Scotland." Holt tried to keep his voice light and free of hurt. After her confessions, he had no idea where he stood with her.

Although her lips curved in a smile, it was weak and more than a little sad. She caressed his cheek. "I wasn't planning on telling anyone who I really am, and now I've gone and told you and Ms. Meadows. Last night started out terrifying and then turned weird and wild and amazing. But if I'm honest—and I want to be honest with you from now on—I'm feeling off-kilter."

"I get it." And he did, even though he would bet her honesty would end up breaking his heart. "I know what will help."

She cocked her head. "What's that?"

"Keeping busy. Come help me with the animals."

"My clothes are dirty."

"You can borrow some of my mom's clothes while we give yours a quick wash."

While he was at the big house rummaging through his mom's dresser for something appropriate, Claire prepared toast and poached eggs. When he returned, his stomach leapt at the smell. They shared breakfast on his couch while watching the morning news and the reports of storm damage.

"A few degrees warmer and it could have been much worse," he said.

"I prefer Scottish mists and blizzards over storms like last night." Claire stood with his mom's clothes in her hands. Holt would be sad to see her out of his thin cotton T-shirt. "I'll be ready in a jiff."

He had just cleared their plates when she returned and did a quick twirl before striking a pose that made him grin. The jeans were too long but otherwise fit well. The flannel shirt and down vest made her look like she belonged on the farm.

His grin grew brittle and he turned away to give himself a mental talking-to. He could not let himself imagine her belonging to the farm or to him.

She cleared her throat. "What comes first? I've always wanted to learn to milk a cow."

Surprise wiped away the discomfort of the moment. "Have you really?"

"Ever since watching *The Quiet Man*. Maureen O'Hara gave John Wayne hell."

"I've never seen it, but I think my parents have it on DVD."

"Oh, we need to watch it sometime."

"Okay. It's a date." He raised an eyebrow and watched, fascinated, as pink spread from her neck to splotch her cheeks. How could a force of nature like Claire be so easily thrown off-balance?

Guiding her toward the door, he said, "The milking is done by machines these days. A few men work on the farm to herd the cows into the milking barn, but you're in luck. We currently have one cow who needs some TLC. First, though, we have to feed the gluttonous goats."

Holt did so, and Claire lingered to laugh at their antics. "They're natural comedians."

"It's a good thing they're cute and funny because they're not good for much else." Although he said it good-naturedly, it was the truth. His mom had abandoned her idea for goat yoga in favor of traveling, and he wasn't interested in getting into specialty goat milks or cheeses.

She leaned an elbow on the fence and turned to him. "Does every animal have to pull their weight on a farm?"

"Yep. Even the cat has a job." He sighed. "Look, farming is hard work, and the profit margins are slim even in the best years. We went all organic two decades before it got trendy. Our milk fetches top dollar, but it's a tough business. We can't afford to feed animals that don't bring in money."

"That's harsh. Entertaining you and making you

laugh and feel good isn't enough? They have to make you money or you'll throw them out like rubbish?" The tenor of the question was tart.

He opened and closed his mouth, wondering where he had gone wrong.

Before he could formulate an answer, she continued. "Why don't you kick them out to fend for themselves, eh? I'm sure they'll be fine."

Her hands were curled around the top rail of the fence, her knuckles white. He put a hand over hers. "I would never throw them out like rubbish. I'm not cruel. They do make me laugh and keep me entertained. The goats will be perfectly safe and happy with me, I promise."

She closed her eyes and muttered through clenched teeth, "Bloody hell, I'm the Glennallen goat."

"What?" Confusion fed the knee-jerk question.

She turned to meet his gaze. "I'm entertaining, but useless. I'm a bloody goat."

"You do make me laugh and keep me entertained, but you're also immensely talented and smart and kind."

"I'm none of those things." She proceeded to tick off her fingers. "Firstly, singers like me are a dime a dozen. I'm nothing special. Secondly, I didn't even pass my A-level maths. Thirdly, I took the job with Ms. Meadows not because I wanted to help an old lady, but because I needed a place to crash for a few weeks."

"You may have taken the job for your own reasons, but only someone who cares would take off through the woods in the middle of a storm to find help. That took real courage and heart."

"I was terrified the entire time. I'm a coward at heart."

"Quit calling yourself a coward." Holt gripped her shoulders. "Being scared is not the same being cowardly. Doing what's right despite your fears is the actual Merriam-Webster definition of bravery."

"It is?" A flicker of something—hope?—flared in her eyes. He actually had no idea, but she didn't need to know that.

"It is," he said with more force than the question warranted.

She shot him a considering look then stepped away, her back to the goats. "What's next?"

If she wanted to change the subject, he wouldn't probe old wounds. "Next up is our troublemaker cow."

It was cozier in the barn. The sounds of various animals snuffling and shuffling were as comforting as a lullaby, and the earthy scents brought forth nostalgic memories of childhood and adolescence.

Roy, one of the farm's long-standing hands, was hauling buckets of oats to the various stalls. The barn housed animals who were injured or sick or having a difficult labor.

"I'll handle the troublemaker, Roy." Holt waved toward the stall to his right.

"Right-o, Holt. Everyone else is fed. I'm headed to the milking barn unless you need me for anything else." Roy glanced between him and Claire, the deepening of the grooves along the side of his mouth signaling a slew of teasing questions later.

Holt made a shooing motion and waited until Roy ambled out of sight before joining Claire at the stall door. The troublemaking cow chewed on alfalfa, her udder full and hanging low.

The wind gusted through the open door with a bite, and Claire shivered.

"Come on. Let's get this done. We don't want to chance missing visiting hours at the hospital." Holt was almost thankful for the distraction.

"Why is she a troublemaker?" Claire asked.

"She busted through a loose gate and snacked on bitter weeds. Not for the first time, I might add. They soured her milk. She'll remain culled and be hand-milked until she sweetens."

"That seems like a lot of extra work for a repeat offender."

He entered the stall and patted the brown-and-white cow on the rump. "Come on in. She won't bite. Probably."

"A ringing endorsement." Claire sidled inside and the door snicked shut behind her, making her press herself against the wall. "I've changed my mind. I'll watch from here while you do your thing."

"We already established that you aren't a coward, Claire Glennallen." The use of her real name jolted her gaze to his.

She shushed him as if a spy tasked with reporting to her parents was lurking. "I'm still Claire Smythe as far as anyone else in Highland knows."

"All right, Miss Smythe. Come on over and I'll teach you to squeeze some teats."

A laugh stuttered out of her and she took a tentative step toward him and the troublemaker. "That sounded weirdly sexual."

"I promise you there is nothing sexy about milking a cow." Holt grabbed a stool from where it hung from a peg on the wall and positioned a bucket under the cow's udder. "You sit and take hold of a teat."

"That's basically her boob. I can't grab hold of that without an introduction at the very least. It would be rude."

"Would you like me to perform introductions?" His hand flourish was over-the-top but did its job pulling a slight smile to her lips.

"Aye, I would be most pleased to make her acquaintance. What's her name?" She shuffled closer to put herself within arm's reach of the cow in the crowded stall.

"She doesn't have a name. She has a number." He leaned on the cow's flank and tapped the identifying tag punched through the cartilage of her ear like a ring.

"A number is so impersonal."

Claire reached out tentatively and stroked the cow's soft ear. The cow raised her head to bat her big brown eyes. Holt could almost hear Claire's internal *awww*.

"Do you have a problem with me giving her a name?" she asked.

As Holt sensed Claire had already bequeathed the cow a name, he shook his head. "Go for it."

"I shall call her Maureen. That's a good name for a troublemaker." Claire grew bolder and patted Maureen's neck, then shot him a smile. "Her fur is soft. Hi, Maureen. Do you mind if I touch your teats? I'll try to be gentle."

If Claire ever saw the automatic milking operation, she wouldn't worry about being gentle. Maureen shuffled toward Claire, bumping Holt aside. Dangit, he was already calling the cow by her given name in his head. That might prove to be bad news down the line.

Holt adjusted the position of the stool and patted it. "Come on, then."

Claire sat, stared at Maureen's udder, and then poked a teat with a finger. "It feels weird."

"Let me demonstrate." Holt squatted, took hold of the two nearest teats, and expressed the milk, muscle memory taking over. He couldn't even remember learning how to milk, but he did his best to explain how to work the teat from the top down.

"Are you sure it doesn't hurt her?" Claire glanced

over at Maureen's head, but the cow munched on alfalfa and acted like they weren't even there.

"Trust me, we're doing her a favor. It hurts worse
if the milk builds up. Plus, the risk for mastitis in-
creases." He took her hand and helped her get started.
It took a few tries, but Claire got into a rhythm.

"I'm doing it." She shot him a satisfied look.

After five minutes, she began to flag and hunched
her shoulders. He tapped her arm. "Let me finish.
Milking uses muscles you aren't accustomed to using.
It takes a long time to build stamina."

She gave up her seat without protest, and he finished the job, discarding the bucket of milk. He led her
to the barn sink, where they washed up.

"I get it now." Claire watched him dry his hands.

"Get what? Why you shouldn't name farm animals?"

"No. I get why your forearms look like that and why
your fingers are so agile." Her gaze shot to his face,
and a blush burst in her cheeks. "I shouldn't have said
that out loud."

He burst into laughter, threw an arm around her
shoulders, and hugged her into his side. "I knew my
years of farm chores would pay off someday."

She relaxed into him, and they walked side by side
out of the barn. "What's next?"

"Next, we go and see how Ms. Meadows is faring."

"I'm worried." The previous night's anxiety worked
its way into the cracks of her voice.

"Marilee sounded confident that Ms. Meadows will
make a full recovery."

"It's not just that. Everything is changing. Fast."

He stopped and turned her to face him. "Will you
do something for me?"

"What?"

"Don't make any decisions until after Christmas. Will you stick around until then?"

"I don't know . . ." Her gaze drifted off to the side, and he squeezed her hand to bring it back to him.

"Ms. Meadows won't be able to find a replacement for you this close to the holidays." Desperation churned his stomach.

"I should stay for Ms. Meadows?" She tucked her hair behind her ear in a gesture he was coming to recognize as uncertainty. It was good to know he wasn't alone at least.

"And for me. I can't think of anyone I'd rather spend Christmas with than you."

Chapter Fifteen

Claire would say no. It was a simple word. Two letters. One syllable. She barely got an n-sound out before her mouth mutinied. "Yes. Okay. I'll stay," she said instead.

Even as she internally berated herself, tension flowed out as if she'd pulled the stopper of a tub. Right or wrong, staying in Highland was what she wanted, as brief as the respite might be.

The day after the storm remained cool but the blue skies and sunshine injected much-needed optimism. After she dressed in her now clean and dry clothes, Holt ran her by Ms. Meadows's house so she could pack up a small bag of toiletries and a fresh night-gown, a day dress, and underthings.

The hospital was bustling but Holt seemed to know where to go and who to talk to. When he took her hand to lead her down sterile hallways, she was grateful. He had an instinct on when he should take charge or back off.

She counted down room numbers until they reached Ms. Meadows's room. The door was shut. With a deep breath, she knocked lightly and cracked the door to peek inside. Ms. Meadows was propped up at an angle in the hospital bed.

"Come in, girl." Ms. Meadows smiled. "I'm still alive."

"I never doubted it," Claire said even though she actually had.

"Is that Holt with you? Come on in, then. I'm decent." The bed made Ms. Meadows look small and frail, but her hair had been brushed and her cheeks were pink.

A shadow passed over Ms. Meadows's face. "They want to run a few tests and are talking about keeping me another night."

Claire set the bag on a tray on wheels, pulled an armchair over, and perched on the edge. "The doctor told us. What sort of tests?"

"Heart tests and blood work. Nothing to worry about." Ms. Meadows patted Claire's hand, which did nothing to diminish her worry. "The food isn't nearly as good as what you've learned to make."

Pride burst in Claire's chest like a Roman candle. "Only because I had the best teacher. What can I do?"

"You remember what we talked about?" At Claire's nod, Ms. Meadows continued. "Get rid of the magazines and box up the books. The library will take them. There are some nice hardbacks mixed in. You can keep any that tickle your fancy. Something to remember me by."

Claire had to swallow hard against a rising lump of tears. "Yes, ma'am. I'll get started today."

Ms. Meadows nodded and turned to Holt. "Could you give Preacher Hopkins a call? Fill him in and ask him to drop by."

"I'll do that right now." Holt stepped into the hall.

"He's a good man, Claire," Ms. Meadows murmured. Claire jolted around in the chair. Embarrassment she'd been caught mooning at the sliver of Holt she could see through the cracked door mixed with surprise at the rarity of hearing her actual name.

"I told Holt who I really am last night." Claire glanced toward the door. The low murmur of Holt's voice was steady.

"Good. You can't have a relationship without honesty."

Guilt pricked Claire like a needle, but she ignored it. She was closer to her true self than she'd been in more years than she could count. "We're not having a relationship. It can't happen."

"Why not?"

The simple question flummoxed her, and her mind went blank. Finally, she said, "My inheritance. My family."

"You should make peace with your parents, but don't live your life for them."

"But I'm a Glennallen."

"Does that indenture you to work in the whisky business?"

"I'm not qualified to do anything else." A self-deprecating laugh chuffed out. "Of course, I'm not qualified to run a business either."

"You're a musician. Do something with your talent."

"Like what? I'm tired of touring."

"Then teach. I loved my time in the classroom. It was very rewarding."

It was the same thing Holt had suggested. Was that a sign? "I would be walking away from a fortune."

If she didn't return to work at the distillery, she would forfeit everything. Her shares would revert to a trust. Neither her parents nor Lachlan would have control of them. It felt like the ultimate betrayal.

Ms. Meadows made a pishing sound. "What's money worth if you're not happy, girl?"

Claire had done without the Glennallen fortune for years, but in the back of her mind, the safety net had existed. It made the decision to leave the Scunners easy. Her mind was paralyzed at the thought of stepping into the world completely on her own.

Holt returned. Ms. Meadows held Claire's gaze and didn't bother to hide the challenge in her expression. Could Claire give everything up and teach music? It was preposterous. It was laughable. Except she didn't even crack a smile.

"Everything all right?" Holt's obvious curiosity broke the staring contest between the two women.

"Fine and dandy. What did the preacher have to say?" Ms. Meadows asked.

"He sends his best and is praying for you right now. He's doing his hospital visitation rounds this afternoon and will come by for a visit," Holt said.

Ms. Meadows relaxed into the pillows. "If you two don't mind, I'm going to take a little nap. Those nurses woke me up every hour to check my vitals and make sure my heart was still ticking."

Claire and Holt were effectively dismissed and didn't speak again until they were back outside in the sunshine. Claire lifted her face and took a deep breath. The few minutes she'd spent in the artificial lights and sterility had left her dismayed.

"Ms. Meadows mentioned a care facility in town. What's it like?" Claire asked.

"There are a couple of different ones. Surely she's not considering leaving her house?"

"That's why she tasked me with going through her magazines and books. I told her I'd help her organize the house." Claire shot him a glance. "She wants to sell the house and land to you."

He stuttered to a stop under the bare branches of a tree at the edge of the parking lot. "Are you serious?"

"That's what she said. A dream come true, right?"

Instead of pumping his fist or giving her a high-five, he gnawed on his bottom lip. "The farm isn't exactly cash-rich at the moment. We upgraded milking machines last year, and with Mom and Dad semi-retired and traveling . . ."

"Can't you apply for a loan?"

"We already hold a sizable loan for the milking machines." He ran a hand through his hair and fisted the back. "While her place has been a thorn in Dad's side, it's not a necessity to own."

"She was a teacher. Will her insurance pay?"

Holt made a disparaging noise. "This isn't Britain. Her insurance will pay for a shared room in the nursing home. If she's lucky."

"Is the nursing home nice?" The slide of his gaze to the ground and silence were answer enough. "Wait, she mentioned an assisted living place. Is that the same one?"

"No, the assisted living facility is way nicer."

Her shot of relief was short-lived.

"And way more expensive."

Claire hadn't seen Ms. Meadows's bank statements, but it was clear that she wasn't flush with money. Her wealth was in her house and land, which were only worth how much someone was willing and able to pay.

She pressed her hands against her cheeks. "There's no use in worrying about it right now."

"You're right. How about we run by the Scottish Lass for some lunch?"

"Sure." The gnawing in her stomach was more akin to anxiety than hunger.

The restaurant was busy. Holt grabbed two menus off the unattended hostess stand and led her to an open table in the back of the room. She sat and kept her eyes on the menu Holt handed her, but when it became clear no one was staring at them, she relaxed.

After putting in their food order, Claire stole glances around them. The cousins Jessie Mac and Jessie Joe occupied a table full of men around their age.

"Those men are the biggest gossips in town." Holt leaned over the table to smile at her. "I'll bet they already know about Iain and Anna."

"How?"

"They have informants everywhere and know everyone. They're more efficient than the CIA."

She forced a laugh, but his assessment wasn't reassuring.

His smile faded as he leaned closer. "Your secrets are safe with me. I didn't mean to make you worry. I wouldn't tell them anything even under threat of torture."

"I've been living as someone else for so long, it's second nature to watch my back, but I can't hide forever." The thought used to fill her with fear, but now only resignation came with the acceptance.

Holt looked as if he wanted to say something, and by the tight set of his features, it was serious. Claire tensed. Before a word was spoken, Iain strode through the restaurant toward them.

"Mind if I join you for a tick?" He commandeered an empty chair from a nearby table and sat before either she or Holt could respond. "I need help."

Holt leaned back and held his hands up in mock surrender. "Is this about you and Anna, because man, I'm not sure—"

"It's about the Burns Night festival." Iain turned to stare at Claire with his steady, disconcerting gaze until she couldn't help but squirm. "The Jacobites need you."

"Me? Why?" It was a stupid question. They needed her voice. "You guys already have a great blend of harmony. You don't need me."

"Robert has nodules on his vocal cords," Iain said.

"That's bad luck, but I can't help you." Claire fiddled with her rolled silverware.

"One good practice and two performances is all that's involved. You're a professional and already have more experience than the rest of us put together. It'll be a cinch." Iain dipped his head to catch her eye. "Please. This festival is important to Anna. Unless . . . are you leaving Highland before Christmas?"

Her gaze shot to Holt's and his brows rose. "No. I'll be here for a little while longer. I suppose I can sing with the Jacobites, but only this one time."

Iain pumped his fist once. "Thank you, lass. We're practicing in Anna's studio tonight."

"I don't have transportation."

"I'll be happy to play chauffeur," Holt said mildly.

"I know you're busy on the farm, and I've taken up too much of your time already." She tried to sound firm.

"Stuff and nonsense, Holt doesn't mind giving you a lift, do you, mate?" Iain clapped Holt on the shoulder.

"'Course not. What time do you need her there by?" Holt asked.

After the time was settled, Iain took his leave as the waitress arrived with their food. A cheeseburger and chips for Holt, and a chicken potpie for her. It reminded her of the raised pies of her youth except the crust was buttery and flakier.

"Did I overstep?" Holt asked before taking a bite of his burger.

Claire sighed and poked holes in the top of her pie with her fork. "Being dependent on someone—anyone—makes me nervous."

"Look at it as one friend helping out another."

"Friends." She wasn't in a position to question the label. There were worse things than to be sleeping with a friend. In fact, Claire couldn't recall any of her past lovers qualifying. "I suppose you're right. Thank you."

The rest of the lunch passed in discussion of unimportant topics like their favorite movies, music, and books. They had more in common than she would have guessed. Both of them liked action movies and classic rock. Neither of them had time to read, but wanted to.

As Holt was settling the bill, a dapper middle-aged man in wellies with khaki pants tucked in the tops stopped at their table. "Can we move our appointment to after Christmas, Holt?"

"Sure. No hurry." Holt gestured toward Claire. "Have you met Claire Smythe? This is Doctor Jameson, former mayor and local veterinarian."

"Nice to meet you, sir." Claire exchanged a handshake with the man.

Dr. Jameson's eyes brightened. "You're the Scottish lass I've been hearing about. Welcome to Highland. I'm fascinated with Scottish history and genealogy. I'd love to hear about your family if you have time. Dessert is on me."

Claire froze with a smile on her face, unable to think of a worse turn of events.

Holt rose and Claire followed his lead, grateful for the escape. "Claire has work to do for Ms. Meadows. Rain check?"

"Of course! Anytime." Dr. Jameson wandered to the table with the gathered men and took a seat.

"That was a close one," Holt whispered, taking her hand. "Where to now?"

"Ms. Meadows's house. I actually do have work to do. I'm going to organize her den as requested."

Holt had her back to the house in ten minutes. He let the truck idle and shifted toward her, one arm across the steering wheel, the other draped over the back of her seat. "I'll pick you up at a quarter to seven this evening. Why don't you pack an overnight bag and plan to stay at the cabin with me?"

Claire looked to the house and opened her mouth to decline, but did she really want to stay out here all alone when he had such a lovely big . . . bed? "That sounds brilliant. Thanks for the offer."

A charmingly crooked smile spread slowly across his face. "I'm not being strictly altruistic, you understand."

Her answering grin was as inevitable as the end of their relationship. "I certainly hope not."

Claire slid out of the truck and gave him a wave before entering the house. The silence was unnatural. What would happen to the house without Ms. Meadows? Would it be consumed like the old car outside?

She closed her eyes and turned in a slow circle in the den. She could almost hear the clatter of feet and the laughter of a family. Melancholy slashed and burned its way through her chest. She shook herself out of the mood, looked around her, and got to work.

The noise of the telly helped to banish the gloom, and the afternoon sped by. Stacks of magazines were ready to be hauled to a recycling center, and books were separated into hardbacks and paperbacks. With Ms. Meadows's poor eyesight, Claire wasn't sure if she would want to keep any for the sake of sentiment, but she set aside several volumes that appeared to have been enjoyed countless times.

Standing at the kitchen counter, she ate a bowl of tinned soup with white water biscuits and then washed up and placed the chipped bowl on the drying towel. It looked forlorn and lonely. Was this how Ms. Meadows felt before Claire had come to stay with her? And why was the emptiness leaking into her? She had been alone most of her life and had learned to adapt to any situation.

Suddenly she felt like an interloper and missed Ms. Meadows more than she thought possible three months ago. The job had offered a place to stay and seemed easy enough. Claire had planned to bide her time, decide on her next move, and leave with no attachments or regrets.

How had her plan blown up so spectacularly? Instead, she had gained a cadre of friends, a grandmother-like figure, and a lover.

She took a shower, packed a few things in her canvas duffel bag, and waited on the porch for Holt, unable to stand another moment of silence and solitude. At the sight of Holt's truck turning onto the lane, her heart filled with warmth and sped up.

She hopped inside the cab and before she even realized what she was doing, she leaned over and kissed his cheek. She froze at his startled expression.

"Sorry?" she said with a lilt of uncertainty.

"What exactly are you apologizing for?" He caught her wrist when she tried to retreat to the passenger door.

"Was that overstepping or whatever?"

"It was—how do you say it?—absolutely brilliant." His fake Scottish burr was so terrible, it was hilarious.

He returned the favor and kissed her cheek, but

when his mouth moved over hers, any humor disintegrated in a wave of wanting. With more self-control than she could claim, he broke away with a low whistle.

"I wish you didn't have someplace to be. Damn the Jacobites." The look he shot her could melt metal. "To be continued, Miss Glennallen."

She latched the seat belt and thought how natural her real name sounded coming from him. She had reclaimed her identity. Now she just had to figure out who she wanted to be.

The lights were on in Anna's studio, and a muffled cacophony of sound made it all the way to the sidewalk. The tuning of instruments was like hearing a favorite song. She took a deep breath, stretching her diaphragm, and smiled.

"You've missed this," Holt said as he opened the door for her.

"I left the Scunners with no regrets, but maybe leaving the band doesn't mean I have to leave music behind entirely."

Anna burst into the front room and gave first Claire and then Holt a hug. "Iain is super excited you agreed to sing. And so am I. After all, the Burns Night festival is all about music. A bonus that you are well versed in Robert Burns."

"They strip you of your Scottish citizenship if you don't love Burns." Claire's smiles were coming fast and furious these days. Her level of comfort with Anna surprised her. In a good way.

Anna looped an arm through Holt's. "Let's hang out in my office while they get on with things. It's been a while since we had a good gossip."

"I figured all the good gossip was about you and your baby-daddy." Holt tossed her a knowing glance.

Anna shushed him. "We've managed to keep the

news under wraps so far, but that won't last if you go flapping your gums."

Holt and Anna retreated to her tiny office while Claire joined the Jacobites. It took three songs for Claire to find her groove, but once she did, she was surprised at how comfortable she felt with the group. It was a different dynamic than with the Scunners. For one, these weren't professional musicians, but hobbyists who had day jobs in accounting and factories and plumbing, among other professions.

What brought them together and kept them together was a simple love of the music. They were older and more mature, and she observed no battles between egos. Robert helped her and Iain work up harmonies, and soon their voices melded with a sweetness that made her heart long for things she couldn't even name.

Her voice was tired and cracking by the time they wrapped up. She was out of singing shape but there was little time to build her stamina back up. The rest of the Jacobites packed up and headed to their various homes in a fine humor, leaving Anna, Iain, Holt, and Claire alone in the studio.

Anna tucked herself under Iain's arm and looked up at him. "You want to ask Holt now?"

"I proved at an early age that I'm a terrible singer and a worse dancer," Holt said with his trademark grin. "I'll only drive people away from your festival."

Anna waved her hand as if shooing him away. "Nothing to do with the festival. You could help with another venture we're planning though."

"What's that?"

"Our wedding," Iain said.

Claire gasped. "Congratulations! I'm so happy for you."

Anna had tears in her eyes, but a smile on her face.

It was like a rainbow appearing in the middle of a spring shower. "We were thinking sometime between Christmas and New Year. Something small. But . . . I'd like you to give me away. You've been a good friend to both of us."

Holt put a hand over his chest, his smile swallowed by his surprise. "I would be honored. Truly."

The couple visibly relaxed into each other. Anna shifted toward Claire. "I hope you can attend. You were the first one to know I was expecting. You've become part of our story now."

Claire's breath caught. She had felt like a footnote in her parents' lives, but in Highland, she was writing her own story. She daubed her dry lips with her tongue before saying hoarsely, "I don't know yet where I'll be."

The weight of Holt's regard was a physical pull she couldn't deny, and she shifted to meet his gaze. Questions she couldn't answer yet were writ across his face, but he wouldn't ask anything more of her than she'd already given him. She teetered between being grateful and disappointed.

"Yes. All right, then." Iain cleared his throat. "We'll let you two get home, shall we?"

Holt and Claire said their farewells and were in his truck headed toward the farm in minutes. The tension had accompanied them.

"You know things are complicated." Uttering the tripe made her feel like the pathetic heroine in her own romantic comedy. No, a rom-com ended happily. While she hoped things didn't take the tragic turn of Romeo and Juliet, her life was a mess. A mess no one could clean up but her.

"I didn't say anything." Holt's calm pragmatism only increased the flood of what-ifs.

What if she hadn't left the Scunners and stayed in

Highland? She would never have gotten to know Holt. He would have remained the good-looking Highlander she'd watched compete in the athletic games from afar.

She wouldn't have discovered the funny, stalwart, loyal man and most definitely wouldn't be headed to a night of fun and bliss in his bed. She packed up her regrets for another time and vowed to enjoy him while she could.

She reached across the space in the cab and took his hand in hers, linking their fingers. His surprise at her gesture registered, but she didn't acknowledge it. "You are a better man than I deserve, even if it's just for a little while, Holt Pierson."

His puckish grin stamped out the remaining tension. "If I'm such a saint, why do I want to do such devilish things to your body?"

She laughed and snuggled into his shoulder, her anticipation rising to fever-like levels.

Chapter Sixteen

After a night in which Holt fulfilled his devilish prophecy in bed, Claire helped Ms. Meadows settle back into her house. The lengthy discharge process in which Dr. Marilee Ivey had relayed copious warnings and instructions on what to do if Ms. Meadows had another episode had left Claire on edge.

It took all afternoon and evening for Claire not to tense every time Ms. Meadows rose from her armchair to go to the bathroom or to the kitchen. Claire continued to sort through books and magazines. Input from Ms. Meadows made the sorting go faster, and it was clear she was being brutally unsentimental. She was serious about selling and moving into a retirement facility.

"Did you talk to Holt? When is he going to make me an offer?" Ms. Meadows sipped her sweet iced tea. "No. That book goes in the library donation pile."

Claire flipped through an illustrated edition of *Robinson Crusoe*. "I'm not sure the Piersons are in a place financially to offer for your house and land."

"What? After all these years of sniping at me, they

don't even want my land?" Ms. Meadows looked more stricken than angry.

"Holt said they took on a loan to upgrade their milking machines last year." At Ms. Meadows's continued silence, Claire said, "We'll figure something else out."

"I can't afford the assisted living place without selling at a good price, and I don't want to go back to living here all alone." Her despondency was at odds with her usual biting optimism.

"You're not alone. I'm here."

"Not for much longer."

Claire wanted to reassure Ms. Meadows, but couldn't. Her hands tightened on the book, and she hugged it to her body as if it could offer stability. Wasn't it about a man adrift on an adventure? Maybe she should keep it as a manual. She was unwilling to make a decision because as soon as she did things would be put into motion she couldn't undo. It was cowardly and unbecoming a Scottish lass descended from battle-hungry Highlanders.

"I don't expect you to stay, girl. You have a family business to see to in Scotland. After all this time, I'm sure your parents will be thrilled to have you back in the fold. I hope you'll call me every once in a while, though." Ms. Meadows smiled, but her lips trembled with unexpected emotion, and she didn't meet Claire's gaze.

Claire cleared her throat. "Holt is renting a wheelchair from a medical supply shop, and you are coming to the Burns Night festival tomorrow. I insist."

"I'll have to check my calendar." Ms. Meadows winked and whisked away the tension.

By bedtime, they were both tired, but Claire slept poorly, fearing Ms. Meadows would wake with another episode, or worse.

Blue skies and bright sunshine greeted them the next day. The chill that had descended from the clear night warmed into springlike temperatures. It was a good omen for the street party. The Burns Night festival would begin late afternoon to attract families and continue into the evening. The Jacobites would perform twice, early and late. Several other singers and groups would also pay homage to Robert Burns, the patron poet of Scotland. She was unaccountably nervous, considering she'd played bigger venues many times.

A knock on the door had Claire and Ms. Meadows exchanging a glance.

"I'll answer it." Claire rose from the floor of the den where she sorted.

Holt stood on the porch wearing a sheepish smile, a box of Christmas lights tucked under his arm. An evergreen tree was hidden poorly behind him.

"Is that a tree behind your back or are you just happy to see me?" Claire's nerves evaporated.

Holt looked over his shoulder with a fake look of shock. "Well, would you look at that? We shouldn't let it go to waste."

He set the tree next to him and shook it. The scent was heady. It didn't invoke memories—her mother had favored a professionally decorated fake tree—but a fuzzy picture that might have been a premonition.

"It's for us?" She touched a branch, and her fingers came away slightly sticky with sap and smelling like the woods.

"If Ms. Meadows approves." His eyebrows quirked up.

Claire couldn't guess what Ms. Meadows's reaction would be. "Nothing to do but ask. Come on."

In the den, Claire said, "Holt brought a gift." She

gestured behind her but kept her eyes on Ms. Meadows.

"I haven't had a tree since . . ." Ms. Meadows's eyes
went glassy with tears. Claire tensed, ready to bundle
Holt out the door, but a smile broke over Ms. Meadows's face, one that was equal parts happy and wist-
ful. "Somewhere in the shed is a tree stand and box of
ornaments."

"I'll find them. You ladies decide where you want
to put it." Holt handed the tree to Claire and went out
the back door.

"Prop it to the right of the fireplace." Ms. Meadows
pointed with her cane.

The space had already been cleared and organized,
and Claire leaned the tree against the bookcase and
stepped back. It was a short, full tree, and already the
tang of fresh pine cut through the scent of old books
and woodsmoke.

Holt returned carrying a green plastic tree stand
and dusty bin. The sound of sleigh bells and the tinkle
of ornaments accompanied his every step like a sexy
Christmas elf. He had the tree set up in moments, and
Claire filled the stand with water. Holt opened the box
of lights he'd brought and untangled them.

Ms. Meadows opened the bin and stared inside as
if facing a chasm. Her shuddery breath drew Claire to
her knees at the old woman's side. A tear slipped down
Ms. Meadows's cheek as she lifted out a homemade
wooden ornament in the shape of a child's hand. She
laid it on her palm as if she could re-create a time when
her son slipped his hands in hers to cross a street.

With the string of lights draped over his shoulders
and twinkling, Holt stood rooted, as still and silent as
a tree himself.

Claire clasped Ms. Meadows's hand, enfolding the

ornament between them. "Are you sure you want to do this?"

Their fingers entwined like a time-lapse movie, young and old. What would the years bring for Claire, hope or heartache? No, it wasn't so simple. Her time with Ms. Meadows had taught her life would be full of all that and more.

"I should have done this years ago. Samuel and I couldn't bear to decorate after Kevin died, but it's my last Christmas in the house. It's time." Ms. Meadows pushed herself out of the chair, shuffled to the bare tree, and hung the red-painted wooden hand front and center. "Go on and string the lights, Holt."

"Yes, ma'am." His voice was raspy with reflected emotion, but he got to work. Claire helped pass around the lights and then a length of raggedy silver tinsel.

"Sing us a carol, girl." Ms. Meadows banged the end of her cane on the floor like a queen commanding her bard.

Claire would miss Ms. Meadows terribly. She fiddled with the tinsel to hide a rush of sadness. A sad song wouldn't do. She launched into "Santa Claus Is Coming to Town." Before she'd made it to the chorus both Holt and Ms. Meadows had joined her, Holt in a pleasant baritone and Ms. Meadows in a shaky alto.

Claire led them straight into "Frosty the Snowman" and "Rudolph the Red-Nosed Reindeer." She should have saved her voice for her Burns Night performances, but she had no regrets when she saw the happiness on Ms. Meadows's face. By the time she launched into "Hark the Herald Angels Sing," they had most of the ornaments on the tree.

As the sun was setting, Ms. Meadows held out a star made of silver filigree. "Don't forget the most important decoration."

Claire held the star carefully. "It's lovely."

"It was my mother's. I want you to put it on top, Claire."

The use of her given name didn't go unnoticed, but Claire didn't remark on it. Instead, she looked back and forth at Holt and Ms. Meadows. "I've never decorated a Christmas tree. I made ornaments in school, but I don't know if my mother even kept them. She certainly never had them hanging on our tree. I'll—" She swallowed, but her voice still cracked when she continued. "—never forget this."

Ms. Meadows took her hands and squeezed, giving back the comfort Claire had offered earlier. Holt slipped an arm around her shoulder and pulled her into a hug. The three of them stood connected for a long moment.

Finally, Claire laughed softly. "If I cry and get all stopped up, I won't be able to sing tonight."

"Let's get the star on top," Holt said.

Claire stood on a kitchen chair and placed the star on top. Holt turned the lights off, and even with the afternoon sun through the window, the lights twinkled merrily against the tinsel. It would be magical come the night.

Claire hopped off the chair, slipped her hand into Holt's, and whispered, "Thank you."

He merely gave her hands a squeeze. "I'll leave you ladies to get ready for Burns Night. I need to get kilted up, but will be back in an hour to pick you up. Sound good?"

Claire took care getting ready, even though her choice of outfits was limited. She topped her well-worn kilt in Glennallen colors of red and green with a white blouse and cozy woolen jumper. The temperature was likely to plummet as soon as the sun set, and she didn't want to freeze.

She styled her hair into artfully messy waves with drugstore mousse and her fingers. If she'd been playing with the Scunners, she would have molded it into a fauxhawk and applied copious amounts of glitter, but that look belonged to someone else entirely. Someone who didn't exist anymore.

Ms. Meadows dressed in comfortable trousers, sensible orthopedic shoes, and a shirt, jumper, and jacket. A knit hat and gloves poked out of her jacket pocket. Color flooded her cheeks, and her eyes were bright. Barring the hospital visit, it was the first time she'd been out of the house since Claire had arrived several months earlier. The excitement was understandable.

"We're not climbing Mount Everest, Ms. Meadows." Claire shot her a teasing smile while checking out the front window for Holt.

"Come talk to me when you're my age, you whippersnapper." The effect of her arch tone was ruined by her good-natured laugh.

Holt pulled into the drive. Her heart skipped like a stone when he walked toward the house in his kilt, his bare knees flashing. Who knew men's knees were so attractive? She sighed.

"Goodness, you've got it bad, don't you, girl?" Ms. Meadows elbowed Claire aside and twitched the curtains. "My Samuel had nice legs too. I never could get him to wear a kilt, though. Back in our day, the summer festival wasn't what it is now."

Claire opened the front door for Holt before he had the chance to knock. Holt offered his arm to Ms. Meadows and lifted her into the passenger seat of the truck without needing any help from Claire even though she hovered like a mother hen giving him useless directions. After he folded and stowed the wheelchair and Claire settled in the backseat, they were off.

Ms. Meadows pointed at various landmarks with comments on how things had changed. Woods cleared to make way for a small housing development. An old barn replaced by a new house with a stone facade. The creep of commercial businesses around Highland that spoke of progress. Ms. Meadows grew more fretful the closer they came to town.

Holt and Claire exchanged a glance in the rearview mirror. Change came to everything and everyone. Claire refused to transcribe the truth to her own situation or she might become as uneasy as Ms. Meadows.

Ms. Meadows pointed to a white-columned house advertising a law office. "That was my best school friend's house. She died a decade ago. I thought her son was living there."

Ms. Meadows craned her neck to watch the house disappear behind the oak trees. Her melancholy turned the earlier excitement bittersweet.

The traffic slowed as they approached the main drag through downtown. Police barriers had been erected to block traffic. People wandered up and down the street already socializing. Holt lowered his window, and mouthwatering scents from the gathered food trucks called like the Pied Piper. Recorded music played over speakers, but an empty stage sat ready for the live performances.

A spate of butterflies took flight in her stomach. Excitement with just a tinge of apprehension, but from experience, she expected even the tinge to disappear as soon as she opened her mouth to sing.

Holt drove straight up to the police barrier and gave a brief, but piercing whistle. A grim-faced policeman with a prominent nose turned around, adjusted his gun belt, and moseyed toward them. Claire tensed for a confrontation. The policeman put his hands on Holt's window, peered inside, and grinned. The transformation was startling.

"Why, Ms. Meadows! Holt texted he was bringing you to the celebration tonight. You probably don't remember me. Cameron Sackfield. You taught my Sunday school class when I was in elementary. It's awful nice to see you."

Ms. Meadows blinked and patted her hair. "Cameron Sackfield. My stars, but you've grown up to be a fine young man. I'll admit, I had my doubts. I remember having to sit you in the corner a time or two."

Cameron only laughed. "ROTC and a stint in the army got me straightened out. Come on through and park in Wayne's lot, Holt."

Cameron jogged to the barrier and shifted it, waving as Holt inched by to park.

Ten minutes later, Ms. Meadows was comfortably situated in the wheelchair, and Holt was pushing her into the blocked-off street. The atmosphere was festive and fun. Christmas was days away and a roving Santa passed out candy canes to children and adults alike.

Jessie Joe and Jessie Mac stepped off the sidewalk and intercepted them.

"Ms. Meadows!" Jessie Joe rubbed his hands together. "Do you remember us?"

"The Sawyers cousins. My goodness, how could I forget? I'm only surprised you remember me."

"What? You were our favorite teacher, right, Jessie Mac?" Jessie Joe tapped his cousin on the chest.

"Yes, ma'am. You sure were." Jessie Mac's manner was as soft as his cousin's was bombastic. These were the first words Claire had heard him speak, and even Holt's eyebrows rose at the pronouncement.

"Can we buy you a piece of pecan pie, ma'am?" Jessie

Joe asked. "I know of some other folks who'd love to say hello."

"That would be lovely." Ms. Meadows glanced back at Claire and Holt. "You two go and have fun."

Jessie Mac took control of the wheelchair while Jessie Joe walked alongside, chatting nonstop, pointing out the various shops along the way, and waving people over to say hello.

"It's going to be good for Ms. Meadows to be part of Highland again, don't you think?" Claire asked. "She's been hiding out too long."

Holt tucked her hand into the crook of his arm like a gentleman of old as they strolled. "I do indeed. And she's not the only one who's been hiding out too long."

She rolled her eyes in Holt's direction. "I'm getting ready to sing in front of all these people. That doesn't qualify as coming out of my shell?"

"Coming out of your shell is not the same as facing your problems."

Her sadness over the coming day of reckoning, aka her birthday, had grown heavier the closer she'd grown to Holt and Ms. Meadows. Leaving Highland would be unbearably painful.

He pulled her to a stop in the middle of the street and stroked a finger down her cheek. "I understand you have to leave, but don't forget you always have a place to land here in Highland."

Was he asking her to stay? A flicker of hope was smothered by reality. "I'll come back." She tempered the crumbs of a promise she wasn't even sure she could keep with a reluctant qualifier. "Someday."

"What if I come find you?"

Heedless of the festivalgoers streaming around them like a river around a rock, she slipped her arms around him and lay her cheek on his shoulder. Shoulders that bore the weight of expectations and responsibilities with ease.

She closed her eyes against the tension and emotion battling in her chest. Her bruised heart cried out, and her lips moved against the skin of his throat. "I love you."

He jerked slightly against her. "What did you say?"

Her eyes popped open, but she didn't raise her head. She was a total ninny. Why had she said it out loud? What now? Denial or acceptance? Wasn't that one of the steps on the 12-Step program for addiction? Addiction to Holt. That sounded about right.

"What do you think I said?" she asked, buying time.

"I think you said you . . . love me?" On the plus side, he didn't sound horrified.

She knit the threads of her confidence into something she could either hang on to or hang herself with. Lifting her head, she met his gaze head-on. "Turns out the Christmas miracle you promised happened early. You are the best man I've ever met. I didn't mean to fall for you, but it doesn't change anything."

"Of course it does."

"No, it doesn't."

"Yes, it does." His stubbornness in the face of her contrariness only made her love him more.

She opened her mouth, but no words came.

"There you are, Claire! It's time for our first set." Iain stopped a dozen feet away and waved her over.

"You go on. We can talk later," Holt said. "I'm going to find a good vantage place to enjoy the entertainment."

Feeling like a prisoner given a dawn reprieve on the way to the gallows, she slipped out of Holt's arms to follow Iain toward the stage at the far end of Main Street. Iain's excitement was contagious.

The Highland Jacobites were announced and a familiar zip of energy had Claire bounding onstage to take up the mike like the lead singer she had been with the Scunners. They launched straight into "Coming Through the Rye," an up-tempo Burns favorite.

Searching for Holt through the first verse, she finally spotted him leaning against a lamppost on the right side of the stage, his smile proud as he watched her. The warmth flooding her was reflected in her voice as she hit the chorus.

The crowd gathered around and like any good Burns Night celebration, it turned into a sing-along of the better-known songs. The Jacobites put a twist of bluegrass into the traditional tunes that suited the Southern town in the foothills of the Blue Ridge Mountains.

Claire held out the last note of "Green Grow the Rushes, O" before stepping back to make room for Iain Connors to read "Address to a Haggis," a famous Burns poem. Hearing the familiar cadence of the poem recited in a true Scots accent tumbled Claire through nostalgic memories.

No longer the center of the crowd's attention, she studied the town and the people spread out before her. The stately library and the quirky Brown Cow Coffee and Creamery. The Drug and Dime and Wayne's Fix-It shop. Besides Holt, she crossed gazes with Ms. Meadows and Jessie Joe and Jessie Mac and Preacher Hopkins. This was a town where happiness seemed to brush her fingertips, but she feared grabbing hold would be impossible.

She etched details in her memories. The extravagant Christmas tree with the crooked star on top. The lampposts bedecked with red ribbons and bows and gaudy Santas and Rudolphs and Frosties.

Her gaze flitted over a man and woman standing in the back of the crowd before recognition shot ice through her. She blinked rapidly. Her parents were in Highland. It was incongruous. Highland didn't exist in the same world as her parents—or at least, that's what it had felt like these past months. But of course it had only been a matter of time until her worlds collided like a dinosaur-killing asteroid.

Chapter Seventeen

Claire didn't wait for Iain to finish his recitation. Like a robot, she clipped the mike to the stand, descended the stage steps, and weaved her way through the crowd toward her parents.

They stood next to each other but didn't touch. Theirs was a partnership that had lost any affection, if affection had ever existed.

"Mother. Father. How are you?" It was all her dumbfounded brain could come up with.

"Well enough. How are you?" Her mother leaned toward Claire, who awkwardly went in for a hug. Except her mother bussed Claire's cheek instead. Claire's momentum took her into her mother for the world's weirdest hug. They pulled apart, and Claire knew her cheeks were as rosy as her mother's.

Claire tried to study her parents without meeting their gazes. Her mother's face was still unlined—probably due to regular Botox injections—and her hair was the same auburn as Claire's with no trace of gray. In fact, if Claire hadn't lived the intervening years, she wouldn't have guessed her mother had aged a day.

Her father's thin-lipped mouth was bracketed by

lines she didn't recall. His skin was more weathered and his paunch had grown, but his hair was still thick and his clothes well tailored.

Her father cleared his throat in a way that transmitted his discomfort with the reunion. "We watched you sing. You sounded good. Is that your new band?"

"No. I've been singing with the Jacobites for fun."

Her mother ran a practiced eye from Claire's choppy hair to her scuffed boots, cataloging and assigning a value to every square inch. "It's a good thing we came when we did. You need us."

"I don't actually. I found a job, and I've got friends in Highland."

Her parents exchanged a glance. Her father spoke. "You will be twenty-five on Boxing Day. You know what that means."

"I do."

"We've given you as much freedom as you wanted the last few years. Are you ready to come home?" her mother asked.

She darted a look between her mother and father. She would never be ready to go back to Scotland, but she would do it anyway. Before she could formulate an answer, another too-familiar voice spun all three of them around.

"Not so fast. Not until I have a say, anyhow." Lachlan Glennallen strode toward them from the sidewalk and met them in the middle of the street like a scene from some old American Western. His dark-gray suit was rumpled, his hair disheveled, and dark stubble dotted his normally clean-shaven cheeks. He nodded at her parents. "Aunt Mathilda. Uncle Lewis."

"Lachlan." His father's voice was full of familial disappointment. "What are you doing here?"

"My assistant found out about your travel plans."

Lachlan turned his attention to her, his red-rimmed eyes narrowed and suspicious. "Claire and I have an understanding regarding her allegiances."

Her father barred his teeth at Lachlan in the facsimile of a smile. "That was years ago. Situations change. People change. And Claire has every right to vote with me, her father."

The power struggle between Lachlan and her father was a tangible tension binding them.

"What vote? What's going on?" Claire asked.

"Dennison is here with us. Let's go somewhere private to talk." Her father stepped forward, took her hand, and tucked it into the crook of his elbow, the pressure subtle but inexorable.

It was fitting her father's first overture wasn't a hug but a gesture of control. Now that the moment she had dreaded and anticipated was upon her, she felt numb and disconnected.

Over her shoulder, she searched the crowd for Holt or even Ms. Meadows. Imagining Ms. Meadows pulling her shotgun on her father lightened the gathering sense of foreboding. No one was riding to her rescue. And she didn't need them to.

Dr. Jameson trotted over. "Someone has rented out the back room of the pub, but the office at my clinic is available, Mr. Glennallen."

Dr. Jameson flashed a starstruck grin. Claire hated the fact her family name had this effect on people. It had always felt icky to be deferred to for no other reason than an accident of birth.

"It's Sir Glennallen, actually. The queen conferred a knighthood some years ago." Her father spoke with the same amount of bland coolness he'd use to impart how he liked his tea. "Lead on, Doctor Jameson, we would be most grateful for the privacy."

While Dr. Jameson's smile had faltered at the correction in title, he recovered and gestured toward the barrier at the opposite end of the street from the stage. "Right this way."

Dennison, the Glennallen family solicitor, waited at the barrier, carrying a briefcase and wearing a pinstriped suit.

"Dennison. I can't believe I warranted a trip across the pond." She smiled and barely kept herself from hugging him. Such a show of emotion would have embarrassed him terribly.

"The complications of Glennallen Whisky have put my children through university." He winked, slipped a hand into his jacket pocket, and held out a lemon sweet.

She took it and popped it in her mouth. The nostalgia was as sweet and sour as the candy. Throwing propriety to the wind, she hugged Dennison around the neck. He smelled of expensive black tea and shaving tonic.

"I'm glad you're here," she whispered.

When she pulled away, he did indeed look terribly embarrassed but also pleased.

Dr. Jameson fell into step next to her. "I wish you had told me you belong to the Glennallen Whisky dynasty. It would have been a good excuse to host a tasting. Do you think your parents will be in town long enough to—"

"No," Claire said brusquely before softening her tone. "My parents won't be staying in Highland. And neither will I."

Confusion drew Dr. Jameson's bushy brows in. "But I thought you and Holt Pierson were . . ." His voice trailed off into nothing.

Were what? she wanted to ask, mostly because she

was unsure herself. Friends, yes. Lovers, definitely. Could they have been more under different circumstances?

Dr. Jameson fumbled for his keys as they approached the cabin-like building that housed his practice. The clinic sat on a dead-end offshoot from Main Street. Her mother's clacking heels filled the tense silence between Lachlan and her father.

Inside the clinic, animal scents overlay a clean, bleachy smell. It reminded Claire of Holt's farm.

Her mother's nose wrinkled in distaste, but she said nothing. When Dr. Jameson turned to leave, Claire put a hand on his arm, stepped close, and spoke in low tones. "Could you let Holt and Ms. Meadows know I'm with my parents and cousin? Also, Iain. I'm not sure I'll make it for the second set with the Jacobites."

Dr. Jameson searched her face. "I will. You'll be okay?"

She nodded and offered a tight smile.

Dennison set the briefcase on the receptionist's desk, popped the latches, and opened the case. Different-colored folders were neatly arranged in the body, various writing implements in the pockets along with a calculator and a stapler.

"Your hair looks terrible, Claire." Her mother rubbed the ends between her fingers.

Claire jerked her head away from her mother's touch. "I'm growing it out."

"As soon as we get home, I'll make you an appointment with Glennis."

Claire's hand went to her nape before she could stop herself. Ten minutes with her parents and she was already a mass of insecurities. She walked up to Lachlan. "What vote were you and Father referring to?"

Lachlan ran a hand through his hair. "If you checked your email, you would know."

"Well, I haven't, and as you're standing right here, how about giving me the short version?"

"A vote on whether to take Glennallen public." Lachlan's jaw clenched. It was obvious from his defensive posture that he stood against the plan.

"After I inherit my shares, you need my vote to ensure the company doesn't go public?"

"Actually, I just need you not to give your vote to him." Lachlan gestured toward her father. "I've got enough support to hold the company private. For now."

"That's why you came all this way?"

"I couldn't risk they would get your signature on any proxy papers. I left for the airport without a stitch of luggage as soon as I heard they were on their way. I've been traveling for twelve hours."

Her father paced in front of the desk, his hands clasped behind his back. On his pinkie finger, a gold ring with the Glennallen crest winked at her hypnotically on every turn. "Claire, darling, the last years of estrangement have been difficult for your mother and me, but despite everything, you've shown a resiliency that's admirable. Honestly, I expected you to crawl home after being on your own for a summer—after all, you have no skills whatsoever—but you persevered."

Her father had almost given her a compliment. If only he hadn't wrapped it so thoroughly in an insult. "Thank you. I guess."

Her mother took Claire's hands. Claire looked down, unable to stop herself from comparing her mother and Ms. Meadows. Her mother's touch was cool, her skin was unmarked, but signs of aging crept closer. Her knuckles were knobbier and veins were prominent along the backs.

"We want you home for more than a vote, darling. I regret our estrangement more than you know." The sincerity reflected in her mother's voice and face seemed genuine, and Claire fought an age-old longing to connect.

"If I don't return to Scotland to work for Glennallen Whisky, what would happen?" She directed the question at Dennison, but it was her father who spoke.

"You would betray your family name. You would shame your ancestors. You would forfeit your inheritance. No one would be daft enough to walk away from that much money." Her father propped his hands on his hips, his suit jacket flared back over his arms.

A dog from the back barked.

Claire blinked with a sudden realization. Her father was a dog trying to intimidate. Except Claire had seen too much and had learned to deal with all kinds of people on the road. She wasn't easily intimidated. Not anymore.

She turned again to Dennison. "Is he correct?"

Dennison's calm voice was like a balm to the anger crackling around her father. "If you choose not to accept your inheritance, the percentage of Glennallen Whisky you were set to inherit will be put into a trust to be split equally among all owners in five years."

"I wouldn't receive any money at all." She wasn't surprised to hear his soft but emphatic, "None, at all."

"Has any heir refused their inheritance?"

"None have been brave enough to forge their own path." Dennison's brows rose over his glasses as if posing a question he did not ask.

The information cracked a door open. She wasn't sure she should or would walk through, but for the first time since seeing her parents and Lachlan in the middle of Highland, she could take a deep breath.

Lachlan stepped between her and Dennison. Instead of trying to intimidate her like her father, he gave her puppy-dog eyes. "Claire, I need you."

"Do you?" She wasn't asking to annoy him. She was genuinely curious *why* Lachlan needed her.

"Yes. With your vote guaranteed, I could enact my plans and—"

Claire held up her hand. "I can't promise to blindly support every initiative you put forth, Lachlan."

Claire's father poorly muffled a chortle.

Claire swung to look at her father. "I wouldn't ever support taking Glennallen Whisky public. The short-term gains aren't worth it."

With her father on one side of her and Lachlan on the other, Claire had a vision of her future. She would be the pawn in a constant tug-of-war. All they saw when they looked at her were her shares and what those shares could do for them.

They didn't know her heart and dreams and fears. And they wouldn't try to get to know her, not when she possessed something more valuable—a vote. She could use her vote to manipulate her father, maybe even wrest her own piece of power. Or she could do something good with the money and power she'd inherit. She could become a benefactress like her mother.

Claire studied her mother. Was she happy? "I'd like to talk to Mother alone."

Because the two men were trying to make her happy, they obliged, stepping outside. Dennison joined them. Music drifted through the open door before it closed again. The haunting sound of Iain singing "My Love Is Like a Red, Red Rose." It was her song to sing and she was missing it.

"Do you have any advice for me, Mother?" Claire slid onto one of the waiting room chairs.

After a moment, her mother perched on the edge of the chair next to Claire. "Of course you should return and support your father."

It was a regurgitated line. Claire shifted until her knees bumped her mother's legs. "Have you been happy? No regrets?"

Her mother's throat worked and her jaw clenched as if holding back a flood. Finally, she broke. "I was happy at first, but as the years have gone by, I realize money isn't everything. Lewis loves Glennallen Whisky more than he ever loved me. I see the same single-minded obsession in Lachlan. I don't want that for you, Claire."

Claire's breath caught. "You think I should walk away?"

Her mother cast her the briefest of glances. "I dreamed of being a dancer."

"Why didn't you tell me?"

"When you decided not to go to university, a small part of me was glad for you. You were doing something I wasn't brave enough to do. I convinced Lewis to let you be. To let you come to us if you needed help. I hoped you would forge your own path. And you have." Her mother graced her with a real smile that warmed her eyes.

There was that word again. *Brave.* People kept wanting to pin it on her like a medal she didn't deserve. "I haven't forged my own path. I'm currently lost in the brambles if you want to know the truth."

"There's someone special in Highland, isn't there?"

She didn't even question her mother's sudden perceptiveness. "Actually, there are many special someones in Highland, but if you're asking specifically about a man, then yes, there is."

"Do you love him?"

Her earlier confession to Holt was still tender and raw, but she was done lying. "I do."

"Does he love you?"

"I . . . don't know. I hope so."

"Shouldn't you stay to find out?" A challenge lilted in her mother's voice.

"Father will be angry."

Her mother's lips mashed together in a tense line. "Yes, but he'll get over it. The balance of power between him and Lachlan will remain the same. If you returned, they would make your life hell."

"I'd already come to that conclusion." Claire scrubbed a hand through her hair.

"I do regret not being able to let Glennis at your hair, though." Her mother tsked, and Claire found herself laughing instead of getting angry.

"Where are you and Father and Dennison staying?"

"A charming little bed-and-breakfast on the outskirts of Highland called Rose House. Apparently, there is a dearth of suitable hotels in the area." Her parents had a talent for combining compliments and insults until one didn't know whether to thank them or take offense.

"Could you and Father stay on a few days? I'd like to introduce you to my friends. And to Holt." First, she had to tell him she was staying. How would he react? What if he'd only wanted a fling? And Ms. Meadows planned to move into the assisted living facility. She would have no job and nowhere to live. Was taking the leap brave or foolish?

"Yes, we will. Let me handle your father and Lachlan. I'll send Dennison back in so the two of you can handle the necessary paperwork." Her mother walked briskly to the door.

Dennison and her mother spoke outside for a few

seconds before he slipped back into the clinic. Her father's voice had risen to pitch and volume, and Lachlan cast a look that could cut glass through the door to her. She turned her back to the maelstrom outside and smiled at Dennison.

"I'm afraid I've thrown everything into chaos," she said.

"The status quo will be maintained. Don't discount the merits of stability when it comes to running a business." He riffled through the folders in his briefcase and pulled out a black one. "You're sure you wish to renounce? You don't want to sleep on the decision?"

If she waited, she would have a safety net before she talked to Holt. She didn't want to live her life with a safety net another second. She would take the leap and trust Holt to catch her.

"I'm ready to sign." Claire sat behind the desk and signed her life away. No, she was gaining her life. She was signing her burdens away.

Chapter Eighteen

Claire pushed the door open and faced her father and Lachlan. The night had turned crisp and the scent of woodsmoke hung in the air. "I'm sorry, Lachlan. I know I'm breaking the promise I made years ago, but I can't sacrifice my happiness so you can control Glennallen Whisky."

Lachlan threw his hands up, but most of the rancor was absent from his voice. "Bloody hell, I can't believe I came all this way for nothing."

"There is a festival going on. I recommend Big Eddie's barbecue truck. Go enjoy yourself."

Lachlan gave her a dirty look. "Don't misunderstand, I'm fashed, but shoot me an email every once in a while and let me know how you're managing, yeah?" When she nodded, he leaned in for a half hug before stalking off toward the festival.

Next, she turned to the harder nut to crack, her father. "I know I've disappointed you, but I'm still your daughter. Just because I'm not part of the business doesn't mean we can't have a relationship. In fact, it might be simpler now that my shares aren't coloring our interactions."

"I feel as if I don't even know you," her father murmured. A hint of admiration had snuck into the disparagement.

"Then get to know me. The person I am now, not the one you remember. I would like that." Claire smiled at her mother, who returned the sentiment with a decisive nod. "Stay in Highland for Christmas. I'd like to show you around and introduce you to my friends. Please?"

When her father didn't answer, she handed him a piece of paper with Ms. Meadows's phone number. "Think about it and call me, okay?"

Her mother plucked the number from her husband's hand and tucked it into her purse. "We'll call in the morning after emotions have a chance to settle."

With all the awkwardness of hugging a porcupine, Claire leaned in to embrace her father. Her mother's hug was only slightly less awkward. It would take time to build something new. Perhaps they would never kindle the warmth of typical families, but it was a start.

Claire took one last look at her parents and then walked away. Her walk turned into a jog back to the Burns Night festival. Main Street was packed. The festival looked to be a great success. She stood on tiptoe to try to spot anyone she knew.

Iain stood like a lighthouse on the other side of the sidewalk, several inches taller than anyone around him. She pushed through the crowd until she reached him. Dr. Jameson was in conversation with him, but they broke off as she approached.

"I thought you'd be long gone by now," Dr. Jameson said.

Claire ignored him. "Where's Holt and Ms. Meadows?"

"Gone. You missed them by naught more than fifteen

minutes," Iain said. "What's going on? Holt looked like someone kicked his favorite pup."

"He doesn't have a pup. He has a bloodthirsty barn cat named Vlad." Her smile was tremulous. "It's a long story, but I need to talk to him. Why did he leave so early?"

Dr. Jameson made a wincing noise that drew both her and Iain's attention. "I think that might have been my fault."

"What did you tell him?" Claire asked.

"What you told me. That you weren't staying in Highland." Dr. Jameson held his hands out in supplication. "Are you not leaving us, then?"

"No. I'm not," she said firmly. "I need a ride out to Holt's place."

"I'd take you, but I've got to help Anna once the festival wraps up," Iain said.

"I'd be happy to take you wherever you need to go," Dr. Jameson said. "My truck's behind the clinic."

Iain leaned in to kiss her cheek and whisper, "I'm glad Highland is gaining another Scot," before slipping away.

Dr. Jameson took her elbow and led her through the crowd and past the police barrier back toward his clinic. Claire tensed. She didn't want to see her parents again until she'd worked things out with Holt one way or another, but the parking area was deserted.

They were on the road in seconds, but traffic made the going slower than Claire would like. Of course, nothing less than light speed would have satisfied her.

The lights of a Christmas tree lot came into view. A compulsion came over Claire, and she grabbed the dash and yelled, "Stop!"

Startled, Dr. Jameson pulled over into the graveled parking area. "What's the matter?"

"I must have a tree." She didn't wait for Dr. Jameson to respond, but hopped out of the truck.

The trees had been picked over this close to Christmas. She stuck her hand in her pocket and counted her money. Less than five dollars. She went straight to the woman wearing an apron in the back and held the money out in her palm. "What can I get for this? Anything?"

The woman looked from the money to Claire's face and back again, finally taking it and counting it out on the top of a register. "Normally it wouldn't buy anything, but there's a tree over here I could let go for that. Come on."

A single tree leaned against a wooden sawhorse, forlorn and scraggly. Claire stood it upright. It was four feet tall and its crooked branches left gaps, but it was green and its needles sweetly scented. It was perfect.

"I'll take it. Thank you and merry Christmas." Without even thinking, Claire leaned in to give the lady a half hug before loading tree into the bed of Dr. Jameson's truck.

The lady smiled and waved her off. "Merry Christmas!"

After Claire was settled back into the passenger seat, Dr. Jameson smiled and shook his head. "Never pegged you for a romantic, Miss Claire."

"I wasn't one until I came to Highland." She grinned back. "Can we stop at Ms. Meadows's house first? Taking care of her is still my job."

Dr. Jameson nodded. "I like your attitude. Come down to the clinic if you're ever looking for a job. I can use someone reliable at the front desk."

Claire stared out the windscreen and blinked in surprise. A job offered in the most unlikely of circumstances. She was knitting together her own safety net. "Thanks. I'll do that."

When they pulled up to Ms. Meadows's house, Holt's truck wasn't there, but a minivan was out front. "I'll wait out here. Take your time," Dr. Jameson said.

Claire was at the front door in two giant leaps up the steps. The entwined laugher of two women, one recognizably Ms. Meadows, beckoned her to the den. Ms. Meadows was in her favorite chair. All the lights except the twinkling Christmas tree lights were off. As Claire had guessed, the tree was magical at night.

Ms. Coburn, the gray-haired librarian, was half reclined on the couch with a glass of whisky in her hand.

"Ms. Meadows." Claire's voice was croaky.

Ms. Meadows shifted around, her mouth in an O of surprise. "Why, girl! I thought you'd run off with your parents."

"I would never leave you like that." Claire bent over and hugged Ms. Meadows tight. The old woman patted her on the back.

When they broke apart, Ms. Meadows gestured toward the woman on the couch. "Janice, this is my . . . friend, Claire Glennallen. Janice goes to my church. She's staying the night."

"Actually, we met at the library." Claire exchanged smiles with Ms. Coburn. "I should stay and—"

"You should talk to Holt. That boy is heartbroken." Ms. Meadows took her hand and gave it a squeeze. "I'm glad you're still here."

"I'm staying for good. You don't have to move to the assisted living unless you really want to."

Ms. Meadows looked around and smiled. "No, it's time. This has been the best Christmas season I've spent here in too long. Anyway, the Piersons came up with the money to buy my house. They'll probably knock it down, but ashes to ashes and all that. It's time."

Claire's lungs tightened and her breaths grew short with the possibility Ms. Meadows's house would be leveled. It didn't bear thinking about or else she might cry.

"Janice and I are having a fine time. I'll see you tomorrow?" Ms. Meadows asked.

"Yes. Tomorrow." Claire nodded.

Dr. Jameson had tilted his hat over his eyes but popped to attention when she climbed in next to him. "Everything good?"

"Yes." Was it, though? "I might be applying for that job sooner than I planned."

They pulled to the front of Holt's cabin in less than three minutes. Now that the moment was upon her, she needed more time. She sat in the truck and stared out the windscreen.

"I'd offer to help, but I think I'd just be in the way." Dr. Jameson winked and Claire laughed nervously.

She hopped out, retrieved the tree, and stopped at Dr. Jameson's lowered window. "Thank you for the ride and everything else. Wish me luck?"

"You won't need it. That boy is crazy about you."

Claire waited until Dr. Jameson had turned the truck around before she climbed the steps to Holt's front door. She punched the butterflies back into her stomach and knocked. He opened the door and it was all Claire could do not to throw herself into his arms.

"Claire? What in the world? I thought you were leaving with your parents." Holt looked at her as if she was a ghost. Then his gaze fell to the tree and he gave a surprised guffaw. "That is a Charlie Brown Christmas tree if I ever did see one."

"Who is Charlie Brown? Does he live in Highland?" Why were they talking about another man at this very important moment?

"I'll introduce you to him and his gang later."

"I brought the tree for you." She cleared her throat. "For us. You deserve a Christmas miracle too."

Any humor disappeared and his eyes darkened. "What does this mean exactly? Spell it out to me as if I'm the village idiot."

"It means . . ." She moistened her dry lips. "I signed away my inheritance. It will go into a trust, and I won't receive a penny."

"You gave all that up? For me?"

"Not just for you. For me too. For Ms. Meadows. For Highland. I don't want to live as my family's pawn, but I thought I had no other choice." She shifted on her feet. "The papers have been signed and witnessed, and even though I spent my last five dollars on this tree, I feel richer than anyone on earth."

Holt took the tree out of her hands and set it inside the cabin against the wall. Then he took her hands, drew her inside the warm coziness, and shut the door. "I didn't get the chance to tell you something very important today."

"What's that?"

"I love you too."

She smiled and stepped into his arms, holding him tight and closing her eyes. "Is this real?"

"Are miracles real?" he shot back.

"I would have said no before meeting you, but I've become a true believer." She pushed back from his chest. "I stopped to see Ms. Meadows before coming here. She said you made an offer on her house and land. I thought the farm couldn't support another loan?"

"It couldn't. I took out a personal loan. A mortgage, actually. It's high time I moved into a real house off the farm. Ms. Meadows's house is perfect. Close enough to be here fast in case of emergency but far enough away, I won't feel like I'm living with my parents."

"You're planning to live there."

"Yep." His gaze darted away and then back. "With you, if you want."

"Yes, I want. I want more than anything."

"I swore off Christmas tonight, but looks like I'll be celebrating after all. Let's decorate our tree, and then I'll introduce you to Charlie Brown."

Our tree. The simple words brought home to her that she wasn't on her own anymore. She had a partner, a friend, a lover. She had been in search of somewhere she could feel at home all her life. Never had she stopped to consider her destination might not be a place but a person.

She was the luckiest Highlander who had ever come to town.

Epilogue

Holt lay in bed awake with Claire cuddled next to him like a hibernating bear. A cute, sexy hibernating bear. He never lollygagged in bed. Since he'd been old enough to walk, he'd risen at dawn to trail after his mom and dad while they took care of the farm.

From age six, he'd had his own list of chores to complete before school. Chores didn't do themselves on weekends either. In high school, he'd had to drag himself out of bed at sunrise tired and hungover to feed the chickens and gather eggs on Saturday mornings. Rising early had become his routine, and he enjoyed watching the world wake.

Having Claire in his bed moved a to-do item to the top of his list, and it wouldn't be a chore to perform. Turning into her, he kissed her to a sleepy wakefulness and made love to her, slowly and with a tenderness she returned in full measure.

"Merry Christmas," she whispered already snuggling back into the cocoon of blankets. Her tousled hair stuck up at odd angles. She peeked over the edge of the blanket. "I'm sorry I don't have anything wrapped and under the tree for you to open."

"You in my bed is present enough."

While he couldn't see her mouth, her eyes crinkled in a smile. "This Christmas is already the best one ever and the sun is barely up."

He lifted the comforter enough to brush his lips over hers. "I have everything I want and need right here. Why don't you snooze a little longer while I see to the chores?"

"I can help." She pushed herself to her elbows, but he pressed her back down to the pillows.

"I know you can, but picturing you naked and waiting here will motivate me to get everything done lickety-split. Then we've got to get to cooking, and based on my past performance, you will have to take the lead."

Claire's parents had stayed in Highland and were coming for Christmas dinner. Holt did not anticipate a merry, laid-back dinner with Sir Glennallen in attendance. While they had been scrupulously polite to Holt, it was clear her parents were trying to figure out why Claire had chosen him and Highland over the status and wealth she could have claimed. Holt wasn't going to question the luck of the universe.

"As long as we have corn bread dressing, Ms. Meadows will be happy." Claire stretched under the covers and burrowed deeper into the pillow.

"Corn bread dressing we can manage. Maybe. I'll get the coffee brewing." Holt left her, knowing she'd be there when he returned. It was not something he would take for granted.

Wrapping a hand around the hot coffee mug, he toed the front door open and enjoyed the streaks of sun over the trees. The crunch of gravel under tires had him tilting his ear toward the farm lane. He couldn't see who had arrived. The farmhands had the day off, and there were no emergencies for Dr. Jameson to handle.

He pulled on his boots and jacket and hopped into his truck to investigate. He brake-checked when he topped the rise to see his parents' RV parked in front of the main house and then hit the gas pedal so hard, his back tires spun.

He met his mother coming out of the front door. Wrapping his arms around her in a bear hug, he lifted her off the ground. "What in the world are you doing here? You're supposed to be soaking up the Florida sun."

"I missed you and the house and my goats." His mom laughed and returned his hug.

"I'm glad I rank slightly above your goats." He set her back down when his dad emerged from the RV carrying a suitcase.

After giving his dad a half hug, Holt took the suitcase out of his hand and hauled it inside. His mom rolled it toward the laundry room. His dad nodded his head toward the kitchen and Holt followed and watched his dad measure out coffee for the maker.

"You could have called and let me know you were coming. I would have made sure the house was in decent shape." Holt also could have given them a heads-up about Claire and the dinner taking place that evening.

Holt hadn't mentioned Claire yet. At first, it was because he'd thought she'd be long gone before they came home. And later, he hadn't wanted to shatter the fragile happiness cocooning them.

His dad pulled down three mugs. "The closer we got to Christmas, the more restless and unhappy I felt. Don't get me wrong, I enjoyed our travels, but if I'm going to settle down, I'd rather do it in Highland. Two days ago, I put my foot down and told her we were headed home for Christmas and I wasn't accepting any arguments."

"What did Mom do?" Holt climbed up onto one the bar stools.

"I swear I barely got the words out of my mouth before she started packing. She had been wanting to come home too, but hadn't wanted to hurt my feelings." His dad's laugh boomed around the kitchen. He poured two mugs of coffee, slid one to Holt, and leaned over the bar on his elbows. "Fill me in on all the goings-on around the farm and town."

Holt didn't know where to start, but he definitely needed to mention the woman currently in his bed. Maybe not right off, though. "Anna Maitland is expecting and marrying Iain Connors in less than a week. She asked me to give her away."

His mom, who had always had a sixth sense for gossip, came jogging into the kitchen. "Wait for me!" She poured herself a coffee and took the stool on his left.

He told them about the impending wedding and all about the successful Burns Night festival. Tentatively, he dipped his toe in more personal conversational waters. "While you were gone, there were some neighborly developments."

"I heard tell Johnston was looking to sell some of his cattle. Have you given them a once-over?" his dad asked. Mr. Johnston's farm abutted theirs on the north side. The Johnston house was a good fifteen miles down the road, but he was technically their next-door neighbor.

"No, and our fields can't support any more heads. I'm actually referring to Ms. Meadows."

"That old bat? What did she want?" His dad regressed into a petulance that would rival any teenager's.

"*Dad*," Holt admonished. "I'm going to make sure Preacher Hopkins puts you in a sermon if you can't locate a scrap of love for thy neighbor."

"You wouldn't be so quick to judge if that same neighbor pulled a gun on you and told you how far south you could go." His dad set his coffee mug down with a thump.

"Actually, she did pull a gun on me," Holt said blandly. "She doesn't even own bullets. And she happens to be a very nice lady who needed us. We let her down."

"I offered a fair price for her land, and she turned me down flat."

"It's her land and house, and she has every right to tell you no." Holt shifted toward his mother. "You need to tell him no more often. Get him used to it."

"Holt's right, dear. You are partial to getting your way." His mom smiled sweetly at her husband over the rim of her mug before taking a sip.

"She fell over the summer, did you know?" Holt asked.

His dad hummed and rubbed a hand over his mouth. "Preacher Hopkins might have mentioned it. But he said she hadn't broken anything and that he was looking for some help for her. He didn't ask anything of me."

Holt could almost smell the guilt coming off his dad and decided against piling on. "Preacher Hopkins did find him help. Her name is Claire Glennallen."

"Like the whisky?" his dad asked.

"Her great-great-grandfather founded the distillery."

"That's good I suppose. Responsibility averted. We already have enough to worry about anyway." His dad's serenity was restored.

His mom stared at Holt with a more discriminating eye. "How old is Claire?"

"Twenty-five tomorrow." Holt didn't flinch under his mom's gaze.

"You know her birthday. How serious is it?" his mom asked.

"Serious? What?" His dad's gaze darted back and forth between them.

"Claire is at the cabin sleeping in. It's been a crazy week since the festival."

His mom's mouth hung slack for a few disbelieving blinks before a smile wiped away the tiredness of the journey home. "I can't wait to meet her."

"Get ready, because you're fixing to meet her *and* her parents. We're cooking Christmas dinner for them."

"Where?" his dad asked.

"Here." Holt shook his head. "Didn't think you were coming back. Although now that you're here, we could use some help in the kitchen, Mom."

"I made your dad stop yesterday for groceries. We can make them stretch." His mom slid off the stool and pulled down a cookbook with handwritten recipes and flipped through, pulling out cards.

"One more thing," Holt said. His parents stopped what they were doing and gave him their full attention. "Ms. Meadows is coming for dinner too. And I bought her place."

"What?" His parents spoke in unison.

"I know, it's crazy. She decided to move into the assisted living place at the edge of town. They had an opening, and Claire got her settled yesterday."

His dad rubbed his hands together. "No, this is good. We can raze the house and cut a path to—"

"We're not razing the house. I'm moving into it.

With Claire. We've already talked to Iain Connors about renovations."

Shock silenced his parents.

Holt drained his mug and rose. "I've got chores to see to. Want to come along, Dad?"

Holt and his dad slipped into an easy camaraderie while completing the mundane, everyday chores that kept the farm running. It was good to have his dad back, but something subtle had shifted. His dad had started to defer to him. It felt . . . strange, yet right.

Back at the main house, Holt washed up in the sink. "Before you guys run down to the cabin, I need to prepare Claire. We weren't expecting you, and she's already nervous about her parents coming over."

His mom chuffed. "Gracious, we're not going to eat her." Then, more thoughtfully, she asked, "Why would she be nervous about having dinner with her parents?"

"They've been estranged for a few years and are starting to mend things. It might be awkward."

His mom gave him an eye roll. "I hosted a luncheon between the Baptist and Methodist women's groups. I can handle awkward."

Holt smiled and gave his mom a hug. "I missed you. Also, your goats are bored and humping each other constantly."

Holt left them to finish unpacking. Claire was puttering around the kitchen when he returned. She made his plaid button-up look sexy. Bending over to check the crisper, she gave him a peek at her pink panties. He came up behind her, wrapped his arms around her waist, and buried his face in her neck. The scent of his shampoo and soap clung to her hair and skin, heady and provocative.

"That didn't take as long as I expected," she said.

"I hope you didn't shirk your responsibilities for my sake."

"I thought about saying to hell with everything and staying in bed with you all day, but Maureen would get mad and eat stinkweed again." He trailed his lips up her neck to nip her earlobe. "Actually, I had help. Mom and Dad came home early. They wanted to be here for Christmas."

She turned in his arms, the smile on her face stiff. "That's brilliant."

"I know it's a shock."

"What if they don't like me?"

"They'll like you." He kissed the tip of her nose. "Even better, Mom is going to lead the kitchen brigade. I'll take you up there in a bit to introduce you."

"What about Ms. Meadows? Will your father behave?"

"After the riot act I read him this morning for not being a proper neighbor, he better or else I'll make sure Preacher Hopkins rains down fire and brimstone from the pulpit right on his head next Sunday."

Her body loosened, and she pressed her cheek into his chest. He swept her into a cradle hold. Her squeal was half surprise, half laughter. He put on his terrible fake brogue because it made her smile every time. "I love you, you daft woman."

She kissed him with her lips curved into a grin. The bedroom was too far. He dropped her on the couch and settled over her, his hand skating up her thigh. The front door opened with a blast of cool air.

Holt and Claire turned their heads at the same time, breaking the kiss. His parents stood framed in the doorway. Holt scrambled to his feet, feeling like an adolescent. "You two are going to have to start knocking."

"I'm sorry, Holt. We got impatient." His mom looked like she'd been out in the sun too long.

"It's only been like ten minutes!"

Claire tugged at the hem of his shirt and squirmed.

"Claire Glennallen. My parents, Sarah and Robert." Holt gestured between them.

"It's lovely to meet you." Claire had the look of a hunted doe. "I think the world of Holt."

"Then we already have something in common." His mom grabbed the back of her husband's shirt and pulled him out of the cabin. "Claire, darling, when you're ready, come on up to the house, and we'll tackle Christmas dinner."

Claire and Holt remained frozen until they heard the sound of his dad's truck back up.

"Tell me that didn't just happen," Claire whispered.

"Oh, it happened. We need to be sure to lock the doors until we move into Ms. Meadows's house. My parents are used to unrestricted access. Why don't you get dressed while I shower and we'll try not to die of embarrassment together."

The next four hours were spent cooking Christmas dinner. Even Holt's dad pitched in. Any initial embarrassment dissipated under the charm offensive his mom launched to win Claire over. Of course Claire found stories about his childhood and adolescence endlessly amusing. He had a feeling old photo albums would be dragged out after dinner.

Claire and Holt picked up Ms. Meadows, who had moved into a cozy efficiency apartment with a mini-kitchen in the assisted living facility. She'd already been to Atlanta to watch *The Nutcracker* with several of the other residents. Holt got her settled on the couch with a glass of wine. Holt's dad sat in the armchair, and they talked. Holt kept an eye on them but didn't interrupt.

He found Claire setting the table with all the care of a visit from the queen herself. Her nerves were like crackles of lightning all around her. "How does it look?"

"Fancier than any Christmas dinner we've ever had. One year, Dad and I came in after seeing to a laboring horse and ate covered in muck."

As he hoped, he got a small smile out or her, but it was fleeting. She smoothed a hand over her kilt and blouse. "What if this goes horribly wrong?"

"Oh, it's going to be weird and stilted and awkward as hell."

This time he got a laugh. She slapped his arm. "You're supposed to be encouraging and comforting."

"You didn't let me finish. No matter what happens, I'm here and not going anywhere and one day we'll laugh about it all."

The doorbell rang. Claire's hand went to her throat on a gasp. Holt put a hand on her lower back and steered her to the door.

Her parents were on the other side wearing the same strained smile as Claire. They held a bottle of Glennallen Whisky. Holt shook her father's hand. "Lewis. Mathilda."

He'd been tasked earlier to call them by their given names, which seemed like a positive step. Claire gave them both kisses on the cheeks and ushered them inside. Holt led them into the den and introduced his parents. Holt's dad cracked open the bottle of whisky and poured drinks for everyone.

Small talk ensued. Ms. Meadows and his dad had buried the hatchet, thankfully not in each other's backs. Things went well until Lewis asked Holt's dad if Glennallen was his favorite whisky.

"I can't deny your brand has a nice finish, but there's no better whisky than Jack Daniel's for my money."

Claire froze, and Lewis Glennallen's face reddened like a fuse had been lit.

"Aw hell," Holt muttered. "It's Glennallen all the way for me, Lewis. I think the food is almost ready, isn't it, Mom?"

Picking up on the undercurrents like the excellent hostess she was, his mother said, "Indeed. Robert, would you escort Ms. Meadows to the table? Holt, you lead the Glennallens to their places, Claire and I will bring the food to the table, and we'll serve family style."

The rest of the dinner was the typical ebb and flow of a conversation among relative strangers, but by the end the Glennallens were comfortable enough to stay for an after-dinner drink.

"Holt tells us you're quite a singer, Claire. If I play, will you sing?" Holt's dad sat at the piano and hit a note.

Claire nodded and the night ended with everyone joining in on several classic Christmas songs. It seemed to shrink the distance and differences between the two families. Claire saw her parents to their rental car. Their flight left the next afternoon, and it would be the last time she saw them for quite some time.

Holt waited in the entry for her. She returned with tears glimmering in her eyes but a soft smile on her face. He enfolded her in his arms. "Everything all right?"

"For the first time ever, I can answer yes to that question. I don't know if I'll ever be close with my parents like you are with yours—too many years have been squandered—but we aren't estranged anymore. I'm happy about that."

He kissed the top of her head. "I'm happy that you're happy."

Holt's mom offered to put Ms. Meadows up for the night, but she demurred, needing to return to the assisted living facility for her medicine. Holt's dad volunteered to take her back, offering his arm. The two old adversaries were almost chummy on their walk to his dad's truck. Talk about Christmas miracles. Holt shook his head and smiled.

After cleaning up the kitchen, Claire and Holt walked hand in hand to his cabin in the dark. The scraggly tree that Claire had given him decorated with multicolored lights and colorful ornaments in the corner made him smile.

"Best Christmas ever," he said against her temple. "I can't wait to plant roots so deep, you won't regret giving up Glennallen Whisky."

"It was never even close. I will always choose you, Holt."

And Holt would always choose Claire. He spent the rest of the night proving it.